About the Author

She grew up and used to swim at Manly Beach, ninety-eight percent European ancestry. Currently a widow. She loves to venture into her world of Italian and Indian cooking, long beach walks and enjoy homemade picnics of delicious rolls and fruits during summer. She enjoys good adventures/drama movies with her popcorn and non-alcoholic wine. Indulge in books from her library: reading murder mysteries, solving quizzes, shows on T.V. Each Saturday at eight a.m., join the parkrun world-wide group.

She loves watching documentaries on set designers. And going to stage shows and old architecture, she enjoys visiting art galleries, museums and festivals. She listens to all types of music and artists.

She has an over active brain, huge imagination. She is a visual writer, watching her characters perform in the clothing and scenery for storyline.

If she is asked to describe herself, she would say the song *(A Million Dreams)* is me.

Two Hearts Entwined

Lynne Browne

Two Hearts Entwined

Olympia Publishers
London

www.olympiapublishers.com
OLYMPIA PAPERBACK EDITION

Copyright © Lynne Browne 2023

The right of Lynne Browne to be identified as author of
this work has been asserted in accordance with sections 77 and 78 of
the Copyright, Designs and Patents Act 1988.

All Rights Reserved

No reproduction, copy or transmission of this publication
may be made without written permission.
No paragraph of this publication may be reproduced,
copied or transmitted save with the written permission of the publisher,
or in accordance with the provisions
of the Copyright Act 1956 (as amended).

Any person who commits any unauthorised act in relation to
this publication may be liable to criminal
prosecution and civil claims for damage.

A CIP catalogue record for this title is
available from the British Library.

ISBN: 978-1-80439-038-2

This is a work of fiction.
Names, characters, places and incidents originate from the writer's
imagination. Any resemblance to actual persons, living or dead, is
purely coincidental.

First Published in 2023

Olympia Publishers
Tallis House
2 Tallis Street
London
EC4Y 0AB

Printed in Great Britain

Chapter One

The Meeting

One may ask themselves daily or each year what real love is. Is it when your heart aches you're unable to breathe? A desire so strong you cannot deny it? Feelings to belong with another human? Your body heating?

Whether or not we can explain love, the individual is all that matters how one feels towards a person. Lynda is unaware she is about to journey into the world of true love, like every morning she showers, dresses and eats breakfast. Lynda stops at a photo in a timber frame, half torn, of her fiance, who hurt her badly a year prior. She likes the photo of herself; it is a memory to remind herself to tread carefully next time. She pours her tea in a takeaway holder and off she sets to work, taking the lift to the first floor and making a quick stop. Mr. Jones, her neighbour on the first floor. She knocks, waiting for him to open his door. "Good morning, Lynda." He hands her a brown paper bag.

"Thanks, Jim." She hands him back the bag and places the object into her pocket.

"Have a good day, Lynda!" Jim says while shutting his door.

Lynda walks out of her building like every other morning. Peter walks his dog at the same time; he lives on the first floor. The springer spaniel wags his tail on seeing her, and Lynda bends down, patting Max and giving him a treat. Max always refuses to move until Lynda pats him behind his ears and gives him a treat, he wags his tail excitedly.

"You spoil him," says Peter, smiling; he's retired and looks forward to a morning chat with Lynda. She smiles and quickens her step towards the bus station, passing a lady picking flowers. She hands Lynda a yellow rose for her desk. She smells it and thanks Karen; she always seems to be in her front yard each morning, either collecting her newspaper or picking flowers. Lynda notices that she is always in her nightgown and slippers, as it's only seven a.m. It's as if the woman waits for her to pass. Lynda thinks to herself that she is a lonely lady and hopes it won't be her one day.

Lynda notices a new face on the bus today. She smiles and says hello to all the regular acquaintances she has made over the past five years. Lynda looks strongly at the new man; he smiles back and she blushes, being noticed staring at him. She found herself compelled to admire him, a rather striking man. Lynda takes her usual seat beside a high school boy, her best friend's son Jason, who is mute, and she uses sign language to communicate with him.

Jason can hear, just unable to speak from the age of four. Lynda has travelled on the same bus since Jason began travelling along the route by himself five years ago. Jason's mother arranged with Lynda to give Jason some independence now he was at secondary school. Lynda used to drive Jason to primary school due to being on her way to work in the city. Jason likes talking with Lynda, passing the time and making his journey shorter. He talks about school and what he wants to be when he finishes. Lynda signs and speaks out the words so he can read her lips. Jason informs her the bullies are getting him down and would prefer to stay home.

Lynda is aware of his troubles and has been trying to help.

She removes an object from her pocket, handing to Jason. He stares, wondering what it is; Lynda presses a button, it makes a screeching sound. A red-light-shines, Jason covers his ears along with fellow passengers on the bus. Lynda clicks a smaller button, apologising to Jason and her fellow passengers. The new guy stares at her with a smile; Jason laughs, seeing everyone's reaction having the gist of her intentions. Lynda signs she has already informed his principle and teachers of his new alert device. Jason places it inside his pocket, thanking her for signing, preferring the other passengers not to overhear their conversation. Lynda explains Mr. Jones makes many interesting gadgets. She invites Jason to visit and she will introduce him, aware Jason likes making things from scrap metal.

The new man is watching her sign and laughing with the boy, thinking she is a caring woman. Jason says goodbye to Lynda and steps off the bus two stops before her as she goes directly into the city. She smiles at him and watches him heading in the right direction towards his school. She fears he may take the day off as Jason has done it on occasion. He would wander the city shops, avoiding school. On occasions, Lynda has had to go and find him and always knows his favourite place is under the Sydney Harbour bridge. Since that episode, Jason's parents have now placed a tracking app on his mobile, and Lynda has it on her phone, too. She stares down at the screen while the bus moves off from the stop; Jason is heading in the right direction towards his school. Lynda sighs with relief, wondering if she will have to be late for work. The bus moves swiftly along the streets, making good time.

Lynda is writing on her mobile, every now and then glancing up at the new man on the bus, she wonders who he is. The younger woman on the seat across the aisle moves to sit beside

Lynda, as she often does. "I wonder who he is?" she asks.

Lynda shrugs her shoulders and the man beside her says, "Maybe you should ask him!" with a grin. The young woman looks at him, they all know she is always nosy, but they've all come to know each other over the years. To have a new face is interesting and makes everyone curious as he is sitting in someone else's seat who is absent today. Lynda comments maybe Martin is unwell today, and this stranger just happened to take the seat, unaware of its normal occupant.

"Yes, he did jump onto the bus in a hurry!" Alex comments.

Lynda leaves all the curiosity of the stranger to her fellow travellers as she gazes out of the window, watching people coming and going. She half listens to the girl beside her, who always seems to chatter along about nothing, really. The passengers stand up in line as the bus pulls into the main stop, everyone saying goodbye and heading in their normal directions. Lynda notices the stranger amongst the other heads being rather tall, and he is walking briskly in front of her. She quickens her steps, rather curious about where he is heading. Her friends have enlightened her curiosity. Lynda notices he stops at the lights, and she is just behind. He walks across the road and heads straight into the foyer of her building. The elevator doors open and he enters along with another man; she is about to reach it when the doors start to close. Lynda notices a hand stopping the doors; she enters and the man is smiling at her.

"Hello again," he says. She smiles, looking up at him as she moves to one side to press the button for her floor. She's glancing sideways, moving her eyes up and down his body; he has a good build. Lynda normally takes no notice of men in her building; today is different, though – he was on her bus, a new face, a stranger she knows nothing of. Lynda's floor arrives, and she steps out of the elevator and proceeds to the receptionist's desk.

"Good morning, Lynda; the papers are on your desk. Your meeting in the legal department has been brought forward!" Jennifer says.

"What time?" Lynda asks.

"In thirty minutes. Eight thirty; that's early?" Jennifer replies.

Lynda takes a deep breath. Her normal meeting once a month in the legal department is always at ten o'clock. Why earlier today?

"I believe there is a new man starting today and he wants to get the meeting over first!" Jennifer tells Lynda, noticing she's looking at her watch.

Lynda thanks Jennifer and walks across to her office. She puts her handbag away, locked into her desk drawer and proceeds to the kitchen to make a fresh cup of tea. Lynda always stacks the kitchen with her favourite herbal teas, knowing no one else will use them as nearly everyone in her office prefers coffee. She pours hot water over her lemongrass and ginger tea and walks out, noticing women have gathered around Susan's desk. "Anything wrong?" she enquires.

"Did you see the new guy in the legal department!" Susan asks Lynda before she can answer.

"No, she has Fridays off, remember!" another woman says. Susan was so excited she had forgotten Lynda was away and hadn't met the new man.

"He came down to introduce himself to Mr. Gardner and us!" Susan comments, very interested in a new man in the building.

"I wonder how old he is?" says another woman and the others smirk.

"You will be better off working than gossiping!" Mr.

Gardner, the head of the office, stated, staring at the women, and he looks at Lynda. He is aware she tries to avoid gossiping in the office and wonders why she's part of it today. The other women disburse quickly, sitting at their desks and getting back to the tasks they should be performing. Susan is always looking for a man in a good position to provide for her expensive lifestyle. Mr. Gardner disapproves of Susan's pursuit of men, especially in his office. He had to deal with a situation she caused last year. Mr. Gardner had cautioned her, except Susan persuaded her union she wasn't at fault. Mr. Gardner is cautious and keeps a tight eye on her.

"Lynda, a word please," Mr. Gardner says in one of his deep voices of disapproval. He escorts her into his office.

Lynda closes the door behind her and Mr. Gardner hands her a folder with reports inside. "I was given today's by Jennifer," she comments.

"No, these are different. The new lawyer insists on seeing these two from the past six months. The firm wants him to double-check!" Mr. Gardner replies.

Lynda looks puzzled. She regularly had meetings with Peter Jones, now retired. Mr. Gardner informs Lynda that Mr. Jones made mistakes during his last year.

"The new lawyer, Mr. Wilson, is only doing as instructed by the firm, performing his job. It has nothing to do with you. These reports were when you went on holidays, never seeing them!" Mr. Gardner says with a smile. He looks at his watch and hurries her along; she only has two minutes left.

Lynda takes the folder and walks out. Closing his door and entering her office, she picks up the current folder. Lynda leaves her tea behind, never taking it with her, and she heads for the lift now she is late. She enters the lift and presses the button for the

29th floor. The lift moves quickly; she's the only occupant and listens to the music, "if somebody loves you." She sighs and arrives at her destination; the doors open. She steps out and is greeted by Patricia, a long-time friend of hers and personal assistant now to Mr. Wilson. She escorts Lynda to the office

Patricia knocks, then opens the door, stepping inside to inform Mr. Wilson of Lynda's arrival. "Show her in," he says.

Patricia opens the door wider for Lynda, then she leaves. Looking straight ahead, Lynda comes face to face with the stranger on the bus.

"Hello, Lynda. Have a seat at the table," he says while moving towards a long table nearer the large windows overlooking the city.

"I was informed to expect an intelligent, sophisticated woman!" he says.

Lynda stares across at him without answering, feeling nervous and hoping she stands up to his expectations. She straightens her shoulders and walks across to the table; she leans across and shakes his hand.

"Call me Neil, please. I like first names. Surnames seem so formal and old-fashioned!" he states, then sits down.

Lynda takes a seat with her back to the wall, and she hands him the folders he requested. He thanks her, placing them to one side and waiting to hear the past month's reports. Lynda's department is engaged in managing the law firm's accounts, and many of the company's clients Lynda deals with are very large. She opens her folder, noticing Neil has removed the overhead projector. She wonders why? Being young, he must be up-to-date with technology. He notices her eyes moving upwards.

"For our first meeting, I would prefer not to use the computer, as Mr. Jones seems to have changed figures. On paper, it is more solid, and I can write remarks or changes before them being edited on your and our computer systems!" Neil advises her as if reading her thoughts.

Lynda lifts her eyebrows, then continues to give her full report, explaining each page. She notices from Neil's changing expressions he is following, and he asks many questions; this man knows accountancy.

"I wasn't aware of any problems with those reports until today!" Lynda says, looking directly at Neil.

"I have been instructed by the company to check Mr. Jones's work. Not your work Lynda. I am sure your facts are correct!" Neil states, looking back at her. He gives a grin to put her at ease.

Lynda proceeds, and Neil takes mental notes while listening to her, and follows along without asking any questions. "Do you understand?" she enquires.

"Yes, I studied accountancy before I decided to become a lawyer!" he says.

Lynda frowns; maybe he's older than he looks? She continues with her report. Lynda finishes and closes the folders, ready to leave until Neil prevents her by asking if she has Mr. Jones's mobile number. Lynda looks toward him and asks the reason, as Mr. Jones gave her strict instructions not to hand out his new number unless important.

"I found a gold coin in a box with a photo of a young girl in my safe. I thought he might like them back!" Neil replies.

Lynda is fully aware of the significance of the coin and photo. The girl is Mr. Jones's daughter who has special care needs, and the coin is worth a lot for her future. Lynda is surprised Mr. Jones left it behind. She accesses her mobile, giving Neil the number.

Lynda informs Neil he should ring Mr. Jones today because

he is leaving for Fiji on an early flight in the morning. "Mr. Jones is then moving to the Sunshine Coast permanently," she informs him.

"I will have Patricia ring him after our meeting," Neil replies.

Lynda is grateful to Mrs. Jones for moving her husband and daughter away, as she won't be subject to invites to their home for dinner. On many occasions, Mrs. Jones had an ulterior motive to match-make her with a man unsuited to her tastes. Lynda is now free from embarrassing evenings and having to make excuses to leave early.

Neil interrupts her thoughts. "Would you like a lemongrass and ginger tea?" he enquires as he has already checked which beverage she prefers. Lynda is amazed because Mr. Jones, after ten years, never got it right; always giving her coffee, which she dislikes.

"Yes, please," she replies.

Neil walks across to his small kitchen, making her a fresh pot. Lynda smells the aroma, and Neil presents her with a wooden tray with a pot and teacup. He admits he wants to make a good impression by asking Patricia for her favourite tea shop. Lynda visits the tea shop twice a week as they have fresh tea leaves, and she always stocks up while visiting. Lynda thanks him, noticing he has black coffee. She loves the smell but refuses to have one as it tends to keep her up at night.

"Do you like the outdoors?" Neil enquires, sitting back in his seat, more relaxed now the meeting is over.

"Yes, I walk every weekend!" Lynda replies.

"Where do you go walking?" he asks.

"I drive to Lane Cove National Park sometimes or North Head reserve. I like to take long walks and stop to take in the views!" Lynda replies. She notices Neil smiling and she is finding his directness rather refreshing. Lynda is curious about his age, unable to detect it she enquires.

"I'm thirty, and you?" Neil answers and asks at the same time.

"I'm forty, a lot older than you!" Lynda replies, looking at him.

"You know age is just a number?" Neil replies.

Lynda finds his smile captivating. She looks away, pouring her tea, and sips it without saying another word.

Neil asks if she can recommend a good restaurant, as he only moved back to Sydney last week, having been away for ten years living in Victoria. Lynda mentions a few she's been to on business meetings, but she does recommend one at Manly, where she lives, a smaller restaurant that she prefers. Neil thanks her and makes notes on his mobile, saying he lives in Manly, so nice and close. Lynda's eyes widen as she lives there too, opposite the beach. She is now wondering where? Because this morning, stepping on the bus several suburbs away.

Lynda decides to ask him if he goes walking anywhere interesting. He replies he went running at Lane Cove Park as his friend lives nearby. Lynda places her cup down and says thank you to him for being direct and not asking unwanted questions. She is used to Mr. Jones not understanding her reports and has to explain for another hour after the meeting. Today is refreshing not having to do this and enjoying a conversation while having tea. She is feeling pleased it went well.

"Until next month," She speaks.

Neil shakes her hand and watches her leave. Patricia notices Lynda smiling as she passes her desk. She enters Neil's office to remove the cups, commenting Lynda never leaves these meetings smiling and normally has a frustrated expression.

"Really? Is she?" Neil replies while looking out of his windows and down at the busy streets below.

Lynda returns to her office with Mr. Gardner entering, making enquires about how her meeting went. He, too, notices she is smiling while telling him.

"You will find working with Neil more beneficial for both our companies. He is a really nice man and knowledgeable, especially on companies we and his firm handle. This is why he was brought in from their other office!" Mr. Gardner tells her.

"Do you know him?" Lynda enquires.

"Yes, I have known Neil since he was fifteen. I am a family friend!" Mr. Gardner answers with a smile.

Lynda smells a conspiracy. "You could have told me!"

"No, I wanted you to judge him for yourself. He is an excellent Lawyer!" Mr. Gardner says while leaving her office.

James enters Lynda's office, asking how her meeting went with the new man, and if they should expect difficulties like they had with Mr. Jones.

"No, problems with Mr. Wilson," she replies.

James sits in her spare chair, asking questions. Lynda refuses to fill him in, knowing he gossips with Susan. She dismisses him and continues opening up her computer to begin her day. She sees an email.

"I enjoyed our meeting, thank you, Neil."

Lynda smiles, then continues answering her other fifty emails from around the office. The day seems to move along quicker than usual, Lynda being more settled after the morning meeting. All the other office workers say goodnight to her, leaving at their normal time of four thirty p.m. Lynda rides an Uber car home due to it being after seven p.m. and never uses the bus at night.

In her apartment, she pours herself a white wine while waiting for her takeaway to arrive. She listens to the TV taking in the late news, except her thoughts are wandering back to her meeting with Neil. She wonders if he will be on her bus in the morning, thinking he must have been staying with a friend. Lynda answers her door, taking her food. She then locks the door and moves into her kitchen, placing the food on a plate – pasta with basil sauce and cheese. She gazes out of her large window overlooking Manly beach, a view she loves, and enjoys her meal. Lynda's past partners never connected with her on a special level or fell deeply in love.

Men who were attractive, charming and her fiance she rather forgets. Lynda has concluded that she may be single for the rest of her life. She is not fearful of her future. She just sometimes would like to have a companion to talk to on all topics, share special moments and walks with, and just enjoy being in someone's arms on the couch watching TV. Lynda thinks back to her fortieth birthday two weeks ago, lots of family and friends and plenty of gifts. Cards with some wording she would rather forget. Her brother gave her one with an old lady rocking in a chair on the front of his card. "Ha, Ha," beside the picture.

Lynda's siblings are married with kids, except for Simon, the youngest being single like her. She is the second eldest and unmarried, to her mother's horror. Her father always reminds her she is too old now to have children, so forget meeting someone special. The words ring loud in her mind. Lynda reminds her father of many celebrities having babies at fifty, staring back at him, informing him she has stored her eggs. The expression of shock and horror on his face at what she has done she will remember for quite some time. Lynda's mother reminds her she let her last boyfriend go. Unfortunately, her mother is unaware he cheated on her four times. Lynda thought she had found the one until she discovered his indiscretions; her best friend's husband came to her rescue and kicked him out.

Lynda now never goes to nightclubs, feeling she's too old and will find the same insincere type of man. She looks younger than her age but now prefers to lounge at home at night or enjoy a nice meal at her favourite restaurant. Lynda, for the first time, is now missing a connection with someone. Her last single friend married last year and is now having a baby. She's feeling lonely, but is uneasy about stepping into another relationship.

On the morning bus, Neil decides to quickly change seats, sitting next to Lynda when Jason steps off the bus. All the passengers watch his quick actions, beating the young girl who normally moves across to Lynda. She can't help smiling.

"Has anyone ever told you have a lovely smile!" Neil tells her, seeing Lynda blush.

"Wow, that is something you don't see these days with the younger women, blushing with embarrassment. Have lunch with me today!" he says with a smile.

The passenger on the opposite seat nods his head to Lynda. She looks away and whispers to Neil. "I have too much work today. Maybe another time!" she replies.

Neil accepts her explanation. He talks about his weekend swimming at the beach, asking if she ever swims. Lynda nods her head yes; he keeps the conversation continuing until the bus stops.

He steps off first, then turns to help Lynda step onto the footpath in her narrow high heels. Neil is quiet while they walk towards their building and enter the elevator, not to bring attention to himself or Lynda from nosy employees. Susan pounces on Lynda as soon as she steps out of the elevator, waving to Neil. He ignores her, and she follows Lynda into the tea room, asking about Neil. Lynda avoids Susan's questioning by changing the subject back to work, asking if she has completed her task for the morning. Susan always rushes off as she is never on time handing her reports to Lynda.

Mr. Gardner rings Neil, telling him to avoid Susan at all costs. Neil only laughs, saying he already has his eyes on someone, and she's attractive too. Mr. Gardner realises who, as Neil first enquired about her bus timetable, wanting to see Lynda for himself after hearing Mr. Gardner talking at the family meal.

"I always knew you to be sensible!" Mr. Gardner replies on the phone.

For the next two weeks, Neil decides to keep travelling on the bus to get to know Lynda. She makes him curious, as she never reveals anything about herself. Lynda keeps the conversation on work or answering Neil's questions about how she learned sign language and how long Jason has been mute. Lynda explains Jason has been mute since he was four years old. She learned sign language after Jason's parents learned it. She studied for six months, so by the time it came for him to attend school, Lynda had become a linguist in signing. She explains she sometimes goes to the deaf school to assist the teacher. Neil is fascinated, asking if Jason attended the deaf school. She explains to him his parents did for the first two years, but then wanted him to have a normal school. Jason attends a school that supplies a room for deaf children, but they are able to play with other children at lunch times. Lynda states he handled it quite well, and high school is more of a challenge for him, being alone as his deaf friends attend another school further away. Neil enjoys his bus trip as he normally drives to work, but now finds he is more interested in Lynda each day.

Lynda receives an email, "Meet me at the tea cafe at one p.m. Be worth your while! Neil."

Lynda accepts but is curious, wondering how Neil discovered her favourite tea café. She leaves the office just before everyone else goes off, and walking down the street, she stops in front of a very clean shop window. Lynda checks her outfit and fixes her hair as a breeze messes it a little. She takes a breath and continues passing two more shops. Lynda opens the door to discover Neil is already inside, and he stands on seeing her. He is smiling, which seems captivating to Lynda.

She walks across and sits. "I see you found the café?" Lynda says.

"Yes, rather nice atmosphere!" Neil replies as he pours Lynda's tea for her. "It's been brewing for three minutes," he comments.

Lynda sips her tea, "Lemongrass and ginger, how did you know I like this flavour!" she enquires.

"I gave you one at our meeting in the office yesterday!" Neil replies, thinking does she have a bad memory?

Lynda says, "Yes, of course, I had forgotten, been so busy lately!"

"You're not overworked?" Neil enquires with a changed expression of concern.

"No, just my normal workload. Always too much to do before the end of each week!" Lynda replies, and her phone goes off with a text.

She takes a deep breath and replies, frowning, "Anything wrong?" he asks.

"No, just my secretary forgot to have me sign a document. All good, just done it. Thank goodness for mobiles!" Lynda replies.

Lynda is rather surprised he even bothers to ask. Her last boyfriend was never interested in her work. She is curious about Neil, his different, finding him interesting to talk too and comfortable in his presence. Neil sees her expression wondering Lynda's thoughts.

Neil says, "I hope you don't mind; I ordered the fruit and cheese platter!"

Lynda looks directly into his eyes, saying, "That's fine," she normally orders it on a Thursday. Neil keeps his conversation away from work, preferring to find out more about Lynda. He asks how often she comes to the tea café; he is rather surprised she comes every Thursday and buys her tea here each month. He asks which tea she buys; Lynda gives him a full account of herbal and normal tea.

"I like the white tea; it's the tiny tips of the plant. I like English breakfast too!" she tells him.

Neil is quite impressed with her knowledge of tea and listens while she talks about Indian tea plantations, she visited a few years ago. Neil enquires about her plans for the weekend.

Lynda answers she may go for a run and swim at Palm Beach. "That sounds good. What time will I pick you up!" Neil replies.

Lynda nearly chokes on her tea from his surprising reply, and she's looking directly at him. She is starting to realise this younger man is quite forward. She decides why not, what's the harm in going with him. "Nine thirty a.m. okay?" Lynda replies.

"Perfect. Can I have your address?" Neil asks.

Lynda gives him her address, arranging to meet him

downstairs in the drop-off and pickup area out front of her apartment block. Neil is happy, thinking finally he is getting somewhere, as he is confident but nervous too; he just never shows it. He realises having an older woman is different. She is more settled in her ways, but she takes his breath away every time he sees her. Neil likes the way Lynda is aware of her looks, but never flaunts it. Lynda walks across to the counter, ordering a verity of tea for Neil, choosing flavours her brother likes and she thinks Neil may too. The girl brings over a wooden tray with two tea pots and cups placing down on the table. Lynda pours each tea into each cup for Neil to taste test, she pours hot and cold water over the top. Neil watches her curiously as she passes him one cup first.

"You might prefer this one to try first, a mild tea, the second one strong!" she tells him.

Neil tastes it and nods his head. "Yes, quite nice," he says.

"It takes time to have a taste for tea. I see you're a coffee man!" Lynda comments.

"Can you recommend tea for me to try at home!" Neil enquires as he says he prefers the second cup of tea.

Lynda agrees to find some for him. She asks if he prefers strong or mild flavour. "Maybe strong!" Neil replies after tasting the tea Lynda chose for him to try, having no idea as he drinks coffee all day. She walks across to a shelf, removing a set of four mini boxes of all different flavours of tea.

"Try these. If you don't like one, then it's a matter of trying another one!" Lynda expresses.

Neil thanks her and he reads the ingredients. She comments her brother tried them, preferring a strong taste and rather liked the red box and yellow box, Lynda tells him while pointing and nearly touching Neil's hand. He watches her and listens to her describing the flavour. She advises him on which one to have in the morning and after dinner. Neil is very interested, as he never really took much notice when his stepmother took time to brew her tea. He will in the future.

Neil looks at his watch. He's been away from work for two hours and will have to remain late this evening. He thinks it is worth it, as he finally had Lynda agree to have lunch with him; he's only emailed her for two weeks. Neil asks if she is in a hurry to return to her office, and she replies she won't be going back to the office; she has finished work for the week.

"You have your own hours?" Neil asks.

"Yes, I work from eight a.m. to seven p.m. every day and finish lunchtime Thursday until Monday!" Lynda answers with a smile, saying she can achieve things in her personal life by having the time off.

Neil is impressed; being slightly jealous. He too would like to have a Friday off instead of sometimes working till ten at night.

"Very nice. I shall see you on Saturday morning!" Neil says, standing up from the table and going to pay for lunch on his credit card.

Lynda waits until he's finished paying, and she walks with him; Neil opens the door for her. Lynda is rather impressed by Neil's old-fashioned behaviour, wondering if he is just doing it to impress her. She shakes his hand, thanking him for lunch.

"You're welcome, Lynda!" Neil says. "Goodbye."

Lynda watches him walk off. Neil turns his head back, seeing her looking at him; she quickly about turns. Neil smiles, thinking, well, that's a good start. Back at the office, Neil thanks Patricia for organising the lunch and for the recommendation. "Lynda was impressed!" he says to her. Patricia is very keen to have Lynda find a nice man as she deserves one after her last relationships. Patricia has known Lynda for a long time and is a good friend. She is helping Neil to get to know her friend.

Neil rings his best friend at work. He talks about Lynda and how he likes her intelligence, and her smile is captivating. "I am just compelled to know more about her. Have any suggestions?" Neil asks.

"You've had plenty of dates. Just do what you normally do with the young chicks," says Ben, his friend.

"Well, Lynda is not my usual taste. She's older than me and I want to make her feel special," he tells his friend.

"How much older?" Ben enquires, now curious.

"Forty," Neil replies.

"Wow, what really? I need to see a photo of her. Neil, don't use your usual forceful behaviour!" Ben advises.

"I guess you're right, but she is special. I will take your advice!" Neil answers.

Ben is very keen to meet Lynda. He asks Neil questions, wondering what makes her special. Neil answers, saying more mature and interesting conversations, which draws him in. Ben knows why he broke up with his last girlfriend after six months; she was using Neil to be closer to his family and connections. Ben enquires if Lynda knows who he really is, having money and his father owning several buildings in the city. Neil informs Ben it's too early to tell Lynda about his family. He will keep it for when they develop a relationship.

He hasn't invited her out to dinner. It took him three weeks to have her agree to lunch.

"Maybe she already attended one of your dad's parties because of Mr. Gardner's connections?" Ben says.

"No, I think I will have remembered her!" Neil replies and

says he must get back to work.

"She may have been to one while you were living in Melbourne!" Ben replies, asking when he can meet Lynda. Neil tells him maybe in a few months. Neil rings Mr. Gardner and enquires if Lynda ever attended one of his father's family parties.

"No, Lynda always made excuses not to accept the invite. She dislikes large parties. Want my advice? Treat her differently, she's a nice lady!" Mr. Gardner replies and advises Neil not to rush Lynda as she had a bad breakup a year ago.

Neil listens and will take notice. He hangs up, getting back to work and soon the night lights of the city shine through his large window. Neil looks at his clock on the wall; it's eight p.m. He finishes and leaves the office, not realising Patricia remained late too. "I'm sorry, Patricia, you should have left!"

"I always leave when my boss finishes," Patricia says.

Neil escorts her down into the car park straight to her car, making sure she is safe. He watches as she drives off. Neil is always cautious for the women in the office to be escorted if working late to their cars.

Saturday morning

Neil drives up in his jeep, and he stops on seeing Lynda waiting for him. He jumps out of the car, runs around and opens the door for her. Lynda thinks this guy is for real. She never had anyone open a door for her. "Thank you," she says while climbing inside; she places her bag in the back seat. Neil climbs in and drives off. Lynda asks him how he likes driving the jeep, and she comments on the interior. Lynda is making idle chat while Neil's driving along. He does the same, making comments on other drivers and how nice and hot the day is.

"I hope you brought your swimsuit?" he enquires with a

cheeky grin.

"Yes, I'm wearing it," Lynda replies.

Neil turns his head sideways at her, only seeing her jogging outfit, a little disappointed. He is now excited to see her in a bikini, he hopes. The drive is soon over, stopping at the track. Lynda opens her car door before Neil can reach her, stepping out ready for their jog. She removes her water bottle from her bag, handing one to Neil. He declines, saying he normally jogs for hours without water. Lynda looks at him. "Okay, on your head. It's very hot today!" she comments.

Neil locks the car, and off they go jogging beside each other all the way down the track. Lynda stops, showing Neil a shortcut off the track up to the lighthouse; she races Neil to the top. She stands puffing with Neil just behind her; he looks out at the crystal blue ocean. Yachts sail by and Lynda takes in the views, commenting to Neil how she loves it here.

"Yes, I have a beach cottage." He turns Lynda around, pointing it out amongst the other roofs; this one stands out near the pathway and steps. Neil explaining his grandparents on his father's side left it to him in their will four years ago.

"You're lucky," she says while sipping some water, washing her mouth then swallowing.

She offers some to Neil, and he takes a sip handing it back to her. Neil snaps a photo of her sitting on a rock. He sends it to Ben and keeps it for himself. A small breeze just catches Lynda's pigtail, moving it sideways. Lynda turns her head towards him. "Are you taking photos?" she enquires.

"Yes, the view is amazing. I keep a record of everywhere I go for my social media account!" Neil replies.

"Let me take one of you with the view in the background!" Lynda says while moving towards him across the rock.

Neil hands her his mobile. Facing her, she captures a sailboat just behind him. Lynda takes two for him. He persuades her to stand next to him for a selfie; he will send her a copy of the outing. Lynda is reluctant but succumbs, thinking, why not? Neil stands closer to her, and he takes it quickly.

"Thank you," he shows her the photo being of good quality. He has a top-of-the-range mobile with excellent camera features.

Lynda jumps down off the rock, "I'll race you back, and she jogs off. Come on, slow coach!" she cries.

Neil soon catches up to her, making their way back to the car, jogging beside each other. Lynda stops, and she pulls his arm, pointing under a tree at wallabies. Neil takes a photo while the animal just keeps eating. Lynda tells him the wallabies are often here under the tree. She decides to walk instead of jogging as it's rather hot and she's sweating; they soon arrive back at the car. Neil unlocks the car removing two water bottles from a fridge he had installed. Lynda is very grateful for having cold water, and they rest for a bit enjoying their surroundings. "Climb in," he says while holding the door open. Lynda climbs in and he drives down to the beach.

On stopping the car, Lynda removes her joggers and tight pants, showing her legs. She puts on a long white shirt she always wears over her swimsuit. Lynda wears thongs, and so does Neil and they walk down to the beach. He walks beside her all the way to the beach, dropping his towel onto the sand. Lynda unbuttons her shirt revealing her one-piece swimsuit. Neil smiles, seeing her figure and thinking, not a bikini, but she looks great. He strips down to his swimmers and races her into the water. Neil swims off with Lynda close behind; they seem to be having a contest with each other. Lynda soon catches up to him as she is rather a fast swimmer, and Neil teases her.

A wave drags him under, and he comes up for air laughing. Lynda dives under a wave with Neil, both looking at each other underwater, and then they come up to the surface. She swims off towards the beach with Neil following her; both stand and walk back to their towels. Neil wipes himself down as Lynda uses her own beach towel. She applies more sunscreen and he offers to do her back; she smiles, thinking he is really cheeky.

Lynda puts her shirt on, which disappoints Neil. He applies sunscreen to his own body, and both lie in the sun talking. Soon the beach is beginning to get crowded; Neil puts on his T-shirt and stands, holding his hand out to Lynda, "I have a surprise for you," he tells her.

Lynda takes his hand and, standing, she picks up her bag walking beside him down the beach. He approaches a path and stops to put on his thongs along with Lynda. He escorts her up a narrow path to a set of steps. Standing out is a white cottage and Lynda looks at it, thinking it's nice. Neil admits he arranged for groceries to be delivered; his neighbour has a key and put everything inside for them. On the veranda, Neil removes the spare key as he will keep it now. He opens the door, allowing Lynda to walk inside first.

On opening the fridge, he removes all the ingredients and finds a platter he begins to prepare for them both. Lynda is impressed with his skills, "you cook?" she asks.

"Yes, I find it relaxing, one of my favourite pastimes!" he replies.

Lynda asks for plates and cutlery and follows his directions around the kitchen. She watches how careful he is and she asks him for the bathroom. Neil points, giving instructions she follows, taking her bag in with her. Lynda changes into shorts and a white T-shirt, and she brushes her long hair out, which is still slightly wet. Neil calls to tell her there is a hair dryer in the cupboard. "Thanks," she says. She uses it and comes out feeling refreshed and dry.

Neil has changed into long shorts and T-shirt; he notices her legs are slightly burnt. "I have some after-sun cream if you would like?" he asks.

Lynda looks down and takes the cream, applying it while Neil places the food on the table and takes sidelong looks at her. He has only seen Lynda in work clothes which are totally different from her casual clothes. Lynda expresses how she enjoys having company on her day trip. Neil is glad to hear this and agrees; he talks to her about how he likes to sky dive, asking if she has ever jumped.

"No, I'm scared of heights," she replies.

"That's okay; you can jump hanging onto me," Neil answers. Lynda changes the subject toward Jason and his situation at school. She tells Neil her gadget works on the bullies; the noise hurts their ears. A teacher was alerted to him and came to assist him. Neil warns they could retaliate harder. Lynda is now concerned she may have caused more trouble for Jason, she frowns.

"I will be glad to speak with the guys for Jason!" Neil tells her, looking into her green eyes.

"Thanks. I will tell Jason on Monday. His father spoke with the parents and got nowhere," Lynda says.

"You never drive to work?" Neil enquires.

"No, I never bought a new car when my other car was a lemon. I had to get rid of it to a wrecker, so don't trust car dealers any more!" she replies.

"The Uber must be costing you a bit each night!" Neil comments.

"The company pays for it, all covered! How did you know?" Lynda asks.

Neil lifts his eyebrows, thinking her arrangement is better than his company. "You told me on the bus the other day as I missed seeing you on the evening bus!" he replies.

Neil asks if maybe she can go over his contract and get him a better offer. "Yes, I can view it for you," Lynda replies, quite happy to assist him. She has done it for her employees at her office.

Lynda likes talking to Neil about work, something familiar for her. She's out of touch making idle chatter with a man in Neil's age group. Lynda asks if he plans to renovate the cottage.

"Funny you should ask; I just received the plans back from my architect last week!" Neil moves from the table and walks across to a drawer, removing the drawings.

Lynda moves their plates and dishes from the table while Neil spreads the plans out, explaining them in great detail. "You are modernising the place?" she questions his decision.

"Yes, I thought it was about time. It's over fifty years old and has never been updated. Why? Don't you like my ideas?" he questions her.

"No, just you don't want to lose the character of the home and especially as it's been part of your family for so long!" Lynda replies.

She points out some changes using her finger on the plans. Neil listens and rather likes some of her ideas. He is adamant about completely converting the upstairs, liking modern for the master suite and bedrooms. He points out his study at the back of the house, a new addition with a small hallway and doors opening out to a veranda. Lynda likes that idea of being completely separate from the house and shutting it away when finished.

Lynda agrees with the changes upstairs. "Keep the sunroom and kitchen where it is just modernised!" she says, looking up at him.

Neil makes notes on his mobile and will think about her suggestions. He rather likes having a woman's point of view on his cottage. Neil explains he will stay as often as he can and allow family and friends to use it when he's not here. Lynda moves out to the sunroom, and looking out across the ocean, she expresses he should stay every weekend, especially in summer.

Neil stands beside her. "Yes, it's beautiful," he says, looking at her sideways.

Lynda is unaware he's commenting on her and not the view. She turns to him, smiling and agreeing with him. "Want a cup of tea? We can try one you chose for me?" he asks.

Lynda accepts, saying the milder tea with rose petals. Neil makes the tea while Lynda wanders across to his CD collection, noticing some of the artists are older. "I would not have guessed you're a Michael Bolton fan?" she asks.

"No, my mum left them here on her last visit!" he comments but says he rather likes the romantic songs, showing her his collection. More hard rock artists and modern singers. "I will update all the electrics and sound equipment in the renovations!" he expresses.

Lynda asks if she can put on a CD she likes, and he says, "Of course." She puts on the Ten Tenors and tells Neil she loves their music. He hands her a mug of tea and sits opposite her in a chair, sinking. Lynda can't stop laughing, the first time Neil has heard her laugh. He laughs, too, while trying to get out without success. Lynda walks across, giving him her hand. She pulls while he digs his feet in. Neil leans towards her on standing; then he manages to balance, straightening, then smiling, and sits down on the couch beside Lynda.

"New furniture, I think!" he says.

Lynda can't help giggling, "Sorry, it was so funny seeing you sink in the chair!"

Neil is counting this outing as a date, even if Lynda is not. He sips his tea, asking her for suggestions on a colour scheme for the house.

Lynda has many ideas and expresses them to him. She leans toward blue and yellow cushions, curtains or ornaments, and white walls. Neil is fascinated listening to her suggestions; he rather likes her ideas. He especially likes her design for the master bedroom, not too feminine but elegant beach designs. Neil and Lynda enjoy the afternoon together, discussing many topics on the cottage. Lynda feels comfortable in his presence, liking discussing decorating; different from work, she comments to him. Neil explains once he leaves the office, he clears his mind and never takes calls on his weekend or days off.

Neil likes to escape work, preferring to give the person he's with his full attention. Lynda is impressed with Neil's control. Not many men do this; instead, they take all their daily troubles home. She also prefers leaving work at work and concentrating on other topics, and giving her attention to someone. Lynda explains she uses a different mobile on her days off, so work is unable to reach her as they call too often in the evenings, aware she works until seven or eight at night. Neil enquires for her number, and she gives it to him, thinking, 'why not?' She has enjoyed her day with him. And maybe there is more to Neil than she first thought.

"You're not worried about leaving the office late and waiting for your Uber?" he enquires as he always looks after the women in his office, having a man escort them to their cars in the basement car park.

"No, I have Fred, the security guard. He always comes up to my office and escorts me downstairs, waiting until my car arrives. He has done this for the last year, since my new contract!" Lynda replies.

"Oh, that's good to hear. Must protect you, women!" Neil comments, surprised to hear she's only had her new contract for a year.

"Can I ask why you changed your hours?" he asks.

"Yeah, I live alone now and filling in the evenings with work helps the loneliness, and besides, I like to volunteer at the deaf school once a fortnight on a Friday. The other times I go shopping or rock climbing!" she expresses.

"You're scared of heights, you said?" Neil replies.

"Yes, I use the indoor walls, never look down and never a mountain!" Lynda replies.

Neil understands. He says he loves to go mountain climbing and knows of a place not far from here with a smaller climb. "Maybe come with me. I can help you make it up!" he suggests.

"I could try, maybe give it a go one day!" Lynda replies, allowing him closer to her. She has known Neil now for a month on the bus and at work as he sends her regular emails and texts.

Chapter Two

The Bus Rides

Neil catches the bus as usual, except today there is a difference – Lynda is absent. Jason is sitting by himself, and he is curious why. Maybe she is avoiding him? No, they had a good day together. Neil texts her, receiving an instant reply. *Lynda: I have broken my ankle.*

He can't believe it. When could it have happened? They were together on Saturday and she was all right when he left her outside her apartment. He texts her.

Neil: "When did this happen?"

Lynda: "Saturday night, I tripped over a skateboard a kid left in the foyer of my apartment. I was carrying groceries and didn't see the board!"

Neil: "Is there anything I can do for you!"

Lynda: "I'll be okay, just can't catch the bus. I'm on crutches using an Uber to get to work!"

Neil: "You at work?" rather surprised she didn't take the day off.

Lynda, "I spent two nights in hospital; that was long enough. I have work that must be completed by the end of the week!"

Neil says he will email her later at work. The bus moves along quickly and he soon arrives at his office building. Neil stops at the ground floor florist, places an order and then proceeds upstairs to his office. He speaks with Patricia about Lynda's accident, aware they are friends. She thanks him and rings her friend straight away. A girl arrives on the second floor and she walks out of the lift. Jennifer is amused as all she can see are legs. The girl stops, asking for Lynda. Jennifer escorts the florist across the floor, down a passageway passing desks and voices chattering. "Who are they for?" Susan asks, dying to know.

Jennifer doesn't answer; she keeps walking toward Lynda's office and she opens the door for the girl. "Flowers for you, Lynda," Jennifer says, showing the girl inside.

Lynda instructs her to put them on the end of her large desk. The florist is happy to as the vase is rather heavy, being solid glass.

The girl states twenty-four yellow roses, and the vase is hers to keep. She hands her a small envelope with a note inside; the girl says, "enjoy." She hasn't had a large order for a week and is happy to deliver this order, being only upstairs from her shop.

Lynda reads the note. "For a special lady." No name. She places the card into her desk drawer. Lynda receives a text message, *"Did the roses arrive? Neil."*

"Yes, thank you, my favourite flower and colour!" Lynda replies, wondering how he knew.

Patricia is assisting Neil, knowing her friend's likes and tastes. Neil has been told by his boss of Patricia's loyalty and can be trusted with private matters. She wants Lynda to be happy with someone and is rather enjoying helping Neil to pursue Lynda. Patricia, undeterred by his age, believes he may just be the right man for Lynda.

In Lynda's office, Mr. Gardner has provided a special chair for her with a footstool so she can elevate her leg. He also provided her with a moving table to sit comfortably while on her computer. Susan is curious, and she enters Lynda's office on the pretence she is making an enquiry about an email. Lynda is aware of her motives as she is pretending to smell her flowers, obviously looking for a card.

"You have an admirer?" Susan enquires.

"The flowers are from my family!" Lynda replies, telling a white lie to avoid awkward conversations with nosy colleagues.

Susan straightens, a little disappointed. Lynda explains her email. "Anything else, Susan?" she asks.

"You must have had a good weekend; you are sunburnt. Is that how you broke your ankle?" Susan asks, looking straight at Lynda who is looking down at her computer screen.

"No, I tripped over a skateboard in my apartment foyer!" Lynda replies, at the same time dismissing Susan. She has an important email to attend to. Susan smiles and leaves the office, closing the door behind her, not wanting to upset her immediate boss. Lynda is glad she made her leave; she is busy reading an email from Neil saying he will take her home tonight.

At six thirty p.m. Neil arrives at Lynda's office, and on entering he is smiling to her, "I'm here to escort you home!" Neil states while lowering her cast onto the floor and picking up her bag.

Lynda laughs. "That bag doesn't suit you!"

Neil looks down and he too laughs, "Come on, lovely lady, let's get you home in one piece!" He is aware the office is empty at this time, and he takes Lynda's arm to support her to stand. Neil moves the crutches towards her, and she manages to balance, still clumsy with them. Neil opens her office door, and Lynda manages to squeeze out this time without hitting her crutches on the doorway. She slowly makes her way down a narrow passage that had been made for her. Mr. Gardner moved everyone's desk to the centre of the room for Lynda. She is very important to the company and they have allowed special conditions for her injury. Neil is impressed by her skills at the lift; he presses the button and helps her inside. Lynda notices he presses B2 lower basement to the employee's car park.

"Did you bring your car?" Lynda enquires.

"I sent a young lawyer home to fetch my car for me. He drove it back here, somewhere; I'll have to find it!" Neil replies.

The lift doors open and he holds them, allowing Lynda time to exit. He walks off in a rough direction given to him by the young assistant to fetch his car. He uses his key and keeps beeping and pointing in both directions. His jeep should stand out, being red and large. Neil sees the lights blinking; he jumps in and drives to the lift seeing Lynda talking to the security guard on duty. Neil parks and the guard opens the door for her. Assisting her into the seat, he places the crutches in the back.

"Thanks, mate!" Neil says, waving. The guard waves back, saying goodnight.

Neil drives off, asking all about the kid leaving his skateboard. Lynda explains the boy always leaves his skateboard in the apartment's hallways. "I will just have to watch out for it next time!"

Neil tells her he has arranged his times to coincide with hers. "Why?" Lynda asks

"You need assistance and I want to help!" Neil replies while concentrating on a driver running a red light. He brakes just in time and swears. Lynda looks his way and she blurts out, "Bloody fool!"

Neil laughs, "precisely," he says.

"I'm very grateful for you driving me home. Just worried about Jason, he's never travelled the bus alone until today. He video-called me at lunch and disliked being alone!" Lynda tells

Neil.

"I will pick him and you up in the morning!" Neil replies.

"You'd do that?" Lynda asks, surprised by his generosity, something that had been lacking in her life.

"Of course, friends help friends. You are my friend, Lynda, aren't you?"

"Yes," Lynda answers, liking the sound of that.

Lynda tells him she will arrange everything with Jason's parents tonight. Neil escorts Lynda to her apartment, sits her down in her lounge chair and moves a footstool under her cast. He rather likes her scandi-style apartment; the first time being inside. Neil places her bag down. He walks into the kitchen, and on opening the fridge he sees only fruit and yoghurt. He moves to the cups, same thing, a few spices, tea and coffee. He notices a stack of chocolate bars and he laughs, "I thought you went shopping?" he states.

"I dropped everything when I fell over. Mr. Jones threw it all in the bin!" Lynda replies.

"I'll go shopping for you tomorrow just give me a list of groceries!" Neil says.

"You don't have to do that. I'll get takeout during the week!" Lynda says.

"What will you like to order?" Neil asks,

Lynda decides on Chinese tonight and Neil orders enough for them both, telling Lynda he'd like to eat with her. She's happy to have company, and she tells him if it's okay with him, she'll go and have a shower.

"Just nice to know you're here in case I fall over!" Lynda states.

"No worries. Want some help undressing?" he says with a grin.

She smiles at him, hopping on her crutches across to her bedroom and carrying clothes to the bathroom. Neil places two plates on the table; he hears a knock at the door and opens it taking the order. Lynda comes out in her night dress and dressing gown. "Hope you don't mind? Easier to dress for bed than change twice; still getting used to the cast. Unfortunately have to wear dresses instead of suits!"

"Good!" says Neil. Lynda looks at him, asking what he's referring to. Neil explains her dresses are nicer than her plain suits.

He finds a marker and he writes on her cast, "Dinner for two in eight weeks," with a smiley face.

Lynda chuckles as she turns half her body to the table to eat. She is rather hungry, stating she forgot to have Jennifer order her lunch. Neil says he will send Jennifer an email to make sure Lynda eats.

"I'll sort it!" she says.

Lynda points over to her side cupboard. "I have wine glasses on the top shelf and wine on the bench!" she instructs Neil.

Neil removes two glasses and walks across, pouring wine for them both; he sits, handing a glass to Lynda, asking if she's in pain.. A little, she tells him; he asks if she wants painkillers. Lynda declines, not wanting to mix them with wine. He notices she's looking tired and he removes the leftover food into the fridge then washes up, asking Lynda if there is anything else he can do for her. "Need to be tucked into bed?" he asks.

"No, cheeky. I can manage!" she says while grinning and looking up at him.

"Now rest. See you at seven in the morning!" Neil says, closing the door behind him.

Neil feels this gives him a chance to develop a real

relationship with Lynda in the next eight weeks. A new twist instead of having sex straight away, then try to have a relationship. Neil really wants this to work between him and Lynda. A friendship first, then love, he hopes. Neil drives home, rearranging his office hours with his boss and asking for a temporary parking space next to the lift. Neil explains the reason and the boss agrees, he too wants to assist Lynda in her condition. She is respected by the firm, and the boss is fascinated by why Neil has taken it upon himself to make her life easy. Neil refuses to explain his reasons. The boss accepts and talks about work, then hangs up.

In the morning Neil picks Lynda up at her apartment door, making sure the skateboard is nowhere to be seen. Neil packs her into his jeep sitting in the back seat so she can sign with Jason. Lynda tells Neil Jason's address to lock into his street map on his phone. He locks his phone into the holder and drives off. Lynda talks with him as he drives. On arriving at the home, Lynda's friend walks out to thank Neil personally for picking up her son. She speaks with Lynda, checking how's she feeling. Lynda comments her ankle is a little sore.

"Take care, I'll ring later!" she says with a smile, now actually meeting Neil.

Neil drives off on overhearing from the front seat. "You should report this to your doctor!" he states, a little concerned.

"I have a phone video visit with my doctor at lunchtime!" Lynda tells Neil.

Lynda signs with Jason. He needs her help with maths and asks can she video call him tonight. Lynda talks out loud to include Neil in the conversation; he appreciates her efforts. Neil gives his import having some solutions in handling bullies; he has a few tricks. Lynda signs talking to Jason, and he explains the boys are leaving him alone at the moment. Lynda is talking out loud what Jason is saying to her to include Neil. He appreciates her efforts. Jason signs they have another victim. Neil nods his head to Lynda and she smiles, thanking him for his suggestions last week as he's been helping Jason handle the bullies. The jeep stops outside the school, and the boys that normally tease Jason watch. Neil gets out to show how tall he is and stares straight at the boys.

"Have a good day, Jason!" Neil lets the boys know Jason is a friend. He nods his response as Jason can hear, just unable to speak. He walks off through the gates.

Lynda knows what Neil is up to, "That was nice of you!" she says as he drives off.

"That's what friends are for!" he replies.

Lynda remains in the back seat, being more comfortable moving her leg sideways. She enquires about Neil's plans for the weekend. He replies, saying he made special arrangements for Friday lunch.

"To spend the day with you!" he states.

She rather likes his forwardness, assuming she will agree to the idea. Lynda asks where he is planning on taking her. Neil keeps it to himself, saying she will find out on Friday. He parks next to the lifts and Lynda asks how he arranged this spot normally kept for his boss.

"I have my ways!" he says, helping her into the lift; it doesn't matter if anyone from either office sees them together. Neil and Lynda ride the same bus, and colleagues are used to seeing them in the lift at the same time every morning.

Jennifer waits to help Lynda with her bag. She thanks Neil, knowing he is driving and picking Lynda up each morning.

Patricia and Jennifer are aware of the arrangements and enjoying being secretive. Jennifer escorts Lynda to her office as she's rather clumsy on the crutches. She informs Lynda of her schedule for the day, and she has booked a taxi for her hospital visit. Lynda forgot to tell Jennifer she was video calling her doctor this time, that he said there was no need to go to the hospital.

Jennifer says she will cancel the taxi, then she places Lynda's handbag into the cupboard and pours her tea.

"Thanks, Jen," Lynda says, grateful to have a brilliant secretary but also a friend.

Neil arrives at his office. Patricia asks how Lynda is this morning and he informs her. She hands him his new re-arranged client list for the next few weeks, adjusting his diary on his computer, she reports. Neil thanks her and she informs him his boss is already waiting in the boardroom. Neil looks at his watch; Patricia comments, "He wants to discuss a matter with you first."

Neil thanks her, walking briskly and reading at the same time to meet with his boss to discuss their clients' business. Neil enters the room seeing his boss sipping coffee, which is unusual before a meeting. The boss says he needs Lynda's advice on a report he has received from their client. He asks Neil to take everything down to her to discuss the situation with her.

"Something wrong with the report, and she signed off on it. I need an explanation or get Lynda to fix it by four p.m. this afternoon!" the boss states urgently for Neil to visit now with her.

Neil frowns because Lynda checks everything before she hands any report to any firm. Neil texts Lynda he is coming to see her, and it's urgent. He takes the folder and immediately travels down the lift to her floor and firm. Jennifer tells him to go straight in and Neil opens the glass doors entering the main office. Susan sees Neil. She quickly jumps up to escort him to Lynda's office. Susan tries all her usual tricks with flirting, which Neil ignores. He is not impressed, having seen this all before with other young women.

Susan sees Mr. Gardner and she quickly moves back to her desk. He meets Neil, asking about the urgency. Both men enter Lynda's office. All of her meetings are being held in her office now to avoid damaging her ankle. Mr. Gardner pulls up a chair to discuss the matter; Lynda reads the report, handing it across to Mr. Gardner. She checks the folder on her computer and read the entire thirty pages; sometime later she sees the problem.

"I see it!" Lynda admits her mistake and tells Neil she will have it fixed by two p.m. this afternoon.

"No, make it four p.m. You have your doctor's appointment!" Neil comments. Lynda has forgotten for a minute; she nods her head.

Mr. Gardner is pleased with Lynda's discovery of the matter; he always tries to keep their important clients happy. The law firm is the largest amongst many other companies they handle. He whispers to Neil, "I hope you're not distracting my right-hand person!" referring to Lynda.

Neil smiles, shaking his hand. When the boss leaves, Neil says, "Until tonight, winking at Lynda."

She smiles, saying, "Go, I need to work!" she enjoyed last Saturday with Neil and is deciding to ignore his age for now.

Lynda is advised by the doctor to keep an eye on her pain levels, and if she is still having problems, he will arrange for her to attend the hospital. Lynda's pain increases and she makes arrangements to visit the hospital. She texts Neil asking if, after he drops Jason off in the morning, can he take her to the hospital? He replies, "No worries."

At the hospital, Neil waits for Lynda in the waiting room while she has a new cast set. He keeps himself busy checking his emails and working. Inside, the nurse asks Lynda if she wants to keep the message on her cast. Lynda replies she has the date on her mobile with an alert; she had forgotten about Neil's message.

She wobbles out on her crutches and Neil takes her to the office. He helps her out of the lift, and Jennifer is already waiting to assist; he hands her Lynda's bag. Jennifer thanks Neil for taking Lynda as she has a lot of work to finish. Neil says, "No worries."

In the evening, Neil helps Lynda inside and this time he cooks dinner after ordering food on the app for delivery the night before. Neil notices his message has gone, so he quickly puts another smiley face on her cast.

"I have our date written down. Best not to re-write it as I have nosy colleagues!" Lynda says while smiling.

Neil understands and resists writing a verse and date, or anything else. He leans over and kisses her, then makes spaghetti with avocado and cheese. Lynda is impressed with how he can come up with quick and nice meals.

"You'll have to show me how to cook; I have been enjoying your meals. Taste better than takeout!" Lynda comments, enjoying her meal.

Neil says when her leg is healed, he will show her how to cook. Lynda asks if he will stay while she showers. She told him she nearly slipped last night after he left. Neil quickly moves into the bathroom. He places two floor rugs in front of the glass screen and a shower chair Lynda ordered. She thanks him and he leaves, allowing her to shower; she is finding it easier with the chair. She moves out in her nightie, and Neil thinks when they move further along with a relationship, he will buy her sexier nightwear. He kisses her goodnight, saying, "See you tomorrow." Being Friday.

In the morning, Neil's plans include a wheelchair for Lynda. He is arriving at ten to give her time to dress. On arriving at her apartment, he notices she's wearing a long feminine dress covering her cast. Neil approves; he admires her figure as it's a fitted dress. He helps her to his jeep. Neil asks how she is coping with her leg at work, and she comments that it is sometimes awkward not having face-to-face meetings. She is finding getting in and out of bed hard and can't turn like she normally does. Neil offers to stay over to assist – with a cheeky grin. Lynda doesn't answer and notes his expression; she admires the view changing the subject. Neil seems to be taking her somewhere new. He has a special luncheon at an exclusive restaurant on a river. He arranged for them to have the entire place to themselves.

The owner is Ben, his best friend, and he's been nagging Neil to meet Lynda after seeing the photo of her. Once Ben knew of Neil's arrangement, now six weeks away, he offered his restaurant for an exclusive luncheon. Neil accepts his friend's offer to make all the plans thinking it is a good idea, but why wait? Neil pulls up close to the boardwalk, and Lynda mentions she will have difficulties with her crutches. Neil jumps out of his jeep, moving quickly to the back and removing a small wheelchair. Neil opens the passenger door and helps her out into the chair.

"You really thought this through!" Lynda says.

Inside is a table set with white linen in front of a huge window. Neil helps Lynda on to a chair, moving the wheelchair to one side.

"Have you visited here before?" Neil asks.

"No, never knew it was here. How did you find this restaurant?" Lynda asks.

Neil explains the owner is a friend, and the chef comes out to introduce himself, eager to meet her. "Hello, you must be Lynda; I've heard so much about you. I'm Ben, Neil's best mate!"

Lynda looks toward Neil as she hasn't told him about any of her friends except for Jennifer and Patricia. She's keeping all information relating to family out of her conversations with him. Ben gives her his speciality of choices. Lynda likes them all, and she decides to try his seafood platter for two.

"Is that okay for you, Neil?" she asks; he accepts her choice. Ben mentions he has changed it with two special sauces. Lynda tells him she is allergic to eggs and milk; Ben assures her they are herbal and fruit sauces he made specially. Neil already explained this to his friend as he took mental notes during their conversations the past weeks at dinner. Neil tells her how his father sails his boat down these waterways once a month. He has been away for years and Ben informed him of his new restaurant.

"I thought you might like some privacy due to your leg!" Neil comments.

"Thank you for being considerate!" she replies. Neil looks at her, admitting Ben offered making all the arrangements.

"Still nice," she says smiling, while looking out of the large window.

Lynda tells Neil her father used to have a yacht and how, as a teenager, she and her siblings would sail from Manly to Sydney Harbour every Sunday. She talks about how much she used to love the breeze against her cheeks and hair, her brothers diving into the water and always in trouble. Her father would panic due to sharks, and they soon stopped the trips – her father refusing to take them out. She speaks in a casual manner. Neil is listening to the stories; this is the first time Lynda has mentioned her family. He is fascinated as she explains her father used to sail in races.

"Dad sailed in the Sydney to Hobart race, finding it hair-razing but loved every minute of the trip!" she speaks with fond memories.

Lynda explains she was only twenty then; he has sold his yacht and now plays golf instead. Neil expresses he must miss sailing; she admits she thinks her father does but never complains. Ben brings out a large platter; a huge crab sits in the centre surrounded by oysters, prawns, fresh mussels and crumbed fish pieces. He sets down a bowl of salad along with the dressings keeping them in separate dishes for Lynda and Neil.

"Enjoy with my compliments!" Ben says, winking to Neil, who thanks his friend. Lynda states it looks too lovely to eat.

"Please do. I would like your import on my new flavour for my crab!" Ben replies. He opens a bottle of wine, pouring a glass for them both, a special white wine he chose for his seafood.

Lynda takes a small sip saying it is an excellent choice. "I like her," Ben says and walks off back to his kitchen to prepare dessert.

Neil serves the crab for Lynda; small pieces with the selection of seafood she wants to try first. She tastes the crab commenting it's the best she has ever had; Neil is very pleased as his friend designed the luncheon specially for them both. Lynda eats and sips wine talking to Neil about her family. The relaxed atmosphere makes her feel comfortable with Neil. He listens, desiring to know more about her family as she is revealing things about herself too. She is normally very private on the subject of family. Neil asks if she always wanted to be an executive accountant.

"No, I wanted to be a fashion designer!" Lynda looks up at

him with a disappointed tone in her voice.

"What happened, if you don't mind me asking?" Neil asks while looking into her green eyes.

"My parents didn't think I would be able to support myself or pay them back for the courses. You see, I have a sick brother and, at the time, having issues with his health. Medicine being expensive and hospital visits!" Lynda explains, looking directly at Neil.

"Is he all right now!" Neil enquires.

"He has a lifetime health problem and sometimes refuses to take his medicine, causing seizures!" Lynda explains.

Neil places his hand on hers, apologising for bringing the subject up. Lynda is okay with it, and she turns her hand around to hold Neil's hand. He is rather pleased with the movement of affection towards him; Ben walks towards the table. Lynda quickly removes her hand before Ben notices but too late, he does. He asks how she is finding the food. Lynda expresses how marvellous the crab is, never tasting anything better. Ben is very happy; he sits and chats with her asking which sauce she prefers. Lynda comments she likes the lime and mango, "unusual flavour."

"Good, I will use that one on the weekend. I made it specially for you when Neil explained your allergies. I added a secret spice I make for my deli!" he tells her, also asking if she likes the prawns.

Lynda says yes, another surprise, especially with the wine he chose. Ben explains he soaked the prawns in wine and sweet chilli, trying new ideas on her. "Neil informs me you eat out a lot, so I thought to make your luncheon a special treat."

"I am very flattered; your restaurant is lovely. I like the ambiance, and the large windows out across the river are wonderful!" Lynda tells Ben.

He is very grateful for her input; he turns to Neil, asking for him to choose a wine for dessert. Neil excuses himself and walks across with Ben, picking a red wine.

"I like her. You're right, a very interesting woman; she has a lovely smile. Keep her friend!" he touches Neil's shoulder handing him two new glasses for the wine.

Neil is very glad to have his friend's approval even though he has already decided he wants Lynda to become a part of his life. Neil's feelings have increased for her over the past weeks, seeing her every day driving her to work and home again. The conversations they have and her love of books and music, he enjoys listening to and rather likes a few of her love songs. Neil sits again, pouring red wine into their glasses. Lynda mentions how beautiful the view is. Neil agrees while looking at her; he loves her long brown hair.

Neil talks about his family and his younger sister of eleven years. Lynda is surprised at the age difference. Neil sees her expression and then explains she is the daughter of his father's second wife. He tells Lynda he lost his mother quite young due to cancer, and Lynda gives her sympathy. Neil says he only has distant memories of his mother and tells how he loves his little sister; admitting he has spoilt her. Lynda listens to every word, enjoying getting to know a man before intimacy; she suspects this is why her last relationship failed. She is looking for more this time, a friend and real partner, a lover. She finds him refreshing, being younger and so energised and full of life.

Lynda invites Neil to come around on Sunday for a meal if he wants and play some backgammon. Neil accepts straight away so she can't change her mind; she smiles at his being so quick to say yes. Neil is, however, curious about how she is planning on making dinner on her crutches. Ben comes out with dessert, which happens to be Lynda's favourite – pineapple and lime sorbet with chocolate mint leaves surrounded by lychee fruits. The flavour tingles her taste buds, and the red wine is perfect. Lynda invites Ben to join them instead of being alone in the kitchen. He is happy to sit with them and pulls up a chair; he pours himself some wine.

"This happens to be my favourite dessert!" Lynda comments.

Ben winks at Neil because his friend had asked Jason's mother what Lynda's favourite sweet was. She has been helping Neil too, everyone conspiring behind Lynda's back as they all want to see her happy and with a man that appreciates her. Lynda enjoys interacting with Neil's friend; she asks him how long they have been friends.

Ben laughs, "Since year five."

Lynda lifts her eyebrows and thinks this a long time; she hasn't kept in touch with any of her friends since school. Lynda enquires how long he has operated the restaurant, and Ben informs her ten months; still new. He explains he only opens Thursday to Sunday nights; he owns a deli shop, too, making preserves and sauces for that business.

"Your wife must not see you very often?" Lynda states on seeing his wedding ring.

Ben has forgotten he's still wearing it. Neil quickly speaks for his friend, saying she left him a year ago.

Ben says, "It's okay. Our divorce is finalised next week; I suppose I can take this off!" he fiddles with his ring. His wife ran off with a lawyer from Neil's previous office in Victoria.

"You must make everything count when you do find the right person!" Ben says, smiling at Lynda.

Ben removes the dishes, and Neil thanks his friend for a great lunch. Lynda thanks Ben very much for an excellent meal. And if he likes, she can recommend his restaurant to business associates. Ben thanks her, but for now he is quite happy with his bookings as they have booked months ahead. Neil and Lynda sit for a while; she asks for the bathroom and Neil shows her. He walks her over and then enters the kitchen. Seeing Ben cleaning his kitchen he asks, "Did you eat?"

"I'm used to eating after guests," Ben says.

"Bring a plate out and talk with us!" says Neil. Ben thanks his friend but declines saying he has orders he must do, and pack jars for his deli.

"Need any help?" Neil asks.

"Yes, matter of fact, you can start over there!" Ben replies.

Neil turns around, seeing many boxes and a table full of preserves; he walks out of the kitchen to check on Lynda. He tells her Ben needs help with packing boxes, "Of course, we can help!" she says, moving on her crutches towards the kitchen. Neil holds the door open for her. Ben moves a high stool across, just the right height. Ben asks can she wipe the jars and hand them to Neil? Lynda is happy to help and always wanted to sit in a restaurant kitchen. They talk while working. She asks about Neil as a boy and Ben is happy to tell her all about their boyhood and things they got up to. Neil quickly packs the boxes laughing in between with his friend and Lynda. On sealing the last box, Neil says it is time to leave.

Lynda shakes Ben's hand, saying, "Until next time." Ben slaps Neil on the shoulder, nodding. Neil helps Lynda back in the wheelchair to the jeep, and he drives her safely back to her apartment and says goodbye, it now being five in the afternoon. Lynda stands up, balancing herself next to her kitchen bench. She asks Neil to come closer.

He moves in front of her, and she asks him to lean down and gives him a quick kiss on the lips. He places his hand on her cheek and gives her a kiss which she enjoys; she thanks him for a lovely lunch. Neil smiles, asking if she wants him to pick up anything for Sunday dinner.

"No, I have it all sorted!" Lynda replies, keeping her secret. Neil says goodbye.

Neil is not stopping tonight as Lynda's sister is coming over with pizza, being their lady's night in once a month to watch movies. Julia arrives with homemade pizza from her pizza oven with their favourite toppings, garlic bread and a bottle of wine. Lynda chooses a movie on BigPond for the evening. Julia places everything on the coffee table for easy access for her sister. Lynda sits with cushions under her cast, and she plays the movie. Julia is eating a slice of pizza when Lynda blurts out about Neil.

"What? You seeing someone? Tell me all about him!" Julia asks, putting her pizza down. She puts her leg up on the couch, turning towards her sister, eager to know more.

Lynda explains how she met him and travelling on the bus together for weeks. She explains that since she broke her ankle, he's been picking her and Jason up and stays every second night, having dinner with her.

"A great backgammon player, Neil always makes leftovers so I can reheat in the microwave. He is always considerate!" Lynda says.

Julia is very interested in meeting him. She asks what he looks like. "Very tall, dark hair and blue hazel-green eyes with strong looks!" Lynda replies with a smile.

Julia notices her sister when talking about him. Her eyes sparkle, something she has never seen with a man. Lynda opens her mobile, showing her sister a photo of Neil. She admits sneaking it when he was cooking.

"He's gorgeous," Julia comments; saying if she were single, she would go after him. Lynda laughs, aware how much her sister loves John, her husband.

"Well, I wonder if we would have liked that movie!" Julia states as it came to the credits.

"Never mind, I rather enjoyed finally telling you about Neil. I like him!" Lynda lifts herself up on the couch, looking at Julia.

"How old is he?" Julia's eyes open wide after seeing his photo.

"Just turned thirty!" Lynda replies.

"Really, Sis, good for you. You might have better luck with a younger man; and more fun. I bet he's great at sex!" Julia smiles while talking, thinking he looks very sexy.

"Julia!" Lynda says, looking surprised at her sister.

"Don't tell me you haven't thought of it?" Julia replies, moving her leg and sipping some wine.

Lynda replies she did have a good look at his bare chest and legs when they went swimming.

Julia laughs, "He must look good in his trunks, otherwise you wouldn't be blushing." "Nice muscles, too," Lynda tells Julia; they both laugh while having tea.

Julia helps Lynda off to bed now, being one in the morning after talking about Neil. Julia sleeps in the spare room and always stays over so she can enjoy drinking with her sister and a night away from being a mum.

The women wake up at nine the next morning. Lynda wobbles out, seeing Julia already making breakfast. She sits on her dining chair.

"By the way, you have four texts from someone called Neil!" Julia says while grinning.

"Funny, Sis," Lynda says. Taking her phone, she reads the texts, his asking how her night went. She texts Neil back that she only just got up.

Neil: must have been a good night. Did you talk about me?

Lynda: No. Not wanting him to know she did. She smiles as she texts, asking what he is doing today.

Neil: I'm going mountain climbing up in the Blue Mountains.

Lynda: have fun, don't fall

Neil, I won't. See you tomorrow night.

"He's keen," Julia says, eating her toast.

"Yes, he's not shy. A very confident man and, I think, eager for us to be closer. I just want to go slower this time, making sure we are compatible!" Lynda answers, putting jam on her toast and sipping coffee – she always has one after a late night drinking.

Julia showers and dresses, helping her sister; then John picks her up with Zoe, her daughter. The little girl gives aunty Lynda a picture she has drawn of her leg in a cast.

"That is lovely, Zoe!" Lynda says, giving her a cuddle.

Zoe is happy. John asks if they enjoyed the movie, and Lynda looks at her sister but too late. "She has a boyfriend!" Julia blurts.

"No, Sis, not yet. Just getting to know him!" Lynda replies.

John wants to know more, and Julia encourages Lynda to show him the photo. John likes the look of him saying he's younger. Julia says, "Yes, Simon's age, great isn't it," Julia says excitedly, holding her husband's arm.

"Julia and John, don't tell Mum and Dad; I will introduce him when I'm sure we are going to be in a relationship!" Lynda tells them with a serious expression.

John and Julia agree, aware how their mother feels about Lynda not getting married two years ago. Both say her secret is safe with them. Zoe is out on the balcony, never hearing the adults. Lynda sighs, thinking she won't let anything slip. Julia calls Zoe; they're leaving as they have shopping to do. John winks at Lynda smiling, happy she has someone in her life.

Sunday morning

Lynda's friend Brittany is making lasagne and chocolate brownies for Lynda's Sunday evening. Brittany offered due to Neil picking up her son Jason every morning and taking such good care of Lynda. She arrives around four in the afternoon giving Lynda instructions to cook the dish for fifty minutes. And heat the brownies in the microwave to melt the icing and serve with ice cream. Lynda listens and thanks her friend, who is a very good cook. Brittany sets the table with Lynda's best placemats and wine glasses; she places three large candles along the centre. Lynda is very grateful to her friend for cooking the meal and now setting the scene. Brittany lights the candles to help them settle; she helps Lynda zip up her dress – a tighter fit.

"Good choice. Have a very good evening," Brittany says while leaving; smiling. Happy Lynda is finally getting out there again.

Thirty minutes later, Neil texts he's coming up in the lift. She texts him the keypad code as she changes it each week. Neil enters carrying a large bunch of yellow roses. He hands them to her, giving her a kiss and finding her lips warm. He asks where her vases are; Lynda points towards the hall cupboard and on opening the door, he finds two vases. Neil removes the largest and fills it with water; he places the vase at the end of the dining table. Lynda hops across, placing the roses in the vase.

"They're lovely!" she says, smelling one.

Lynda asks him if he can turn the oven knob on. She tells him the dish is already in.

"How did you manage to prepare the dinner?" he asks while pouring the wine.

Lynda admits Brittany made the meal for them. She wriggles in her seat, feeling a little guilty about not being able to cook. She admits that it is a little difficult.

Neil grins, already knowing she has trouble balancing still without her crutches. "It's the thought that counts," he says, looking at her.

Lynda sits up straight, moving her leg back, wanting to be able to face Neil instead of slouching. Neil sits beside her on the couch and enquiring what activities she would like to do when her mobility comes back

She mentions she will like to go for walks and swim before summer ends, placing her hand on his. Neil is pleasantly surprising typing it on his mobile, saying that would be easy. She smiles at him, "Just keeping notes." Neil says, switching his mobile off and placing it on the coffee table. Lynda quickly tells him she will organise their first outing in appreciation of him helping her. Neil sits back against the couch, placing his arm around her shoulder. He notices Lynda is comfortable sitting close to him.

"I've enjoyed driving you, and our evenings together. I feel we understand each other!" Neil exclaims, picking her hand up and kissing it affectionately, with his eyes on hers.

Lynda says she also likes getting to know him, and is looking forward to the official date he wrote on her cast. Neil is, too, as he's arranging a lovely evening for them both. Lynda tries to get it out of him, but no luck. Neil picks up his wine, sipping it, not telling her. He's keeping it secret – he likes surprising her. Lynda asks Neil if he can remove the lasagne from the oven and serve it for her.

"The salad is in the fridge!" she tells him

Neil serves, placing the plates on the table and moving quickly over to help Lynda to the dining chair. She leans on his arm, wobbling across a little smoother now. She tries not to use her crutches around her flat. Lynda fears she will trip herself over and have no one there to help her. Neil pulls out the chair for her, helps her to sit, then sits opposite.

"How did you know this is my favourite dish?" he enquires, looking at her.

"I have my muses too!" she replies, as she had asked Patricia.

Lynda suggests they play backgammon after dinner. Neil accepts her challenge after him winning two games to her one the previous time they played. He comments on how nice the lasagne is, saying Brittany is a good cook. Lynda nods her head as she's chewing.

"Yes, very!" she manages to say after swallowing.

Neil asks which dish does she want to learn to cook first; Lynda looks at him. He remembers her asking him, "Curry, I love chicken curry, sweet, not hot!" she states, sipping her wine and keeping eye contact with him.

"Can do," he replies, serving more salad on to his plate. He's rather hungry as he went jogging that morning to keep fit.

Neil tells Lynda he's been playing backgammon since he was twelve; that's why he is a good player. Lynda decides to bring out the monopoly; she is skilled at this game, always beating her siblings.

"I must warn you; I play this game with my sister once a month!" stating he's rather good, seeing through her plans and smiling.

"That wasn't long ago!" Lynda laughs, looking at Neil's face.

"Who's the banker?" he asks.

"Me, of course," Lynda jumps in quickly, being the accountant.

The couple play well, buying up houses and hotels to try and bankrupt each other, and the game goes late. At eleven thirty Neil calls it quits, commenting he better leave, otherwise he will fall asleep. Lynda offers her spare bedroom, amazing Neil. He is eager to stay but would rather be with her. He declines, not trusting himself alone with Lynda. She sees him packing up the game and tells him to leave it as it's late and he must get home. Luckily, he only lives four blocks away.

Neil kisses her goodnight and she holds onto his arms, this time balancing and giving him a responsive kiss. He quickly places his arms around her back, holding her tightly and having a longer kiss. She loves it; he makes her feel alive inside

The next weeks seem to move along quickly. Neil has been keeping a list of all of Lynda's likes and dislikes for future ideas. He is grateful to Patricia for helping him. She asks for Friday off and he gladly gives it to her, aware it's Lynda's day off too. Lynda walks into the café in her colourful new shoes she bought for herself online as a reward after being in a cast. Patricia notices, commenting how nice they are. Lynda says how she is enjoying walking around without crutches.

Patricia asks whether she likes Neil, "Yes," Lynda replies, being cagy and not wanting to allow anyone in on her affections towards Neil. She orders tea when the girl comes over, and Patricia orders coffee.

"Come on, tell me all about him and you!" she grins.

Patricia has been friends with Lynda for ten years, and both women share their inner thoughts and opinions with each other. She is only four years older than Lynda and happily married and believes Lynda can benefit from her experiences as a wife and full-time worker. Lynda admits the last eight weeks have been wonderful having someone to talk with in the evenings. Neil is very knowledgeable on many topics and enjoys similar tastes on outdoor activities. Lynda says she enjoys Neil's unexpected luncheons and outings to include her when she was in her cast.

"Neil is very considerate to my needs, and without him I would never have done anything, just sit around feeling sorry for myself. I am having fun with him!" Lynda tells her friend while sipping her tea.

Patricia is happy to hear noting Lynda's voice going up when saying Neil's name, and she smiles each time. Lynda continues explaining her doctor has advised her to take it easy until strength comes back into her ankle. Patricia asks Lynda what her perfect romantic evening is. She mentions candles, wine, chocolate and a sexy man. Lynda grins; Neil's on her mind.

"Is that your plan for Neil? You two haven't?" Patricia enquires, not giving Lynda time to answer her first questions.

"No, my ankle made it impossible. I want a real relationship this time, getting to know Neil before intimacy. I like to think it is working this time!" Lynda replies.

"I don't think you have to worry about Neil's affections towards you!" Patricia states.

"Has he said something?" Lynda asks quietly.

"Doesn't have to, seen change in him, and he re-scheduled all of his meetings to accommodate you!" Patricia answers.

"I'm still concerned about our age difference and I haven't met his parents yet! I wonder if he's told them about me?" Lynda speaks softly to her friend to prevent anyone overhearing.

"Neil couldn't care less about your age. Wow, you have a younger man besotted with you. Who cares? Enjoy having fun and develop a relationship with this man!" Patricia advises.

The girl comes and both women order. Once they leave, Patricia emails Lynda an entire list she's been collecting on Neil. Lynda gazes down at her screen, saving the information. Patricia guides her friend on how to pursue this man, giving advice; she really wants Neil and Lynda together. Lynda tells Patricia she can't wait till Saturday and seeing Neil again in his swimmers.

"What does he look like?" Patricia enquires, smiling.

"Very handsome and trim!" Lynda replies.

"At least you see him half-naked!" Patricia answers, watching her friend as she sips her coffee, smirking.

Lynda just smiles, ignoring that comment; her face seems to light up when mentioning Neil. Patricia asks if she has told anyone in her family yet.

"Yes, I told Julia!" Lynda comments, taking her food from the girl servicing and thanking her.

Patricia raised her eyebrows, thinking if Lynda confided in her sister, she really does like Neil. This makes Patricia happy – she cuts into her food.

Lynda's mobile vibrates on the table and she looks, smiling; a text from Neil. He sent a yellow rose to her, making Lynda feel special. She shows Patricia, who smiles; after all, it was she who informed him about Lynda's favourite colour rose. Patricia asks if Lynda's workload is easing after being behind with all of her meetings. She replies yes, businessmen have stopped complaining and everything is back to normal meetings in the office.

"Jennifer is arranging all of them for the next two weeks.

That should keep the men happy!" Lynda comments.

"I suppose you'll go back to wearing those awful suits!" Patricia says, and Lynda looks at her friend. Patricia mentions how much nicer she looks in her dresses and could at least buy stylish suits. Lynda says she is trying to keep the men on business, not on her looks. Patricia says she has a special bank card today, and they are going shopping for more stylish suits and colours.

"Orders from my head boss, the lawyer's clients prefer you to wear more colour and not go back to those drab suits!" Patricia states.

Lynda raises her eyes, looking straight at her. "Your head boss, not Neil?" she enquires.

"Yes, and Mr. Gardner, everyone in the building liked seeing you dress better during your injury!" Patricia replies, looking at her friend.

"It's fine. I'm shopping with you!" Patricia says aware her style is nicer and smarter, she smiles at her friend. "The four companies in the building you deal with have a bet going you will return to your formal clothing. Neil and I took that bet. So see? can't lose!"

Lynda can't believe all her colleagues disliked her clothes as she thought she was being professional. Patricia says you can be business-like, just a little more feminine. They finish lunch and walk off down the street. Patricia stops Lynda at a very stylish, expensive store, "in here!"

"Can't bill this on the card!" Lynda says, a little hesitant, but always wanted to shop in the store.

Patricia tells her Neil insisted he has good credit here and a discount. Lynda looks at her friend. "On his salary, how?" she raises her voice slightly.

Patricia laughs, enquiring if Lynda is aware of who she is dating? Lynda gives her a blank expression. "His father built most of the buildings and owns four in the city; he comes from wealth!" she states.

Lynda looks across at her friend. "Really?" unaware of that fact, never looking him up on google, just thought he was another lawyer. Patricia escorts her up the stairs seeing a white blouse with a collar and see-through sleeves. She asks the girl to try this style choosing pink, Navy blue and emerald suits with feminine blouses. The assistant rushes off to the rack, searching for Lynda's size; returning and placing them in the fitting room. Patricia chooses medium heel shoes for Lynda, after her ankle break doctor insisting she stop wearing her stilts. Lynda changes and comes out. The girl and Patricia choose many other blouses to try until they find the one.

"Perfect!" Patricia says when happy.

"The clients won't take me seriously!" Lynda complains.

"Yes, they will. Stick to your business head. Anyway, might get more clients wearing these!" Patricia replies, taking photos and sending each one to Neil for his approval. He sends back yes on this one.

Lynda tries on four more dresses, fitted in an elegant business style in the latest fashion. Lynda likes the dresses and navy and emerald suits but declines the pink one saying more for a wedding than an office. She chooses another style of skirt and shirt with a design, liking it more in light blue. Patricia likes the style but changes the shirt to pink. Lynda agrees it looks nicer. The sales assistant folds the twelve outfits into nice bags, including matching shoes, handing them to the women. Patricia gives Neil's credit card and number for the discount, making a big difference to the price.

Lynda feels rather spoilt by these bosses offering to buy her a new wardrobe, not seeing Neil has paid for most of the outfits. Patricia, keeping it secret as advised by him; he doesn't want Lynda to know, aware she hasn't fallen in love with him yet. Neil is in love already and will spoil her a little as he's never done in a relationship until now. Lynda is special to him and he's been wanting to splurge since meeting her.

Chapter Three

First Official Date

The dinner date finally arrived after Lynda's shopping trip yesterday. She is looking forward to having a formal dinner with Neil. The couple has driven down to the beach cottage, Lynda and Neil enjoying swimming at the beach; both diving under the waves and swimming out far before racing back to the shore. Lying on a towel, Lynda places her sunnies on, admiring Neil standing beside her. He spreads his towel beside her, taking in the sunshine. After two hours of swimming and sun baking they make their way back to the car and Neil drives to the cottage. Lynda has brought a garment bag with her and he carries it for her, opening the door to the cottage. Inside, Lynda takes the bag and goes into the bathroom. She showers and dresses, applying makeup and perfume while Neil showers and changes.

Neil moves into the lounge room; Lynda is standing waiting for him, wearing tight jeans and high heels. Her see-through blouse is long and frilly with a low frontline. She looks lovely, taking Neil's breath away on seeing her lacy bra. He moves towards her placing his arm around her back, taking a kiss from her and whispering. "Hello, beautiful!" as if seeing her for the first time.

Neil's never seen her looking so trim and able to wear jeans because of her cast. He moves his eyes from head to feet, admiring her figure; he is unable to resist his affections any longer. The plan tonight is to express himself, thinking about it for eight weeks. Neil pours wine for him and Lynda, handing her a tall glass; she takes a sip.

Neil puts on music. "I haven't been with a man for a year," she says.

"Don't worry, I've got you covered," he whispers, moving slowly towards her. Neil takes her in his arms while holding his glass behind her back. He shuffles around the room, moving Lynda closer and pressing her body against his. Neil moves back, takes Lynda's glass and places it and his on a table. He removes his shirt, standing and holding his hand out to her. Lynda places her hand into his, breathing rather heavily on seeing Neil's chest.

Neil gently moves her hand down his warm chest; Lynda's heart begins beating faster, feeling his muscles. He moves her hand down his body to his groin, pulling her closer towards him and kissing her gently. Neil moves her back slightly, unbuttons her blouse, and it floats to the rug. Neil places his hands on her back. Lynda's body is warming and she unclips her lacy bra dropping it. She then moves closer, unzipping his pants. She then removes her panties and he, his jocks, now both standing naked in each other's arms. Lynda moves close, pressing her breast against his warm chest.

Neil lifts her off her feet while moving her across the floor, slowly lowering Lynda onto a wide couch. He leans his body over hers and kisses her lips, neck moving down her breast and waist caressing her body. Neil is arousing Lynda's sexualities; her sensation is overpowering, never feeling like this ever with a man. Neil makes his way back up her body, now looking down into her eyes. Lynda pulls him down onto her kissing his lips; she is enjoying his touch. Neil gently rolls her over in his arms on top of him. Lynda kisses his chest moving downwards. Neil's body stiffens, her hair is wet from sweat. Lynda moves upwards, lowering herself onto Neil's body, making love to him, both moving to a rhythm. Lynda moves beside Neil, still wrapped in his arms, puffing slightly.

"How do you feel?" Neil asks.

"Very wet," Lynda replies while smiling.

"You're a beautiful woman," Neil tells her while using one hand to move her hair back from her face. He keeps her firmly in his warm embrace.

Lynda and Neil lie together for some time. He suggests they have some dinner; his appetite has increased after making love. Lynda sits up on the edge of the couch, and he runs his finger down her back. She looks over her shoulder at him, smiling.

"We better have some wine," she says while putting her shirt on, showing her body.

Neil gets up and puts on his pants, lighting large round candles. Then Lynda throws cushions on the floor, pouring red wine for them both. She loves the way Neil sets the scene, the candles are the only flicker of light in the room. Neil prepares the food in the kitchen, then he returns, carrying two plates with food. He lowers them both onto the coffee table and sits beside Lynda.

"This looks amazing," Lynda comments as she hands him a wine glass.

"Stay with me tonight?" Neil asks.

"All right," Lynda replies, surprising Neil by answering so quickly. She's watching his reaction. He's grinning.

"You have no idea how beautiful and amazing you really are!" Neil says, taking her hand and kissing it.

Lynda looks into his eyes, "You could have any young woman! Why me?"

"I've had them. I am looking for more in a woman. Besides, I am attracted to you!" Neil replies, taking her wine and kissing her softly.

Lynda blushes; she has never had a man so considerate and interesting. She wants to get to know him more.

"What will your parents say when they discover my age?" Lynda asks.

"I'm not worried about their opinion; I want to live my own life and who I choose to have that with!" Neil replies.

Lynda smiles, leaning against Neil's shoulder. He moves his arm around her back, holding her close to him, both enjoying listening to the music. Lynda enjoys being close to Neil, especially eating his meals as he is an excellent cook.

"You certainly know how to please a girl!" she says while taking another bite.

"Oh yeah, which one are you referring to? My sex or cooking?" Neil says with a cheeky grin.

Lynda nearly chokes on his statement while sipping wine. She clears her throat in reply, leaving it up to his imagination. She changes the subject by asking when the renovations will begin. Neil tells her next week; this is why he arranged their evening at the cottage to say goodbye, ready for the new style.

"By the way, I related the suggestions you made to my architect and builder, both saying you have good taste," Neil comments.

"You didn't have to do that; it's your house. Make sure it's what you want!" Lynda replies.

Neil assures her it is and really likes her suggestions for making more of a beach style. "Ben agrees with your suggestions to keep it a beach house instead of changing it into a modern house!" Neil tells her, knowing she likes his friend.

Lynda asks if Ben will organise a table for six for a special client she has to entertain next month. Neil says he will ask, enquiring who the client is, and Lynda tells him.

"Mr. Simpson from America. Mr. Gardner likes to entertain him somewhere different each time. I told him about Ben's lovely meals and atmosphere. He asked me to enquire if Ben would be able to arrange the dinner!" Lynda sees Neil's expression change, wondering why. She is unaware Neil knows this man and his reputation; he is in his forties. He enquires if she entertains him often.

Lynda assures Neil she never entertains Mr. Simpson, not liking him or his attention. She thought that by using Ben's restaurant, Mr. Gardner could entertain him this time. Lynda states she hopes Ben's food and wine will keep them satisfied, preventing them from drinking too much.

"Don't worry. I make sure I'm never alone with Mr. Simpson. He gives me the creeps!" Lynda grins as she looks at Neil. She leans across, kissing him on the lips.

Neil holds her in his arms, leaning her to the floor and holding her close to him by candlelight; their bodies together. She embraces his attention and kisses him. They make love again and she suggests they enter the bedroom. Neil sleeps soundly with Lynda by his side for the first time. In the morning he is lying sideways, watching her sleep. Lynda opens her eyes, smiling at him and saying she has never slept better.

"The sea breeze made me sleep!" she whispers, smirking.

"Oh, is that so!" he tickles her, making her laugh uncontrollably. He stops on seeing she can't stop. Neil rubs her back, helping her to stop; she gets up and showers changing into the spare clothes she brought with her. Lynda was prepared in case Neil asked her to stay overnight, which he did so it came in handy. Neil is preparing breakfast, fruit and yogurt – Lynda's favourite. He looks up and sees her in a floral dress.

"I like your clothes. Are they new?" he asks, aware she went shopping with Patricia, and this is one of the casual dresses she bought after receiving a photo.

"Yes, you like?" she enquires as it's rather tight-fitting and showing off her figure.

"Sure do!" Neil says, handing her a bowl of fruit.

Neil tells her it's perfect for meeting his parents. Lynda's face turns red. "Today?" she asks.

"Yes, springing it on you so you can't get out of it!" Neil replies.

Lynda accepts, saying she is looking forward to meeting them as he's spoken often about his family. Neil expresses they have two hours as they slept in and were invited for lunch by his Dad, who is looking forward to meet her.

"Did you tell your dad?" she enquires, taking a bit of a banana.

"No, Mr. Gardner filled him in as he's often mentioned you on his visits. Dad has always been interested in meeting you. Dad would like to show you his business plan, but don't feel obliged on my account." Neil drives to a florist for Lynda; she wants to buy some flowers for his mother. Neil thanks her for being thoughtful. He drives on, and two hours later they arrive in Bondi. He pulls up a long driveway to a very large house. Lynda is impressed by a modern house with large windows; he opens the door for her. She picks up the flowers and removes a bottle of wine from her beach bag. "When did you buy that?" Neil enquires.

"I have my ways!" Lynda replies.

Neil opens the door and, on entering, calls his parents. Two people come out of a room down the hallway. Lynda holds Neil's hand tightly, and he whispers, "Relax." She tries to smile.

Neil's parents had been peeking out of their large window to see the woman he has chosen to introduce to them. Both of them stare as she's nothing like the normal girl he brings home. She is older and his father thinks she is rather attractive.

Neil introduces Lynda. She smiles while shaking their hands. "Dad and Mum, meet Lynda!"

"Call us Robert and Donna!" they tell her, smiling.

Lynda hands Donna the flowers and Robert the wine, "I am very glad to meet you both. I was told the wine tastes nice with a barbeque!" Lynda says.

"Thank you." Donna kisses her on the cheek, thanking her for the flowers. Neil notices the wine label is the same one Ben has at his restaurant, thinking Lynda takes notice of everything. She notices Neil looking as they follow Robert outside, and Lynda whispers. "Ben recommended it after I asked him what your dad liked!" Neil places his arm around her back, walking onto the terrace.

Robert shows Lynda his pride and joy – the largest barbeque she has ever seen. He talks about how much food he's able to cook at one time, especially when entertaining clients. Lynda thinks that for a successful man, he's very casual and relaxed. She listens to him talking while her eyes travel around the garden.

Donna comes out asking Lynda if she'd like to see her garden, and both women walk off. Lynda is very impressed, especially with the perfect roses. Donna asks Lynda for her favourite flower, "Yellow roses," she replies.

Lynda admires the garden, thinking she should have bought chocolates instead. Donna walks her back up to the terrace to join the men, and Neil hands his mum and Lynda a glass of cold white wine. He stands, placing his arm around Lynda's back. Donna smiles, hoping Lynda is the one Neil will finally settle down with.

Donna comments she hasn't seen her stepson so happy as he has been lately. "You must be good for him!" she says.

Lynda blushes and sips some wine. Robert invites Lynda to come over, and she walks over, rather pleased to leave Donna, in case she asks a difficult question.

"Neil tells me you're good with figures and business opportunities. Would you be willing to go over a proposal for me?" Robert asks.

Lynda agrees to look but can't make any promises to go further until viewing the documents.

"Good, looking forward to your opinion. I trust my sons' opinions on people. Let's enjoy our lunch!" Robert says, hoping she likes hot food.

Lynda excuses herself moving across to Neil. She asks him to walk with her. She asks him what he's been telling his father about her, especially about her job. She says his father told her he trusts his son's opinion.

"Really? Did he? I only mentioned your job with my law firm. Dad must have been talking with Mr. Gardner about you!" Neil replies.

"Sorry, just took me off guard!" Lynda replies, holding Neil's hand.

"Don't worry. My dad is okay. He just takes his business ventures seriously!" Neil smiles while saying not to worry and do what she thinks best.

Lynda keeps her hand in his, walking back to the terrace to join his mother. Donna tells Lynda she has good cheekbones and would like to paint her. Neil shakes his head 'no,' to Lynda. She thanks her but explains she is very busy at the moment, maybe later in the year. Donna moves across to fill her glass from the ice bucket built into the bench.

Neil softly tells Lynda his mum is not a good painter; no one looks like themselves, and they are strange paintings. Lynda nearly laughs; she sips her wine to hide her expression so as not to upset his mum.

"She looks too young to be your mum?" Lynda whispers.

"She is ten years younger than my real mum was!" Neil replies, watching Donna walking back to the table with a bottle to half-fill Lynda's wine glass.

The meat smells delicious. Lynda is feeling rather hungry, only having fruit late for breakfast.

"Robert likes barbequing and has enough for two days. Watch his chicken, Lynda. It's hot in chilli flavours," Donna comments.

Lynda finds it rather relaxing around Donna and Robert, not what she expected after Patricia informed her about their wealth. She was a little worried about meeting his parents. Neil has his arm around Lynda's chair, totally relaxing and happy with his parents' reaction to Lynda. Neil notices Donna is not asking her normal questions, like with his other girlfriends. Lynda notices how Neil is showing his affection towards her in front of his parents. She is a little concerned because she's not in love with him; they are just friends at the moment. Lynda is concerned Neil is rushing in too quickly, even though they've had a relationship developing over the past nine weeks. Lynda has had bad relationships and wants this one to work, and for Neil to be the one forever.

Neil is aware of her nervousness. Patricia has already explained not to rush Lynda and take it gently with her. He is just letting his parents know he really likes Lynda and wants it to work. A young girl of seventeen walks out onto the terrace. She stares at Neil crossly.

"Where were you? I looked for you. My practice race was this morning!" she stands, staring wildly.

"I explained last week that I wasn't coming today. You knew why. Come over and meet Lynda!" he says while looking at her.

"Lynda, this is my younger sister, Morgan," Neil says. "Morgan, meet Lynda, my special friend!" he looks toward his sister.

"She's old," Morgan says, slumping into a chair on the opposite side of Neil at the table.

"Morgan, don't be rude! Apologise at once!" her mother says, rather cross with her.

Neil gives her a disapproving look; Morgan takes a can of drink, sipping it loudly. Her mother stares at her, frowning, thinking she is being unpleasant because she is annoyed with Neil. Morgan tells Neil all about her rowing team and Lynda enquires how often she races. Morgan refuses to answer; everyone notices the girl's rudeness. Lynda decides not to worry, just taking mental notes of Morgan's conversation.

Neil walks across to help his dad carry the platters, both placing them in the centre of the table. "I was told you like seafood, Lynda!" Robert states, and he places two large prawns on her plate.

"Yes, thank you!" Lynda says, seeing how large they are.

Neil whispers to try a piece, and Lynda tastes a little, saying she likes the flavour. Robert is pleased, sitting down he tells everyone to dig in. Neil warns Lynda not to eat the chicken, knowing she dislikes really hot, spicy food. She places her hand on his leg looking Neil in the eyes, whispering, "It's fine," smiling. She wants to make a good impression on his family.

"You're right. She does have a lovely smile!" Robert states.

Lynda is beginning to wonder how many people Neil has told of her smile as Ben made the same comment.

"Neil has a lovely smile too!" Lynda states, looking at Robert and Donna.

"Oh, come on, she's trying hard!" Morgan says loudly.

Neil stops Morgan from saying anything else by giving her a disapproving look. She eats the chicken, "Give her some chicken, Dad!" Morgan says with a smile, about to stand and walk away.

"NO, you finish your chicken, Sis!" Neil replies, pushing her back down in her seat.

Robert places a small piece on Lynda's plate before his wife can stop him. Donna looks at her and Neil as if to stop Lynda from tasting the meat. Lynda thanks Robert and she takes a small bite, which instantly makes her mouth feel like it is on fire. Lynda asks where the bathroom is, trying to make a quick escape.

"I'll show you," says Morgan.

Neil stops his sister. He escorts Lynda into the house, taking her straight to the kitchen and pouring her some cold water from the fridge door. Lynda snatches the glass gulping the water, spilling some down her shirt. She asks for another glass. Neil can't help but smile and worry seeing Lynda turning bright red in the face.

"You're a good sport," Neil says while handing her another glass of water with ice.

Lynda sucks on one cube dissolving it in her hot mouth. "How much chilli did your dad use?" she asks, waving her hand across her face.

"The hottest chilli you can buy!" Neil replies. He opens the freezer, taking a teaspoon of ice cream and places it into her mouth. Lynda sucks on the spoon. Removing it she thanks him, feeling the coolness of the ice cream in her mouth. She leans her head on his chest, saying that is the hottest meat she's ever eaten.

"I'll make it up to you later!" Neil tells her, giving her a quick kiss on the lips.

Lynda laughs and they both return to the table. Robert comments she can leave the chicken. Donna tells him and Morgan off for forcing hot food on their guest; she mentions Neil obviously likes this woman. Lynda sits down again and Neil makes sure he is next to her; he hands her the seafood platter suggesting the fish flavours are sweet. Robert tells her about the spices and sauces he uses, talking for half an hour. Donna interrupts her husband, stopping him from boring Lynda. She asks how her ankle is now. Lynda says she is improving every day; she's glad to be off the crutches and expresses how grateful she is to Neil for helping during the past nine weeks.

"I wouldn't have ever done anything!" Lynda states.

"Yeah, neglected us!" Morgan speaks up.

Donna tells her to hush, aware of her dependence on her older brother and resenting him for finding someone special in his life. Robert invites Lynda to his office, if now is okay to come with him. Lynda gets up, releasing Neil's hand, and she walks off talking with Robert. He opens his laptop showing her several folders of business deals he may invest in. Lynda reads, recognising the name of the company and the director's name. She's seen these documents before

"Did Mr. Gardener share this with you!" Lynda enquires.

"Yes, I asked for his advice. I am unaware he discussed this matter with you!" Robert replies.

"No, he asked me to peruse the papers. I haven't had the opportunity to read the work!" Lynda answers, making eye contact. She agrees to read it now.

Robert thanks her. Donna enters the office carrying a tray with a small teapot and cup; she places it on the desk beside Lynda. "Neil told me peppermint might cool you!" Donna says, smiling.

"Yes, thanks!" Lynda says, watching them leave the office and goes back to reading the file.

Outside on the terrace, Morgan is talking with her brother, trying to organise him for next weekend. Neil tells her to give Lynda a chance; he really wants Morgan and Lynda to be friends. Morgan replies she's not interested in one of his girlfriends; they never last anyway.

"That's where you're wrong. I'm serious about Lynda. I want her to be part of my future!" Neil replies, looking at his sister seriously.

"We'll see!" Morgan answers, staring up at him. Her mother overhears and tells her daughter to take the dishes inside. "Put them in the dishwasher this time!" her mother calls.

"You have yourself to blame, Neil. You spoilt Morgan by giving her your attention and buying her anything she asks for!" Donna speaks the truth firmly.

Neil never realised this until now; he will need to fix it and asks for suggestions. Donna advises to maybe include Morgan on one of his outings with Lynda so they can get to know each other. "It may help."

"Morgan must sort this situation out for herself!" Neil replies, disappointed in his sister.

Donna shakes her head. "I like Lynda, a sensible woman for a change! How old is she?" Donna enquires.

"Forty!" Neil replies with a grin.

"Really? She doesn't look it!" Donna says, surprised at her

age.

"Yes, but I have never met anyone like her. She is old-fashioned in some ways and modern at the same time!" Neil grins, speaking of Lynda.

"In what ways?" Donna asks, being rather curious about this woman that has captivated Neil as he is hard to catch normally.

"Lynda is shy in showing her affection. We are opposites, but enjoy each other's company!" Neil informs her.

Donna smiles, seeing why he likes Lynda. She hopes having someone older will settle him down. She comments age isn't important. "Look at your dad and me, just the opposite way round!" Donna states.

Neil never thought of that. He tosses his head thinking he must have subconsciously been attracted to the same age group. Donna watches how Neil expresses himself on his outings with Lynda, getting her outside while in her cast.

"Don't know how Robert feels. I guess he will express his opinion tonight!" Donna says.

One hour later, Lynda emerges from the study feeling rather tired after having wine and doing business. She feels better after her tea asking Neil for another cup. He tells her she will find his dad in the lounge room. He walks off to get her tea, and Lynda goes down the hallway, finding the lounge with a large window overlooking their driveway and out to the ocean. "Great view!" she comments.

Robert invites her to sit and Lynda does, on a large chair with room enough for two people. Donna uses her remote control to turn down her music, and Lynda advises Robert she is unable to advise him without further investigations.

"If you give me three weeks, I should know more then!" Lynda informs Robert.

"That long?" he replies.

"I can recommend someone else; my workload is heavy at the moment!" Lynda replies, looking straight at the man, as she is a straight-talker when it comes to business.

"No, I can wait. My good friend Mr. Gardner speaks highly of you. I will go by his recommendation. Besides, Neil tells me how respected you are in his firm!" Robert tells her.

Lynda blushes slightly at the praise, and Donna sees what Neil meant. Robert is grateful to Lynda for taking the time to read the documents considering Neil invited her to meet them, not work. Neil enters, placing his hands on Lynda's shoulders. She gently touches his hand with one hand. It's four p.m. now and he tells his parents it's time for them to leave; he has an arrangement with Lynda. She thanks Donna and Robert for the barbeque and she says goodbye to Morgan, seeing her standing in the doorway. Morgan refuses to look at her or say goodbye. Neil gives her a disappointed expression and says he will phone her later.

Back in Lynda's apartment, she suggests taking Morgan out the following weekend. She is organising a special outing.

"You going to tell me?" Neil asks while placing his arms around her waist. Kissing her neck, knowing she finds it hard to resist.

"Behave," she tells him.

"No, you are a sexy woman!" Neil replies.

Lynda advises him to wear outdoor clothing and good footwear for next Sunday and says she will send him an app on Friday. He says he will ask Morgan when he rings her tonight.

Neil asks her to relax and Lynda spins around, kissing Neil and runs her fingers through his hair. Lynda's other hand is on his back; she stops kissing him and whispers in his ear.

"You need to go or order food for dinner!" Lynda says.

Neil holds her waist, stating he is staying the night.

"Really?" Lynda says.

"Yes," Neil replies, picking up his mobile to order pizza, half vegetarian and half meat lover. He orders a bottle of wine from a bottle shop he arranges for delivery. Neil walks across, removing cards.

Lynda says, "No, DVD tonight; too tired to concentrate on a game."

"Change into something sexy!" he calls.

Lynda ignores him, walking into her bedroom to change. Neil moves to the cupboard removing an action DVD, aware she likes these types of movies. He leaves the apartment to park his jeep for overnight parking on the street, returning with a bag. Lynda walks out of her room wearing long black tights and a very long T. Shirt. Neil laughs; he wears his undies and nothing else. Lynda admires how he's not self-conscious, giving her a chance to see his muscles. Lynda looks; she loves his casual manner; he is never self-conscious, unlike herself.

"I hope you realise we're sleeping naked tonight, beautiful!" Neil states.

Lynda grins, aware he likes to stir her; she slumps on the couch with her legs up. The delivery guys arrive together and Neil takes the pizza and wine. He places them on the coffee table and he goes and gets the corkscrew and glasses. Neil buys expensive wine, preferring corks, not screw tops. Neil enquires about her opinion on his father's new investment. Lynda informs him she thinks it may be a scam, unsure until she investigates further. She has a business acquaintance overseas and will ask for her help from one of John's friends, a detective.

"Don't go to all that trouble. You have enough to catch up on!" Neil says, feeling guilty about his father asking.

Lynda tells Neil she will solve it, otherwise it will annoy her. Besides, she needs to know in case her office receives the same business contact. Neil thanks her and warns her not to get caught up in his father's dealings. His law firm had to represent his father last year due to a client suing. Lynda sips some wine, saying she likes the way he protects her; she assures him if Robert doesn't send any money, he will be okay. Neil had no idea his father was in a serious situation; he is normally very careful in business deals.

"Besides, he has a good lawyer," Lynda states while picking up a large slice of pizza and looking at him. "I may not say it, Neil, but I respect your knowledge and skills in the courtroom!" Lynda says in a softer tone.

Neil grins at her, thinking he never knew she had seen him in the courtroom and respected him as a lawyer. She admits after their first meeting, she attended one of his cases, being her client too. Lynda did her own detective work investigating Neil as a lawyer, being curious. A new man at the firm after appearing out of nowhere and was not informed of his arrival. Lynda is keeping her information up to date in what spare time she has now. With Neil in her life, he keeps her busy along with her heavy workload. Neil presses the button playing her DVD and sits back with his arm around her shoulder, sipping wine with his other hand.

"You know you can watch it on your app on TV!" Neil states.

"I'm aware, but this is the extended version!" she replies while smiling at him and moving closer to him; she leans against his arm. All ready to watch her movie placing cushions under her feet, both enjoying their wine, she uses her remote control to dim the lights. "Theatre mode," he whispers, liking the romantic atmosphere.

In the morning, Neil returns from the bathroom and sees

Lynda is awake, looking at him naked. He holds his hand out to her, "Let's shower together." Lynda hears the water running. She slips out of bed, passing Neil and he admires her naked form. Neil moves in behind her. Grabbing his soap, he leans Lynda back against his chest as he soaps her breasts and down her body. Neil kisses her neck, knowing this stirs Lynda; her body is tingling inside.

"I must warn you, water turns me on!" Lynda says.

"Excellent," he replies.

She breathes heavily, loving his touch. She turns around, kissing his lips and moving her hands down his back, clutching his buttocks. Lynda caresses his body; she cannot resist this sexy man. Neil moves Lynda against the tiles, gently entering her warm body and holding her in his embrace. Steam and body heat fog the glass screen, and Neil thinks Lynda is a very sexy woman in water. He moves his hands down her waist to her hips, holding her. Their hair is totally wet, dripping down their faces. He turns off the water, leaving her embrace and stepping out. Lynda steps from behind the glass screen, and he places a towel around her body.

"You are an amazing and pleasurable woman!" Neil says.

"I'm attracted to you and like being in your arms!" she replies.

Neil is pleased and he leaves her alone in the bathroom while she dries her hair. He has strong feelings for her, wanting to spend more time with Lynda, and coming up with different ways to interact with her. Neil is preparing fruit when Lynda walks out in her shirt and nothing else. She moves towards him, seeing the knife unsteady in his hand. This is unlike him.

Lynda takes a bit of toast, watching Neil. "Anything wrong?" she asks, fearing he didn't enjoy their shower together.

"Holiday with me at the end of the month. I have a week off!" Neil replies, moving closer to her and handing her a bowl of fruit.

"Is that all? I thought you didn't enjoy my sex!" Lynda whispers, showing her insecurities.

Neil places his hands on her waist. "Don't be silly. You're amazing!" he replies, kissing her forehead.

"Have you decided where!" Lynda asks while taking a piece of fruit.

Neil asks for suggestions about where she would like to visit and the kind of accommodation. She looks at him eating, thinking of places to see. She comments she likes wineries and loves romantic places to stay. Neil looks at her, taking it all in while sipping some coffee.

Neil tells her he will come up with a surprise trip for them both. Lynda is happy for him to make arrangements, giving her time to organise her work schedule. She sits in front of her large window, enjoying the sun's warmth. She enquires about his renovations at the beach house. Neil reports they started last Monday and will take eight months to finish; if nothing unnecessary happens, the builder informs him.

"Sorry, we won't be able to use the house until then!" Neil comments, watching her closely for a reaction, letting her know he wants her in his life long term. Lynda smiles, looking up at him and thinking he's making plans. She walks across removing one of her books, Pride and Prejudice by Jane Austen, one of her favourite books. Neil startles her, walking softly up behind her, nearly spilling her tea on the floor.

"Sorry," he quickly checks her hand for any burn, aware tea is hotter than coffee.

"My mum's favourite books too," he comments. "Have you

read the book?" Lynda asks him.

"Yes, at school," he replies.

Neil explains his dad didn't want the books or CDs after his mum died. "I asked my aunty to keep them for me while I was living in Victoria. She gave them to me when I moved in here!" Neil comments.

Neil removes a CD of Michael Bolton from his pants pocket he brought for Lynda aware she likes this kind of music; he prefers something more upbeat. He finds Lynda puzzling sometimes because she likes love songs but prefers action movies. He likes romantic movies but reads sports magazines and geography. Lynda reads a title out loud. "Alice in wonderland,"

"Not mine," Neil says quickly.

Lynda laughs; she removes a book of Rudyard Kipling, sitting down on her couch and starts reading a verse. Neil sits beside her, still in his undies. . He enquires, does she find the book interesting.

"Oh yes, have you ever read a verse? My copy is at home." she eagerly asks.

"Once, not my taste," Neil answers.

Lynda reads a verse to Neil. She shares her views, having an in-depth conversation about the verse. Neil likes when she becomes enthralled with a subject. He shares his views; both have differing opinions yet still respect each other's. Neil enjoys these talks getting to know Lynda; she was never forthcoming about herself during the eight weeks driving her home and to work, except for Lynda's conversations with Jason in the back seat.

At night, they played board games; she never revealing anything about her family and close friends. She never likes talking about herself; he always using clever ways to find out details about her likes and tastes. Neil is compassionate in bringing Lynda out of her protective shell. She hides behind her books are a deal-breaker for him. Lynda tells him to go and get dressed, and he walks off, returning to find her still enthused with her book. She lifts her eyes to see him in shorts and a tight T-shirt. He notices, so sits with her looking at the verse. Neil walks across, grabbing a book he hands it to her. "Your favourite book, I believe?"

Lynda takes the book, "how did you know? Before she can finish, he states that Brittany, her friend told him. She moves across placing her book back then returns sitting on Neil's lap, she kisses him. He runs his hand slowly along her leg, and she jumps. "Don't."

Neil whispers, "You're sexy in that shirt and nothing else; thanks for a lovely morning!" he's running his hand up her shirt.

Lynda moves, saying she better dress, wiggling as she walks off, and he takes a deep breath, resisting. Neil washes the dishes, and she returns in shorts and T-shirt; she tells Neil she is surprising him with a special outing. He asks if it's far. Lynda nods. "Yes, two and a half hours' drive," she replies.

"We better leave then," giving a grin.. Neil removes walking shoes and cap from his overnight bag. Lynda looks over his arm, asking what else is hidden in his bag.

"You come prepared?" she says, returning to the bedroom to grab a hat and sunscreen.

"Do you have swimmers in your bag?" she asks.

"Yes, I packed encase we go swimming!" Neil replies.

Lynda returns carrying everything, placing them her backpack, including Neil's towel and items. Neil removes his car keys from his bag, handing them to her and trusting her to drive as she does not want to give directions. At the car, Neil places the backpack in his back seat, fills up his fridge with water he has stacked in a box and jumps in. Lynda drives off to the local deli and parking, she walks briskly across the busy street. She returns with a white box and wine bottle; Neil watches curiously. "What do you have there?" he asks.

"You will find out later!" Lynda says while placing it into his fridge, removing six bottles of water and stacking food and two bottles of water. She places the wine bottle into a special fold-out protective bag sitting it beside the fridge. Neil is fascinated watching. Lynda drives off into traffic again, heading towards the highway. Neil reads the signs as she drives, making light conversation. Lynda talks about his parent's house wondering how long they have been living there.

Neil tells her twelve years, they built it as their dream home and retirement for his dad one day. She says how nice the house is. After an hour, Lynda stops, parking in a township with several cafés, stating Neil better have a coffee, knowing he likes to have one every hour. Sounds of chatter fill the café, some talking about cars, a group gossiping and a couple speaking quietly. The noise takes over, Lynda finding it hard to hear Neil thanking her for stopping; he loves his cappuccino. He notices Lynda's face as she drinks a fruit juice, aware she dislikes loud cafés. He drinks quickly to avoid her getting a headache.

Lynda hands Neil the keys saying her ankle is a little sore as it's only been a week out of the cast. Neil is happy to drive the rest of the way and very curious about where she's planning on taking him. Lynda types the coordinates into his mobile, and Neil looks at his phone – Jenolan Caves.

"Great, I haven't been there since I was a kid!" he is rather excited to visit.

Lynda explains there's a walking track down to a blue lake,

a lovely place to have their picnic. "Oh, that's what you bought," Neil says.

"Yes, a surprise for you." Lynda grins, letting it slip. Happy she managed to make an arrangement instead of Neil.

She tells him about the walking trail, and he shall enjoy the scenery. She bought a special thermo pack to carry their picnic. Neil is a little concerned about her ankle. He enquires if she will manage the track.

"Yes, if I go easy besides, you can always carry me!" she says, laughing it off.

"Yeah, I can do a fireman's lift!" Neil replies while concentrating on driving, gazing sideways at Lynda to see her reaction.

She's holding her hand across her mouth near the window to avoid laughing. "By the way, we both have Monday off. Your boss is rewarding you for your efforts and caring for me!" Lynda tells him.

"Really? My boss agreed to that?" Neil replies in a surprised voice, as his boss is strict about people taking time off.

Lynda explains she has known his boss for ten years and has her ways of persuasion.

"Really? I hope not in the same way you do with me?" Neil states rather seriously.

Lynda hits his knee, thinking after the time he has spent with her, he should know what she's like. She is a little shocked he suggests such a thing, especially with his boss, as Lynda keeps it professional in the law firm.

The main reason Susan is never allowed to deliver papers to the firm is due to her indiscretions with the men. Neil says sorry, only kidding, as he rubs his knee while holding the steering wheel with his other hand; she hit him rather hard. Lynda ignores him for ten minutes and then tells him of her plans. She comments she has a bag for him and her.

"How and when did you manage that?" Neil enquires.

Lynda admits she asked Ben to pack his bag for her, placing it in his jeep last week. Neil is now very impressed with Lynda. She tells him she's booked a room at the historical hotel, which looks nice on the internet.

"We have all day and night to enjoy ourselves!" Lynda states.

"I can take that two ways, you know!" Neil says.

Lynda chuckles, and she places her hand on his leg gently; he likes the touch of her hand. He pulls into the car park, parking his jeep he jumps out, opening the back. Lynda removes the food from the fridge, packing it into her backpack, along with water bottles. The wine is for tonight in their room, she tells him; saying he can watch whatever movie he likes, being his turn. Neil's smiling, thinking they won't be watching a movie if he has anything to do with it. He lifts the backpack with food and their towels as Lynda transferred everything for him.

Neil holds her hand, following directions on his mobile. Lynda leads him straight to the public toilets. She suggests that Neil change looking down at his shorts. "Into what?" he asks.

"Your swimmers," Lynda replies handing him his trunks and informing him there's a section where they can go swimming. "Nudity not allowed!" she whispers to him.

He grins and rushes off to change. Soon returning, Neil places the backpack on his right shoulder. People push past, nearly knocking Lynda sideways. Neil quickly takes her hand with his left to prevent her from falling. Lynda tells him to wait and listen. A bird with a pretty sound is high up in the trees. She loves wild birds, she tells him. He admits Donna has an aviary in the back yard, and Lynda mentions she dislikes captured birds preferring them to be free. Neil listens, never knowing this fact. He says captured birds may not be able to defend themselves.

"Yes, I'm aware, just like birds to fly free," she squeezes his hand.

Neil stands looking at the sign saying not far, only one and a half hours return. People and children are pushing past them as they are standing admiring the scenery. Lynda tells Neil there is no need to rush; he agrees.

The pair stroll down the track, keeping to the left to allow other people to rush past them; Lynda points ahead to a bridge they must cross. Neil tells her to stand while he takes a selfie of them both with scenery behind them. At the blue lake, Lynda removes her picnic: cheese and fruit, and she hands Neil a massive sandwich.

"Steak, spinach leaves and tomato on thick sourdough with mustard." He looks it over, stating it is his favourite. He takes a bite saying it's delicious, Lynda is pleased.

She admits Ben recommended the deli having his sandwich, and she is enjoying a vegetarian sandwich. Neil opens the water bottles handing one to Lynda. She sips it slowly, enjoying lunch; she slices the cheese handing Neil a piece. He expresses how he's enjoying the walk, asking how often she visited here. Lynda looks at him, admitting once or twice. Not telling Neil the last time was four years ago when her last partner proposed to her. Lynda loves the place and now wants to make a new memory with Neil; he asks where they are going to swim.

"Further down, below the waterfall." They continue enjoying their picnic. Neil snaps photos of the lake and Lynda on his mobile. She watches as she prefers to capture memories instead of photos. Lynda packs up, telling Neil it is time to go if they want to swim. He walks back and takes the bag and her hand.

She leads the way taking it easy. On arriving, Neil is captivated by the wild beauty; the waterfall is lovely, he states. Lynda removes her shirt and shorts, slipping off her shoes. Neil strips down, admiring the swimsuit she is wearing – a nicer suit in pattern with a lower back. Lynda notices he's wearing swim shorts this time and she smiles. He takes her hand as they enter the water. Neil lets go so they can swim; he dives under, coming up close in front of her; and she splashes water at him.

"Oh, you want to play!" Neil says. Knowing she is an excellent swimmer, he pulls her under, kissing her.

Lynda escapes, coming back up to the surface and treading water. Neil comes up too, smiling. "That will teach you!" he says. She places her arms around his neck, pushes him under, then swims off. Neil swims after her, soon catching her; he grabs her around the waist. He states she is frisky today; Lynda replying she is feeling relaxed after last night and the morning shower. The sunlight shines on them both as someone nearby dives into the water, and youngsters laugh, playing around in the water. Neil and Lynda swim off towards the sides, back to their bag. Lynda walks out, removing towels and lying them down on the ground.

Neil comments she needs sunscreen on her fair skin; otherwise she will burn, and he doesn't want their evening spoilt. Lynda hands him the tube and he applies it to her back, rubbing slowly, covering her entire back and shoulders. Neil has olive skin, so never uses sunscreen, even when she advises he can still burn, but rejects it because he loves a tan.

"Great spot will have to do this again," Neil says, lying down beside Lynda and holding her hand.

She is glad he is enjoying her outing. Knowing he likes the outdoors, she thought Jenolan Caves was the perfect weekend getaway. Lynda tells Neil she's already checked into their room by mobile but suggests they better move along; seeing it's now four p.m. and they must make their way back. She wants to settle into their room. Neil turns sideways, looking at her, and with a cheeky grin, asks if she's in a hurry to get to their accommodation. Lynda runs her finger down his nose, saying, "It's getting late, and I want to enjoy our time together!"

She stands up, taking his hand and trying to pull him to his feet without success. He gets up, and Lynda rolls the towels, placing them into the backpack. Lynda dresses while Neil throws the bag over his shoulder. Neil takes her hand, walking quicker back up the track.

In the car park, Neil puts the backpack in his boot, removing their overnight bags instead. He locks the car while Lynda moves as cars drive out of parking spaces. Neil calls her towards him; she jogs slightly towards him. Lynda leads the way towards their accommodation. At the hotel, they take their key card, making their way to their room, which is elegant, both admiring the furnishings. Neil checks the bathroom returning, stating there is plenty of room for them both. Neil's way of letting Lynda know he enjoyed the last shower together, she kisses him.

In the morning, Neil books two cave tours, including the river cave. He's enjoying the caves and seeing all the beauty, including Lynda. Both enjoy the time away from work, seeing something new together and making new discoveries. Neil takes water bottles once again and they go back to the swimming spot, this time staying longer. Neil packed a lunch, and they swim and sunbake; Lynda wears a shirt to stop her burning. They have the place nearly to themselves, with only one other couple who keep hugging and kissing, not enjoying the ambiance.

"Must be honeymooners!" Neil states, looking directly at

Lynda. She smiles, touching his hand.

Following Sunday outing

Neil arrives to pick Lynda up with his sister in the back seat, "Hi Morgan," Lynda says. She keeps her head down, ignoring her. Neil goes to say something, but Lynda stops him by placing her hand on his leg, shaking her head 'no.'

Lynda explains geocaching to Neil and Morgan, she now has headphones in her ears to avoid making conversation. Neil tries to get her to take them out, but she remains with eyes down, and Lynda whispers not to take any notice. He stops in the car park, and on getting out he opens the door for his sister, who refuses to get out until he grabs her arm. Neil can be forceful when he wants; he whispers to Morgan to behave, and she pulls away, removing her headphones. Lynda explains what geocaching is. Neil is quite excited he's uploaded his mobile.

Morgan says she will go with Neil, and Lynda agrees it would be a good idea; he stares at her. Neil enquires if Lynda will be all right? Aware she gets lost easily and finds riddles impossible to understand. She kisses him, which annoys Morgan.

"Go, have fun. I will look down here. Don't forget to sign your names!" Lynda says.

Neil smiles, taking his sister Morgan. Voices can be heard as she talks to her brother. Lynda hopes Morgan will find treasure hunting interesting, and she tries to understand the riddle. Lynda walks around for half an hour before becoming frustrated, so her feet seem to be leading her towards the café. Lynda's been watching the time, and twenty minutes later her mobile rings.

"We found ours. Where are you?" Neil asks.

"Café," Lynda replies. He laughs and says, "Wave to your right." She looks and sees Neil waving to her with Morgan beside him. Lynda laughs.

"I thought you gave up!" Neil says on his mobile she asks him what type of drink to order for Morgan.

A guy takes Lynda's order, one mug of cappuccino, energy drink and tea, including cake. The guy writes it down and then walks off with the order. Neil sits down with his sister and Lynda asks if Morgan is enjoying their outing so far. She ignores Lynda, asking Neil to take her home after her drink. Lynda takes a deep breath placing her hand on Neil's smiling, so he remains calm.

"I'm not cutting our outing short. You can address Lynda when she talks to you!" he states, rather annoyed with his sister.

Morgan gives him a look and she rings her dad to come and get her. Robert agrees. Neil gives his sister a look of disapproval; luckily, his coffee and cake come out. Morgan opens her drink bottle and drinks from it. Lynda enquires about what type of music she's listening to.

"You won't know the artist at your age!" Morgan says abruptly.

She takes her earplugs out so Lynda can listen to the song. Lynda smiles, saying the singer is new, but the song is old. "I listened to that song as a teenager!" Lynda comments, keeping eye contact with the girl.

Morgan is annoyed and she puts her earplugs back in again. Lynda asks Neil to walk with her; she discusses they have to wait for his dad. "We can have lunch here!" Lynda says, looking at Neil. He apologises for his sister's attitude.

"She needs time to accept you're with an older woman!" Lynda says, holding his hand. He looks at her, goes inside to get a menu and walks back to the table. Neil sits down showing Lynda the menu. She chooses a chicken sweet chilli wrap; Neil a steak salad and he goes and orders.

Lynda enquires if Neil would like to meet her family soon, his eyes open wide quickly, saying, "Yes," before she can retract her invite. Lynda touches his hand, happy he wants to meet them. She asks him to stay the night and Neil whispers, "I was planning to," with a grin.

Robert turns up before their food. He says hi to Lynda, enquiring how things are going with the company. Lynda informs him she thinks it's best for now not to do any transaction with them.

"I believe it's fake," Lynda tells him. Robert turns slightly red. "You asked me to investigate. You didn't go ahead?" she enquires.

Robert says no; he waited. He just feels foolish. Lynda sighs with relief and tells him it comes across as real.

"My friend in America assures me it is a professional scamming team, and the FBI is looking into it!" Lynda explains she has sent him an email of her progress and is trying to find the real company for him.

"Do you want me to continue?" she asks.

Robert says, "Yes, if not too much trouble!"

Neil goes to intervene, but she touches his leg; a signal not to. She can handle it. Lynda advises it will take her another two weeks and asks if he can wait. Robert says yes, looking at people eating.

"The food looks good," after his hour's drive, Robert decides to sit and eat with Lynda and Neil, which annoys Morgan.

"What you having, Chick?" he asks his daughter; this being Morgan's nickname as she chased the chooks as a toddler. She grunts, ordering a pie that is on offer.

Robert asks how their day is going so far. Neil says he's enjoying the geocaching, and they will continue after lunch to the next location. His father is interested, asking all about it. He loves the outdoors. Neil inherited this from Robert, who explains he used to take Neil camping with his mother to wilderness locations once at Alice Springs. Lynda asks questions, interested in knowing what Neil liked as a child and teenager. Neil gets a little embarrassed and Robert laughs.

"Shall I tell Lynda about when you dived into the river, and it nearly took you downstream? I had to dive in and save you!"

"Well, Dad. You just did. I was only eight at the time!" Neil says while taking a bite of his food.

Robert's food comes out with Morgan's. "This looks great," he takes a bite of his burger, saying the flavour is really nice. He asks if it's one of Lynda's favourite cafés.

"Yes, I come with my brothers and sister." Neil looks towards her, thinking that's how she knew where the café was and why they were coming here.

"How many in your family?" enquires Robert.

"Five, I'm the second eldest!" Lynda replies.

Robert enquires about their ages if she doesn't mind. Lynda replies her eldest brother is forty-two, her sister thirty-eight, and brother thirty; he's the youngest.

"You can't count. You missed one!" Morgan says cheekily.

"Yes, you're right. My younger sister died!" Lynda replies.

Neil places his arm around her shoulder, squeezing her arm and letting her know he is there for her. He understands now why Lynda is hesitant about mentioning her siblings to him.

"I'm sorry, Lynda!" Robert says, looking at his daughter crossly.

"It's okay. She lived to twenty!" Lynda replies, her eyes moving downwards.

Neil looks at her, and Lynda looks up. She tells Robert

Amanda was a joyful person, always finding something to laugh about and helping other cancer patients.

"My sister liked the group you listen to!" Lynda says, looking at Morgan.

She looks away then, at her food, eating in silence. Lynda tells Robert and Neil she and her family run in the cancer fund race each year. "The race is in two weeks!" she tells Robert and Neil.

"A good cause, I'll donate for you! If that's okay?" Robert asks.

"Of course, the more money, the better for a cure. You can put in Amanda's name!" she gives him the webpage.

"Will you run with me, Neil?" she asks, looking into his eyes.

"Of course, beautiful!" saying it aloud, normally keeping it between them.

Morgan stands up, urging her father to leave, and Robert stands. "Have fun, you too. Nice seeing you again, Lynda!" he walks off, talking to his daughter.

Neil enquires about Lynda's brothers, asking about their careers. She explains Brian is an engineer with three kids, Julia's a housewife with one kid, and Simon is the one having medical issues; he is a school teacher.

"The one you told me about?" Neil asks.

"Yes," Lynda replies.

Lynda says her mother is an architect and her father a builder. Neil now realises why she understands his cottage plans and making suggestions.

"Pity I didn't know your mother when I was looking for an architect!" he comments.

Lynda smiles saying his firm is a good one and she likes the designs. "I look forward to seeing the progress on your beach house!" Lynda says, looking longing into his eyes. Neil grins. Finally, she is responding and getting closer to him, a big improvement. Lynda suggests they better get to their next destination or it will be too late. Neil goes and pays for the meals. He returns, walking back to the car park he suggests maybe they should go and have some fun instead. He sees Lynda's smile has gone since talking about her sister. Neil wants to cheer her up.

"What's your idea?" Lynda enquires, being rather curious.

"Luna Park, I bet you haven't been there for a long time?" Neil says, looking at Lynda.

"You're right, not for a long time!" Lynda accepts his suggestion.

Neil drives off, heading for the park. Lynda talks nearly all the way about her parents and siblings. Neil's listening and asking questions while driving. He parks and they continue to walk to Luna Park; around the corner, he removes his mobile to show his annual pass. "Come here often?" Lynda whispers.

"Yes, I bring Morgan here three times a year!" Neil replies, taking her hand and walking inside.

Neil walks Lynda over to the Ferris Wheel; she tells him she's scared of heights. He insists she will be fine with him. As the wheel goes up, Lynda closes her eyes. Neil wraps his arm around her shoulders, making Lynda feel safe; she feels his strong grip.

Lynda's stomach has other ideas, doing somersaults; she's feeling sick. Back on the ground Neil steadies her, seeing Lynda's pale face.

"Sorry, beautiful," Neil says.

Lynda leans against his chest, asking for some lemonade. He sits her down and rushes off, soon returning. Lynda takes sips and after thirty minutes, she's feeling better. Her stomach has settled and balance returned.

"I told you I'm scared of heights," Lynda says, looking up at him.

Neil is so insistent sometimes, trying to convince her when she's unsure. He apologises, feeling guilty for not realising how badly she suffers. Neil is very sorry, showing in his expression his concern for her.

"Okay, my turn to choose!" Taking Neil by the hand across to the Dodgem City, Neil goes to climb in the driver's side. "No, I'm driving," she tells him, slipping in beside him. He has to walk around to the other side.

The cars set off. Lynda's moves off quickly, jerking Neil's head slightly and he hangs on tightly. Neil soon discovers Lynda is a daredevil at driving. She spins around with her hair flying out. She drives around other drivers, and one bangs into their side. Neil is not impressed she quickly moves out of the way of other cars. The cars stop and Neil jumps out, holding Lynda's hand and helping her climb out. "I told you I was good!" she says, grinning at Neil.

Neil laughs, asking how her stomach is. "Okay now," Neil thinks it must be the way she drove. He walks her across and tries his hand at basketball, playing four games, and wins her a toy. Neil takes Lynda by the hand, walking across to Rotor. Inside, Lynda is unsure, and Neil explains the time capsule spins and makes you stick to the wall, and the floor vanishes. Lynda goes to leave but too late, it spins and Neil holds her hand as they are lifted up and drop back down. Lynda screams along with all the other girls inside. When it's over she tries to balance. Neil wraps his arm around her back, helping Lynda outside.

"That's it, the last time you choose!" she says to him rather pale again. Neil thinks he better stop forcing Lynda onto fast rides or high ones. Neil has been choosing the rides he goes on with Morgan.

Lynda sits to regain her posture. She just looks up at Neil, "You're a dare devil!" Lynda tells him.

She uses her mobile to look up all the rides at Luna Park and she finds one she is happy with. "Slides," she states.

"Are you sure?" he asks, aware it's rather fast, and knowing Lynda doesn't realise this, he does try to change her mind. She is determined to conquer one of Neil's favourites. At the top, Neil goes first, arriving at the bottom before her.

Neil quickly jumps out of the bag, ready to catch Lynda as she arrives, screaming. Neil helps her up and out of the bag. He laughs; he can't help it. "I did warn you!" he says.

Lynda wraps her arms around his neck, and he holds her tightly, enjoying the cuddle. Lynda sees kids with fairy floss and comments she might try one. Neil stops to buy her one, and tasting it she comments it is sweeter than she remembers. Neil eats it instead, he has a cast-iron stomach. Having fun. Lynda grabs his hand, running him across to the Carousel.

"I have loved riding a horse since I was a kid. Come on!" she says, climbing aboard a white horse. Neil sits on the one beside her with his legs dangling, being tall. He laughs, feeling a little silly. Kids stare at them; lovely music plays while the horses move up and down. Neil holds her hand as they go around. The only adults without kids, Lynda loves the ride and is disappointed when it stops. Neil looks at his watch, suggesting it is time to leave. It's now six p.m. and they have been there all afternoon.

Outside the park, Lynda stops Neil. "Let's take the ferry over to Circular Quay and eat at the rocks!"

Neil looks at her, thinking this is a good idea, walking down to the wharf and boarding a waiting ferry. Lynda stands near the side, looking across the water as they go under the Harbour Bridge. "The bridge is spectacular. It makes Sydney!" Lynda states.

Neil stands beside her, seeing she likes the architecture. Lynda points to an apartment block. She tells him she rented the front one in her thirties for six months; Neil looks, stating what a view. "Very expensive!" she comments.

Neil places his arm behind her back. They are watching the other ferries, both enjoying the boat ride. On docking, Neil helps Lynda off the ferry and they walk hand-in-hand, heading towards restaurants; now all they have to do is choose which one. Lynda points to one facing the harbour and he likes it too; on entering, Neil asks for a table. The waiter looks around, seeing one available for two people. He escorts them across, handing them a menu each.

"This is nice," Neil says. She agrees, feeling a little underdressed as people arrive slightly dressed up.

"We're a bit casual!" she states.

"Doesn't matter. My dad built this restaurant. The owner knows me; he won't throw us out!" Neil tells Lynda.

"Is that why we got a table?" she asks.

Neil nods his head, "Yes."

People's voices soon take over the restaurant, and Neil orders red wine for them both. Lynda likes his choice sipping it slowly as the waiter takes their order, both asking for crab between them. The waiter suggests their chef's speciality salad. Lynda accepts his choice, saying it sounds nice. A man walks towards their table and Neil warns her the owner is coming over.

"Hi, Neil. You are well?" he asks.

"Yes, James. I would like you to meet Lynda, my... friend!"

he hesitated, wanting to say girlfriend but prefers not to make Lynda embarrassed.

"Hi, glad to meet you. Neil, nice you're visiting my restaurant. It's been a while!" James says, looking at Lynda. She smiles up at him.

"Say hi to your dad and enjoy your meal!" James says, shaking Neil's hand. He wanders off to speak to some other customers.

"He's nice!" Lynda comments.

Neil tells her about the restaurant and his family using it for clients and special occasions. A large platter arrives with crab, surrounded by salad. "Enjoy," says the waiter.

Neil serves Lynda and takes a bit of crab, saying it's not as good as Ben's. She likes the salad flavour. Neil comments it's their first restaurant since her accident.

"Yes, must remember this place and time!" Lynda replies. Neil realises she is an old-fashioned romantic wanting to remember the date. Neil types it into his mobile, listening as she describes how she likes the candles and décor. Neil comments it took ages to choose, holding up the opening of the restaurant. James is very particular, he comments. Lynda says it was well worth it; she likes it very much, feeling comfortable even though she's not dressed up.

"Pity I'm not wearing a nice dress considering it's our first restaurant together!" she says, touching Neil's leg under the table.

"Let's come again to see the lights on the water, and we will dress up!" Neil says.

Lynda nods her head, thinking that will be nice. Enjoying the food, she smiles at Neil, thinking he is definitely making plans for them both.

Chapter Four

Family

One week onwards, Neil drives Lynda home after spending a day together. She leans across the seat and gives him a kiss saying she had a really good day and hasn't laughed so much for a long time. Lynda tells Neil she wants an early night, signalling no sex; she wants to relax. Neil grins, saying goodnight, and Lynda heads off into her apartment block; she texts she's inside. Neil drives off, always waiting when he doesn't walk her upstairs. Lynda takes a bath, dresses in her PJs and decides to make a cheese toasty. Lynda puts on one of her action films sitting on the couch with legs crossed.

Neil rings around eight, "Which movie are you watching?" she laughs, telling him.

"Miss me?" he asks.

"No, what. Go around," Lynda yells.

"I better hang up then," Neil says.

Lynda is not concentrating on what Neil is asking, watching her movie. "Sorry, you rang at the crucial point. What did you say," Lynda asks.

"Do you miss me?" Neil enquires again.

"Maybe, miss your smile," Lynda replies.

"Okay, you're watching that action one again. You know it scares you!" Neil states.

"I know. I'll leave the lights on!" Lynda replies.

"Or I could come over and cuddle you!" Neil answers.

"Okay, come quickly," Lynda replies.

Neil hangs up and arrives in ten minutes. He texts to let her know he's arrived. He knocks; Lynda unlocks her door and practically jumps into his arms.

"That movie always scares you. Better stop watching it," Neil says.

"No. I heard a noise outside my bedroom window." Lynda replies, holding him tightly.

Neil moves her back, grabs the torch and opens her sliding door; he shines his torch. Neil is cautious; he looks before walking out and stepping onto her balcony. He sees a pot plant fallen over. A cat is walking along the balustrade going back home next door. He closes the door, locking it, "Just a cat," he tells her. Neil turns off the TV, removing her DVD and instead plays music to settle Lynda, her heart still beating hard.

Neil makes peppermint tea for her and she sips some, then places it on the coffee table; he sits beside her, and Lynda cuddles up to him. Neil wraps his arm around her shoulder. She places her hand on his recognising she is really scared.

"Thank you for coming over. Sorry for pushing you away!" Lynda says.

"Why did you?" Neil enquires.

"Just Morgan's attitude upsets me. I don't think she's going to give me a chance!" Lynda says.

Neil thinks about it. He, too, has concerns about why his sister is not trying to get to know Lynda. He tells her he will talk to Morgan.

"No, give her time. I'm an older woman, unlike your other girlfriends, and different. I'm a threat, taking you away from her!" Lynda comments.

Neil did not realise this. He tells Lynda he's made arrangements for their holiday in two weeks. She reminds him not the weekend of the cancer run. "No, it's the next weekend, the only starting date I can get from work! Will the dates suit you?" Neil says.

Lynda is pleased because she never misses the run and won't let her family down. "Mr. Gardner will be glad I am taking a holiday; been nagging me the last two years to have one! "Neil squeezes her shoulders, kissing her head. She turns around with her back against his side and he holds her tightly. Neil discusses how to involve Morgan; he suggests Lynda come with him to watch her rowing practice the following Saturday. She thinks it a good idea, reminding Neil they are having lunch at her parents' home.

"Are we?" Rather surprised, not remembering her mentioning it before.

"Yes. I told you, didn't I?" She is sure she told him.

"No, you didn't. I would remember!" Neil tells her she has sprung it on him, but he's happy to meet everyone at long last.

Neil asks what wine her dad likes, "Red," naming his favourite brand. "He's a little particular. Mum loves chocolates!" she replies while snuggling up to him.

"No worries!" Neil whispers in her ear, then turns off the music and takes Lynda off to bed, considering they have to wake early for work in the morning. Neil brought his folding bag with his suit, all organised for work.

In the morning, Neil prepares breakfast ready for Lynda. She walks out wearing one of her new suits and blouses.

"You look amazing, very feminine and businesswoman too!" Neil comments. "Thanks, one of my new ones!" Lynda states, remembering he hasn't seen her new clothes yet. She and Patricia planned to launch her new clothes this week. Her dear friend wanted to win the bet about how she will dress for the office, so they waited.

Neil smiles, aware as Patricia sent him photos for his approval. "Thank you, handsome, for allowing me to buy some casual dresses too!" she kisses him, aware he paid for them, giving Patricia his bank card.

"I still like your swimmers best!" he winks, walking off to organise his overnight bag.

Lynda smiles and does her hair in the hall mirror. Putting her long hair up into a bun, she applies her make-up. She pours her tea into her container; Neil states he's taking his jeep to work today, picking up Jason on the way. Lynda is happy, not wanting to rush for the bus and walk; she's been having trouble with her ankle but keeping it to herself. At Jason's school, Lynda moves into the passenger front seat to talk to Neil as he drives. Neil comments he must learn to sign. She's happy to teach him; it just takes time. Lynda has lots of messages on her mobile she is checking each one. Neil gets her attention when mentioning their meeting at ten, and his boss is eager to see her report. The company they are dealing with all depends on her report; his boss is attending. Lynda looks at him rather surprised; she had forgotten all about their meeting.

"My mind been distracted lately!" she whispers.

Neil looks at her rather amazed because she is always so organised and reminds him of their meetings. "Can it be at eleven a.m.?" she asks in a rather serious voice.

"I'll fix it!" Neil replies, thinking he will keep their client busy with his own legal matters for their company. He speaks to his phone, writing a text to Patricia, "Contact the boss of changes, eleven a.m. now for meeting with Lynda!"

"Thanks, Neil, you're too good to me!" Lynda says, putting her phone away. She touches his hand gently and he places his finger on hers.

Lynda rings Jennifer. She reminds Lynda she has an important client coming in at ten. "Really? Who!" Lynda asks.

"Patrick!" replies Jennifer.

"Okay, can you ring him asking if he can manage nine a.m. instead? And find the folders for Neil's meeting at ten!" Jennifer replies she will get on it straight away.

Neil hears the urgency in her voice, asking if everything is all right. She states she just has an important client coming into the office. Neil tries to ease her concerns by reminding her of her expertise in business matters.

"I have never met anyone like you in a meeting. You'll be fine!" He holds her hand.

"I was ready until you reminded me of our meeting at the same time!" she says, taking a deep breath.

At the office, Jennifer is waiting for Lynda, informing her Mr. Patrick is happy to come in early as he has another meeting straight afterwards. Jennifer escorts Lynda to her office, talking the entire time she places contracts on her desk to check later.

"I have set up the boardroom with the folders and transactions for Mr. Patrick's meeting!" says Jennifer.

"Thanks, Jen. You need a bonus this year!" Lynda states.

"That would be nice. I don't think Mr. Gardner will agree!" Jennifer replies.

"Leave it with me. After helping with my injury, staying late at the office and assisting Neil, you deserve it!" Lynda states.

Jen is a little embarrassed but does think, yes, she has done a lot this year. Jen leaves, closing her door behind her and walking briskly back to her office to organise Lynda's workload.

Lynda sits at her desk, and on opening up her computer she sees an email from Neil. He sent a smiley face with hearts. She smiles, sends him a heart back, saying, "Stop distracting me," and then gets back to work. Jennifer just sent all the work for Neil's meeting. Lynda starts working on it immediately, getting it completed before her meeting with Mr. Patrick.

Mr. Gardner steps into her office, checking if she's ready for Mr. Patrick. "You know how difficult he can be!" he is rather anxious and has always disliked the man; but he brings a lot of money into the company.

Lynda performs beautifully during the meeting, impressing Mr. Patrick. He leaves happy everything he organised is settled.

"Thanks, Lynda, once again. I'm satisfied with our agreement with your company. By the way, I like your new outfit; much nicer!" he shakes her hand and walks out of the office, being escorted by Susan.

Jennifer asks how it went, and Mr. Gardener says, "Very well, thank goodness. You handle that man better than me!"

Jennifer is glad she starts to put everything away, reminding Lynda she has twenty minutes to go upstairs to Neil's law firm. Lynda returns to her office and saves everything to a USB, phoning Neil about changes to her presentation. He gets Patricia on it immediately. Lynda runs five minutes late and on arriving at Neil's office, she sees his boss; she apologises for being late. He is not happy but accepts Lynda's explanation, aware she's only been at full strength for two weeks after her ankle injury. He listens to Lynda; Patricia takes the USB, places it into the computer then transfers it to the large screen on the wall in the law firm's boardroom.

Lynda proceeds to explain their client's concerns. She points out many discrepancies, and changes need to be made. The boss is displeased; they are preparing to go to court in three days.

"Can you have it all ready by Friday, Lynda?"

"Yes, I will work on it today and tomorrow. I am aware your case depends on these documents!" Lynda keeps eye contact, aware of how to handle this man.

He rises from his chair, "Friday eight a.m. No later!" he says, puffing as he leaves the room.

Neil congratulates her on getting to work on it, saying he really needs everything by Thursday. Neil is representing the company that is connected to Lynda's firm.

Lynda tells Neil she will work through lunch too. He understands as his day has been interrupted by re-arranging her clients' appointments. Lynda walks from the boardroom, except Neil escorts her down another corridor passing all the office staff.

"Why are you taking me this way?" she enquires.

"Showing off your outfit, they have a bet going you will remain in the same dull clothes. I want Patricia to win the bet!" Neil whispers to her.

Lynda stops, pretending to get some water from the cooler. She sips, letting everyone see her outfit, then smiles, saying hello to everyone as she walks past.

"I want her to win too!" she whispers back to Neil.

The look on everyone's faces is a picture! A lawyer hardly recognises her; her hair is more feminine too. "Wow, Lynda. You look great," he says.

"That's enough," Neil says, seeing his colleagues with smiles on their faces.

One lawyer standing in his doorway comments. "Now I see what you see in her. Quite sexy!" Neil pushes him back into his office.

Lynda states she better get back to her company to start work on his documents. Around one p.m., a delivery boy arrives at Lynda's office, delivering her a lunch and speciality tea with a note. "Compliments of Neil." Lynda thanks the boy and she rings Neil, thanking him, saying he is so considerate to her. She says she will have to stay back until nine tonight, so he should go home, and she'll catch an Uber.

"No, you go early. Can't have you being late due to my mistake!" Lynda replies.

"No, I need to work too. I shall order dinner and come down to you at seven tonight. All my work is on my laptop!" Neil says he dislikes her going home so far by car with a stranger; too dangerous for a woman at night.

Lynda relinquishes, having too much work she must get back to and says goodbye until later. All afternoon Lynda remains at her desk with Jennifer giving her cups of tea, knowing she neglects herself when consumed by her work. All afternoon Jennifer works on re-arranging Lynda's meetings so she can finish the work for the law firm. Lynda informs Jennifer she won't be able to take Friday off as there is too much to catch up on. Jennifer says she will stay until Lynda leaves and informs the security guards they are working until nine. Lynda tells Jen to leave as Neil is keeping her company tonight.

"Goodnight, Jen, order an Uber. I will cover the cost in my budget. I don't like you catching the bus at night!" says Lynda.

Jennifer is grateful; she too preferring not to travel alone as her friends left an hour and a half ago. "Thank you, Lynda. See you tomorrow!" Jennifer says.

Time moves along quickly and Neil arrives just before the delivery man with their food. He meets him at the elevator, thanking the guy and carrying the food into Lynda's office.

"Thank you. I'm hungry!" Lynda tells Neil, smelling the

food, her favourite Indian curry with rice, "Did you get the papadums?" she asks.

Lynda is still upset about having missed her report schedule, as she never missed one in the entire ten years of doing them. Neil tells her she's being too hard on herself, needing time to get back into a rhythm.

"How is your ankle?" Neil asks, seeing it looks a little swollen. He frowns with concern.

Lynda sees him looking and she moves her foot under the table, saying it's just been sore the last few days. Neil is a little annoyed with her for not saying anything, especially going for long walks.

"Is that why you gave up searching last weekend, and I found you at the café?" he enquires, keeping eye contact with her.

"Yes, and no. I became frustrated at not working out the clues!" Lynda replies, eating a fork of food.

Neil watches her carefully while eating. They both talk about work and having to stay back to catch up. "Maybe see the doc again!" he replies, a little worried about her.

Lynda places her hand on his saying her doctor said it would take time to become strong. "I just want it ready for the race!" she tells him.

Neil says he will jog with her at lunch to help strengthen it, at least having someone with her just in case she needs help. Lynda thinks that's a great idea, never thinking about it and asks to start tomorrow. "Stay with me tonight?" she asks, which surprises Neil. Of course he says yes, as he packed enough clothes for three days on the off chance of staying longer at her apartment. Lynda returns to her desk, having eaten and her brain working properly. Neil packs up the leftovers placing them in Lynda's bar fridge, where she keeps water and iced tea. He opens his laptop, working at the table, he sets an alarm, so they both don't stay too late as it takes an hour to get home. At least the traffic will be less in the evening, he hopes, it being unusual for him to remain so late.

Lynda smiles, looking at her computer to finish the day's work so she can start fresh in the morning. Neil hears his alarm telling Lynda it's time to leave. She looks across at him and closes off her computer, being tired. She rings the security guard to inform him she and Neil are leaving the office. He thanks her informing the other guards they are going to the basement car park. The security guard meets them at the lift, and he escorts them to their car, then runs and gives Neil the code to open the roller door.

"Goodnight, you two!" he says, waving and watching Neil drive off.

Neil uses the code up at street level opening the roller door. Once cleared of his roof height, he leaves, pressing the button on the street side. The door closes again. He drives off, moving down the streets to the highway taking them home. He was right; less traffic. Lynda closes her eyes as she is always tired after working so late. Neil touches her shoulder in her garage, waking her. Lynda had given Neil her key as she has two car spaces in her garage.

"Hello, beautiful, we're home!" She opens her eyes and then opens the car door.

In the apartment, Lynda flips her shoes off and she goes to the bathroom, turning the taps on and filling her bath with crystal salts to relax her. Neil enters the bathroom; Lynda is already getting in the bath. She smiles at him, and he climbs in behind her. Lynda moves to make room for him, then relaxes back onto his chest, being rather tired. Lynda closes her eyes; Neil turns the taps off and rubs her forehead as she has a slight headache.

"That's nice. You have a gentle touch!" she whispers, nearly falling asleep.

"You stressed too much today!" he says to her while soaping her back.

"I know. Just haven't had any meetings for eight weeks, and now all the clients are demanding to meet in person!" Lynda explains to Neil. He had no idea how difficult her work has been trying to keep clients happy. Mr. Gardner dislikes having meetings; that's why he has her.

"I will always be grateful to you, Neil, for helping!" she says.

"That sounds like we're parting!" he replies in a low tone.

"No, handsome, just so glad you have been part of my life these past months!" Lynda replies, kissing his hand.

Neil kisses her neck then climbs out, taking her hands and helping her out of the bath. He passes a towel to her, rubbing her back.

"What about your jogging outfit? You're staying here the night?" Lynda asks, walking out into the lounge.

Neil tells her he keeps an outfit at work in his office; he often jogs at lunch. Lynda is amazed by Neil's resilience; he's always prepared for the unexpected. He states he will go home tomorrow night. Lynda wraps her towel around her body, kisses him, then goes and gets into her short PJs. Neil is in his shorts and singlet top. His phone rings and he walks out after hanging up. "It was Ben," Neil tells her.

"That reminds me, the business lunch is next month at Ben's restaurant. I must ring him and organise everything!" Lynda states in a panicked voice.

"No need, that is why Ben rang. He received an email from

Jennifer, and she's organised it all!" Neil explains to her.

Lynda says she must give Jennifer a really nice present this Christmas. Neil enquires if she gives gifts to everyone at work. "No, only Jennifer. She's my personal office manager!" she replies. Neil never knew, understanding why she was so helpful to him with suggestions for Lynda. Neil expresses he has never given any gifts to his office staff.

"You better. Patricia always received one each year from her last boss!" Lynda states while looking at him as she's her best friend.

"Okay, I'll put it on my calendar alert!" he replies while sipping coffee.

Lynda suggests maybe she should organise a luncheon on a Saturday with Jennifer and Ben. Neil lifts his eyebrows, enquiring why. Lynda looks at him, saying Jennifer is lonely and the same age as Ben. She feels they will get along. Jen is an excellent cook; she created several meals for her mum's café.

"I just feel the love of food may be something in common for them both!" Lynda replies, rubbing her foot against his ankle.

Neil smiles, thinking she's a romantic for other people, just more cautious of her own life. He agrees to sort a date with Ben but will make it casual and invite others, so it is not obvious. Ben dislikes blind dates.

"Okay, let's book the café at the beach shore," Lynda replies.

Neil likes that suggestion as they can swim afterwards and he can see her in her bathers and relax on Manly beach. He hears the waves rather loud tonight; he opens the sliding door, standing on the balcony, listening.

Lynda walks up behind him, placing her arms around his waist, smelling the sea salt. Neil moves her around to the front as he's tall and likes to look at her. She comments how she likes seeing the lights from the houses and apartments around the shoreline. He kisses her forehead, asking if her headache is gone; she nods 'yes' and cuddles up to him, both enjoying the breeze. Lynda states she will wear a dress tomorrow, too hot for her suit. Neil likes that idea, "One of your new ones," he whispers.

Lynda smiles, saying yes, the yellow one with a white frill on the bottom. He likes that one but doesn't let on he's already seen a picture of it. "Let's go to bed. Long day at work the next two days!" Neil says. Lynda nods her head; she's very tired, he turns off the lights, and they go to bed.

Over the next two days Lynda completes all the work for the law firm, making Neil and his boss very happy. She hand-delivers the documents personally at five that night, handing them directly to the boss. He is very grateful to her, the documents will help the company he is representing. He comments he likes her new clothes as she's wearing a blue dress today.

Lynda thanks him then walks into Neil's office. "We have a date tomorrow; use the bus in the morning and meet me outside the office building at three p.m.!" she smiles at Neil. Who is wondering what is she up to? "Don't forget I have court tomorrow!" Neil replies.

"I know. I assure you the other company will settle instead of going to court!" Lynda replies.

"How can you predict that?" questions Neil.

"I have dealt with this company before you arrived this year. Once they read my report, they will!" Lynda replies, handing him a USB. Read it for yourself at home.

Friday at three p.m., two Harleys arrive, pulling up at the curb. Lynda takes Neil's hand, walking towards them. "This is your surprise!" she states while opening up her mobile to show the booking to the men. They read it, then hand them both a helmet and a backpack. Neil puts his on his back as per instructed by Lynda. The bike ride takes them to the spit bridge marina, Neil and Lynda climb off, saying thanks.

"That was amazing. Thank you, beautiful!" Neil says he has wanted a ride for years, never having the time.

"It's not over yet. This is your reward for helping me the last months!" she says, looking up at him.

Neil holds her hand as she leads him down along the boardwalk towards a beautiful large yacht. Lynda tells Neil she asked a friend to sail them around the harbour for him, a friend of her father's. Neil is very impressed, seeing how lovely the yacht is. They climb aboard, up some steps waiting for them.

"Hi, Mark!" Lynda says to a handsome, tall man approaching her. He leans down, kissing her on the cheek. Neil looks at her and him, thinking, "Ha, hands-off, she's mine!" Lynda sees Neil's shoulders and feels his hand tense.

"Neil, this is Mark, my dear friend; we grew up together as our fathers used to race each other down the harbour!" Lynda states.

"Hi, Lynda. This must be the Neil I've heard so much about!" Mark states, shaking Neil's hand firmly.

She whispers to Neil, saying he's not her type. Mark invites Neil up to the front as he steers the yacht out. The bridge lifts, allowing them to move out; he's using the motor at this stage. Mark assures Neil he never dated Lynda; she's like his little sister, and he looks out for her. Neil looks up at him, asking his age. Mark states he's forty-six and happy being single. Neil settles his shoulders, feeling more secure. Lynda calls Neil to come downstairs; she has clothes ready for him to change out of his suit. Jeans and T-shirt with a jacket. "You will have to show me one day how to get so much in your small backpack!" Neil says, seeing her removing shoes.

"I learnt a technique off the internet on how to fold things into small parcels!" Lynda replies she is already in her jeans and T-shirt, and she puts on her colourful floral jacket.

On deck, the sea breeze is fresh but nice. Mark has set the sails now going out to sea to sail along then into Sydney harbour. Mark has dinner in the kitchen for them all. He organised his chef; he picked him up along the way with food. Neil is very impressed; Lynda informs him that Mark uses his yacht for business meetings and bookings each summer. She opens her mobile to show Neil. He asks what kind of business he's in as the yacht is very expensive.

"The building trade, larger buildings and industrial!" she informs him, explaining her dad and Mark's father meet at the sailing club. Neil sits enjoying his dining along the beautiful harbour; the Opera House and Bridge look spectacular at night. He sneaks a kiss thanking her for a wonderful evening. She is happy Neil's enjoying his special surprise after he has been arranging everything to suit her needs. Lynda is smiling at him as he often spoke about going sailing and having a Harley ride, both boxes ticked off.

Saturday morning

Neil picks Lynda up, driving to where his sister trains for her rowing, and he waves to her. Morgan sees Lynda and she tells her friends, "He's brought her," the team all look towards Neil and Lynda on arriving, and he introduces Lynda to the girls. She is polite to the girls; they nod their heads to her without saying a word and Neil walks off to speak to the coach. Morgan and her friend call Lynda a bitch as they walk past her, forcing Lynda to move; the words are upsetting, considering she's done nothing to deserve it. She now realises it's going to be more difficult than she thinks with Morgan.

"Have a good practice!" Lynda says. She's not going to let them change her ways; she gives advice.

Morgan tells her team to take no notice. Neil overhears Lynda on his return; he asks how she knows to instruct.

"My sister rowed for her school and won a NSW championship as a single rower!" she comments.

Neil looks at her, unaware of this fact. She whispers to him she's lived a life through her twenties and thirties. He chuckles; Lynda loves his huge smile. She kisses his cheek in front of everyone, which is a big improvement. Neil is thinking Lynda is becoming more comfortable with them as a couple, showing affection in public. The couple move across, sitting on the grass and watching the rowers until they disappear out of sight. Neil stands, saying they will be gone for an hour until coming back again; he helps Lynda to her feet. He walks her along a path to a coffee van which opens early, he comments. Lynda smiles as Neil always knows where to get his fix; she orders a long black, surprising Neil.

"I need one this morning!" she comments.

"Is everything okay?" aware she only has a coffee when stressed or upset. She states she's fine and just wants one.

Neil hands it to her as they walk back. She discusses Morgan, asking which type of music she likes and her interests. Neil tells her a few things she likes to do, enjoys sports and her favourite celebrity. Lynda takes it all in and they sit again, enjoying the morning with their coffee. On seeing the rowers returning, Neil stands watching; he walks down with Lynda by his side as the scull is being lifted out of the water, and the girls place it back inside the shed. Morgan walks out towards Neil, and he gives instructions on her performance, being rather firm and critical. Lynda touches his hand and gives him a look to ease up.

Lynda comments, "Rather good job."

"Not interested in your opinion!" Morgan says under her breath so Neil doesn't hear. Lynda just walks off back to the jeep. Neil talks to his sister and then enters the car speaking with Lynda. They talk about Morgan's team performance. Lynda suggests not to be so hard on her.

"She has to learn; been rowing for four years and still no improvement. They lost the last two years against their opponents!" he replies bluntly.

Lynda is now seeing another side to Neil; he's very competitive. He talks about his basketball team. Neil mentions the training twice a week to achieve their goals and won their finals.

"The girls worked hard but listened. Morgan doesn't like being told when she's wrong!" Neil comments.

"Maybe a gentle approach will suffice!" Lynda replies, saying it worked with her sister. That is why she won many races.

Morgan slumps into the back seat, placing her earplugs in. Lynda suggests she sit in the front to talk to her brother about her training. Morgan stares at her, "okay," she mumbles. Lynda climbs out, swapping places. She talks all the way home; Neil lets her out, saying goodbye; he and Lynda are off as he's meeting her family today. Morgan is not happy being left on the driveway without him coming inside to spend some time with her. Morgan thinks her brother never dated other women this long or met their parents, a signal he's serious. Morgan is not happy; she stomps off into the house.

Lynda watches her as she climbs into the front seat. Neil drives off, asking questions about her siblings. Neil likes to be prepared with all information, asking for details about their lives. Lynda advises waiting and judge for himself. He drives to the liquor shop to buy the wine for her father. Lynda already bought the chocolates for her mum to help him. Neil looks a little nervous and she suggests they stop at the café, her favourite and more personal.

"Good morning, Lynda," says the girl. Neil watches as they all seem to know Lynda; she escorts him across to her favourite table. A good view of the street and people walking by.

"This is nice. How did you find it?" Neil enquires.

Lynda explains she stops when travelling to her parents' home as they live in Mosman, a distance from Neil's parents' home in Bondi. "I like the Scandic style atmosphere and it's quieter!" she replies.

Neil has to admit it's very friendly; the sounds of other voices do not echo. Lynda enquires if he speaks about her to Morgan, and he says he does. Lynda advises him not to – just keep his conversation about her. Neil looks at her, asking why? Lynda explains Morgan has been part of his life without sharing him.

"Might make the transition easier. You have been dating me longer than your other girlfriends!" Lynda states. "How do you know that?" he asks.

Lynda informs him she has been speaking to Donna when recommending wine for her ladies' days. "She shared some information with me to help me understand this is different!"

Neil agrees to keep Lynda out of the conversation when speaking with his sister. Lynda informs him her parents are different from his parents, her father more conservative and her mother wanting to marry her off to anyone. She's warning him so as not to be embarrassed and preparing him for questioning by her mother and brothers.

"I apologise now if Mum asks too many questions about your intentions!" Lynda says, sipping her tea while keeping her eyes on him.

"No, need!" Neil answers, smiling at her.

Lynda is a little uneasy as she hasn't introduced him to her family. She likes him immensely and has some feelings but has not fallen in love. Lynda is unsure about being together long term, especially with a sister that dislikes her. Lynda prefers to step carefully and slowly into a relationship as her past has been difficult. She talks about her brothers and how they love their football. "What's their team?" he asks.

Lynda looks rather surprised at him, and she grins, "Seagulls of course!" As they all live in the area.

Neil sees her expression, stating he's been living in Victoria for the past ten years, so he hasn't been following football. Neil explains his parents live in Bondi, so barrack for a different team, all wondering why he chose to live in Manly. Lynda asks why too. Neil tells her he bought the flat before he left as an investment.

"I have been renting the flat to pay for mine in Melbourne. I renovated the flat last year just before I returned!" Neil tells her.

Lynda shakes her head, makes good business sense, Neil aware she thinks in figures.

Lynda talks to Neil about Amanda. Neil touches her hand, knowing it is upsetting to her when talking about her youngest sister.

"When did she die?" he asks in a soft voice. "Five years ago, last Monday. Yes, my two younger siblings are closer to your age!" Lynda replies, knowing the date.

Neil squeezes her hand, nodding his head. "You have a

young mind and are very active. Stop thinking about our ages!" he says, looking into her green eyes.

Lynda holds his hand tightly, drinking her tea. She looks at the time on her watch and tells him they better make a move; otherwise her dad will say she's late again. "Mustn't upset the folks!" Neil says, finishing his cappuccino and making a move, he pays on the way out. He buys a cake each for Lynda's niece and nephew and she thanks him, "Will they like these?" he enquires.

"Any kind of cake, never matters as they're kids!" Lynda replies while walking out. The owner says goodbye with a smile, looking at Neil. A man is pointedly staring at them both. Lynda smiles back, making the man feel self-conscious. She is aware these days age difference is accepted, but some younger people still comment, like in her office. Susan is trying to find out more about Neil, saying she's the right age for him. Susan is very curious and stops Lynda each morning, enquiring if she knows Neil's mobile; due to the fact they travel on the bus together. The girl is clueless, unlike some others who have noticed a difference in Lynda.

Last Tuesday, Lynda nearly let it slip; she's dating him in her mind, she thought. 'Bloody keep your hands off him!' If only she had the courage to say it out loud to Susan.

Neil asks what she is thinking. "Nothing." He looks at her while driving and sees she's frowning. "Stop worrying about your folks!" he says.

She laughs, saying she's not thinking of them. "Susan in the office is asking questions about your interests and mobile number!" Lynda says while touching his leg softly. "Don't bloody give it to her; I can't stand that girl. I have a real woman and keeping you, Lynda!" He touches her hand, looking at her quickly.

Lynda gives him directions and soon they're pulling into her parent's driveway. An old home, Lynda tells him it's a 1930s house her parents renovated ten years ago. A little girl is standing at the door.

"Hello, Zoe," calls Lynda, and the girl runs down to cuddle her. "This is my friend, Neil!" she whispers to Zoe.

"Hello," she says, looking up at him. "He's tall," she says. Neil hands her the bag with the cakes. "Thanks," Zoe says, looking inside.

"One for Liam," says Lynda. Zoe runs into the house calling, "Lynda and Neil are here."

Lynda looks at Neil saying they are announced. He walks beside her on entering and the entrance is a nice size. He can see her parents kept some art deco features and he rather likes them, now understanding why Lynda wanted him to keep some old structures at his cottage. She says it looks like everyone's out on the deck and she escorts him. A smaller home than Neil's parents', but nice brick with a large deck. Everyone is sitting or standing, looking towards Lynda.

"Hi everyone, this is Neil," she says in a casual manner. She goes around the table introducing him. "Jack, my dad and Ava, my mum," Lynda says. Her father walks across, shaking Neil's hand firmly.

Neil hands him the bottle of wine, "He's going to work, my favourite wine," he comments, looking at his kids.

Julia laughs along with her husband while Neil hands Ava the box of chocolates. She thanks him taking them into the kitchen to speak to her husband, "He looks younger than Lynda said, good looking though!" Ava says. Jack comments he will wait until the end of the day after getting to know him a bit before making a judgement; looking towards his wife, he uncorks the wine.

On the deck, Brian steps forward, shaking Neil's hand and looking at him. Julia asks what he's drinking. "A beer is good," Neil replies, seeing the men are having one and wants to try to fit in today. Simon walks up the stairs; on reaching the deck, he walks straight across.

"Finally, someone my age instead of these old guys Lynda dates. Big improvement on the last one, Sis!" Simon states.

Lynda blushes. Neil holds her hand tightly signalling it's fine; he takes the beer from Brian.

"You can't say that!" Julia says, correcting her younger brother.

"Why not? You guys always go against me. I will have something in common with Neil!" Simon says, taking a beer.

John asks Neil about his career. "I'm a lawyer," he looks towards Lynda. "Lynda has been keeping you to herself, refusing to let us in on what you're like and your job!" Brian states.

"Don't question Neil, you guys. Like you normally do!" Lynda says, just letting her siblings know to tread carefully.

Neil takes a gulp of beer, now nervous. He preferring Lynda would have told her family something about him. Julia invites Neil to sit beside her. She whispers never mind my brothers; they're always looking out for Lynda.

"They gave John a bad time too nine years ago when we dated!" Julia tells Neil as he stares across at her. Lynda goes into the kitchen to find some wine glasses and wine for Neil, aware he prefers wine to beer.

Julia hands Neil some chips and he takes a few. He is being questioned by Brian about whether he has other women on the side. John is as shocked as Julia and Simon that their big brother is saying that.

John quickly jumps in, saying. "Don't mind Brian. Being the eldest, he takes it upon himself to protect the girls. We are just all looking out for Lynda after her fiancé cheated on her; she broke off the engagement eighteen months ago. She was badly hurt!"

Neil is unaware Lynda was engaged not that long ago. She walks out carrying wine glasses and a bottle of red, and she sees Neil's expression. "Okay, what have you guys done to Neil? He's pale!" she comments. Everyone looks at him, which makes him go red.

"Nothing, Sis. Just giving him some advice!" states Brian.

Lynda takes Neil's beer can, handing it to her brother Simon. She gives Neil a glass, filling it with red wine. She kisses his cheek in front of her siblings. All looking at her, she has never done that before,

"Leave him alone, none of your questioning. Remember Neil's a lawyer and can handle you lot!" Lynda says, staring around the table at her siblings.

Neil sips some wine, more to his liking. Lynda slips her hand into his, ready to protect him against her brothers and sisters. Mia enters the house calling she's got the salads; Ava takes them, telling her to go and meet Neil. Mia walks out with her son, and she gazes towards Lynda,

"Mia, this is Neil. Neil, meet Mia and Liam her son. Brian's wife!" John says introducing his sister-in-law. Neil stands to say hello, shaking her hand.

"Wow, Lynda never said you were so tall and good-looking!" Mia says while walking across to Brian, asking if he's been behaving.

Lynda says, "no." Mia punches his arm, a signal not to give Neil a bad time as they did with her when first introduced to the family.

"I have a question, Neil. How did you fit in accountancy and a law degree, being only thirty?" Jack says, sitting down at the table. Lynda gives her dad a stern look. Neil replies he only studied accountancy for one year and switched the last term to study law.

"You must be smart, ha?" Liam asks.

"Just work at it!" Neil replies, smiling at the boy.

Neil's hand is sweating from the family questioning; Lynda squeezes it to let him know she's with him. She excuses herself, saying she's going to show Neil the playroom; at those words the kids run ahead. Neil places his glass down, walking beside her down a set of stairs to a lower level. The house sits on a sloping block.

"Sorry about my brother and dad!" she whispers to Neil.

Neil tells her not to worry about it, he's had worse in the courtroom, just never met a girlfriend's family until today. He is now aware why he avoided a long-term relationship, except this time he wants it to work. Lynda is giving him time to breathe, and allowing John and Mia to handle the family, as they are in-laws too and will sympathise with Neil. Lynda steals a kiss on the stairs whispering she will protect him, aware he is nervous. Neil smiles at her; the kids are already in the room. Zoe sits with her tablet playing a game, and Liam is playing on his uncle's old PlayStation. Lynda gets out backgammon to take Neil's mind off her family; he sets it up and they begin, then Simon comes down. "You don't play that do you?" he yells, thinking it's an old person's game.

"I'm not old!" replies Lynda.

Neil looks up at her. It's the first time he's heard her defend her age, considering she worries about his age being too young.

Neil is beginning to know why after meeting Simon, a little immature and being her younger brother. Neil talks to Simon while playing the game with Lynda, and he still wins.

"Not again," Lynda says, shaking her head.

Simon laughs, "Now let's talk about football!" he says.

"No, no, you're not. Give Neil a chance to get to know you first!" Lynda says, interrupting Simon and taking Neil back upstairs by the hand.

She calls Zoe and Liam, saying food is ready; the kids race past them on the staircase. Neil laughs, having never been around little ones before, he rather likes it. Simon follows behind. The food has been spread on a spare table at the other end of the deck. Lynda hands Neil a plate staying behind the others. Neil notices a wide variety of dishes to choose from, something different for a change, no barbie. Neil takes a little of each, sitting down beside Lynda. She is making sure none of her brothers are sitting next to him as she places Zoe on the other side. Julia smiles at Lynda as she's been through this before, too. Ava, her mother, speaks up, asking Neil and Lynda if they are planning being a permanent couple. Lynda nearly chokes on her wine.

"Let us just be comfortable with each other!" Lynda says.

Neil looks towards her as he has other ideas. He is falling in love with her and thought she was aware of this; obviously not.

"Gee, Mum. Lynda's obviously getting serious. Otherwise she would never bring him to meet us all, especially Brian!" Julia says, winking at Neil.

Lynda places her hand on Neil's leg smiling, letting him know she cares but has no intentions of letting her family know her true feelings.

"No wedding plans then?" enquires her mother tactlessly.

Neil gulps his food quickly. Julia laughs, "Don't worry,

Mum. Lynda will tell you after she's eloped!" Julia says, making everyone look towards Lynda, who is now blushing.

"I hope you made the pavlova. I told Neil all about how nice it is!" Lynda says, trying to change the subject.

Neil looks at everyone and he speaks up. "I will put a ring on Lynda's finger when it's time. I am taking good care of her!"

Ava and Jack look at him with serious expressions. Neil's way of letting everyone know he has no intention of losing Lynda.

He lifts her hand up onto the table, holding it tightly, showing everyone he means business. Julia looks at her husband with a smile.

"I like him," says John. He likes a man that's down to earth, a real Aussie and obviously knows what he wants.

"Has Lynda told you she's frozen her eggs!" Jack yells out, silencing everyone at the table.

"What? You did what?" Ava cries, staring at her daughter, shocked.

"Yeah, good idea, Sis. You're getting old to have babies!" states Brian.

"That's enough, my eggs. I can do what I want with them!" Lynda says loudly, looking mad at her dad for starting the conversation, especially in front of Neil. Jack has never forgiven her for doing it after Lynda revealed her plans for her future.

"I'm sure it's Lynda's business, not mine anyway. Good to have a backup!" Neil says in a strong voice, his lawyer's tone silencing the entire family.

Lynda looks at him. She's seen him in action in court and she thanks him, whispering. Julia quickly asks Lynda and Neil to help in the kitchen with desserts to give them a break. "Sorry about that, Neil!" she says to him. He tells her he's fine, saying something for him and Lynda to discuss in private, not with her family. Julia agrees; she tells Lynda and Neil that is how she was able to have Zoe, she too froze her eggs at thirty.

"I know. That is why I froze mine, after you not falling pregnant. I wanted security, in case!" Lynda touches her sister's arm and the women hug.

Neil watches as he picks up the pavlova. "Don't drop it!" Julia says, grinning.

Lynda takes the pavlova, seeing his hands are a little shaky after the shock of finding out about her eggs; not a discussion for them yet. Lynda thinks her family is trying to ruin her relationship with Neil. Simon comes into the kitchen and Lynda hands him the pav, telling him to go. Lynda hands Neil the bowls while she carries the strawberries and cream. Julia brings out the ice cream being her kids' and Lynda's favourite. "Vanilla. Mum never gets this one!" Lynda comments.

"NO, I bought it for you!" Julia replies, telling Neil it's Lynda's favourite flavour. He smiles, not knowing that yet; surprisingly, he has never bought her an ice cream during the entire summer of their being together. Lynda opens a package of lollies filling a bowl. She fills three others, one with strawberries already cut up and cream. Neil watches; she tells him everyone likes their own toppings. "What will you like?" Lynda asks Neil.

Neil just says fruit and ice cream is fine. She gets out a bowl of mixed fruit placing it on the tray.

"Are you ready to go back into the slaughter?" she asks Neil.

He kisses her on the cheek, saying, "Yes, it's fine." All eyes are fixed on the desserts, especially the kids and men all loving their sweets. Ava serves the pavlova in slices. The adults dig in, choosing their favourite toppings, along with the kids all talking at the same time. Lynda has strawberries with ice cream, the kids lollies and cream, Brian with chocolate and banana, Simon has a little of everything. Lynda serves Neil placing fruit and ice cream on his pav and handing it to him. Neil watches everyone relaxed in each other's company with no topic being off limits, as he found out. Lynda's family is so different from his own. Neil mentions he's been invited by Lynda to join them on the cancer run day.

"Great, one more for the team!" says Simon.

"That's nice of you, Neil!" Ava says.

Neil smiles at her, making them aware he is supporting Lynda and her family. "Are you any good?" questions Brian.

"Yes, he's fast!" replies Lynda, giving her brother a look.

Jack pulls him into line, stating it's just a fun day to raise money. Everyone wears either pink or dresses up; anything goes.

"What about your ankle?" asks Julia.

"I'm here to help Lynda. I can carry her across the line!" Neil quickly speaks before anyone else can answer. Lynda nods her head, telling her brothers how strong Neil is, unlike them being weak.

"You, saying I can't carry my wife? Not strong enough? That's fighting words, Sis!" Brian says. Lynda laughs along with Julia, both aware that he has never done any exercises or attended a gym.

"Julia's stronger than you, Brian, due to her rowing!" states John with a half-laugh.

The afternoon is spent playing cricket; two teams are formed. Neil, Lynda, Julia, Liam and Simon on one team, against Brian, John, Jack, Mia and Zoe. Brian's team batted first, as he knows what a good hitter Lynda is. She whispers to Neil, saying he should go first, knowing he's an excellent bowler. Brian is out quickly along with Jack which amuses the girls. Neil discovers

Lynda is talented at batting, giving them home runs. One and a half hours later, Neil's team wins, making Liam happy as he's never on the winning team. Liam gives a high five to Neil; the boy is so happy he tells Neil he can come and play anytime.

Neil looks, thinking the kids like him. Julia tells him if you make it with the kids, you're in.

Neil looks at her. "Okay, how about you?" he asks softly.

"You are making Lynda happy, that's all I need. Don't hurt her!" Julia replies.

"I have no intentions on that, just want to be part of her life forever!" Neil answers, giving Julia a smile as they walk back upstairs to the house.

Lynda rescues Neil thinking he's had enough of her family. She says goodbye to everyone. Neil says goodbye with his arm behind Lynda's back; everyone notices his affection towards their sister and daughter. This is a new experience for them all. Lynda's other men never showed it, and defending her, they like the way Neil speaks highly of Lynda.

In the car on the way home, Lynda apologises to Neil for her family mentioning her private matters. He shrugs his shoulders and is unusually quiet. Neil stops the car outside her apartment; he has a serious expression.

"Come on up. You obviously want to ask me something?" Lynda says. Neil remains in the car and he asks about Lynda's engagement. She is shocked he found out. "Was it Brian?" she enquires.

"Doesn't matter who. Is it true?" Neil asks.

Lynda tells Neil. Since he's been in her life, she is now finding out for the first time he is compatible with her.

"My last relationship, terrible kisser and sex, he never liked anything I did. He always brought work home or would be somewhere else. I discovered why, being with another woman. I broke it off. I'm glad he's out of my life!" Lynda looks at Neil.

"You never have to worry. I will never do that, ever!" Neil says.

"I trust you, Neil. This is better; we have something more and special!" Lynda replies, looking Neil in the eyes, allowing him to see he means a lot to her.

Neil decides to think about everything. He tells Lynda he will contact her later. Lynda understands after springing a past engagement on him and her father mentioning her eggs being frozen. She climbs out of the jeep, waving to him and watching him drive off. Lynda rings Brian, yelling at him for telling Neil. "You had no right. It's up to me, not you!" Lynda is so annoyed with her brother.

Brian tells her he's looking out for her and saying she'll see if he's a man or not to take it. "You need to keep your mouth shut. I was going to explain when we were further along in our relationship. I might lose him now!" Lynda yells back, hanging up on her brother.

In the morning Lynda dresses in something nice. Neil doesn't ring her and she's a little concerned. She stops, picks up his favourite coffee and morning bun, and she walks to his apartment, only four blocks away. On arriving, she rings his doorbell. After a few moments, he opens the door standing bare-chested and in shorts.

"Do you always open the door like that?" she asks, handing him his coffee. He looks her up and down in her floral dress with sandals.

"I thought I would surprise you! Is that okay?" Lynda says, looking at him with concern as he looks serious.

Neil allows her to come in and, on closing his door, follows her. "Are we all right?" she asks in a soft voice.

"If I thought you never had a husband or fiance in your past, I would be foolish, Lynda; your past is yours. I only want a future with you. Don't worry, I'm not going anywhere!" Neil replies, looking at her.

He steps forward, taking her tea and placing it on his bench; he pulls her close to him, kissing her. Lynda places her arms around his neck with one hand in his hair. Neil loves the way she kisses, and plays with his hair. It excites him.

Lynda steps back, whispering, "I was just a little concerned about your reaction yesterday!"

Neil expresses his feelings are strong and developing each day with her. "I only ask you to trust and come on the journey with me!" he says, holding his hands on her waist in front of him.

Lynda looks at Neil, thinking this younger man must be the man she has been searching for. The fear of losing him makes her realise her feelings for him are getting stronger. He is amazing; nothing seems to deter him.

"I don't compare you to anyone else from my past. I will come along if you'll have me!" Lynda replies, looking longingly up into his eyes.

"That is all I ask!" he says, holding her close to his chest and kissing her head.

Chapter Five

Fun Race

The entire family has assembled, and Simon is wearing a pink curly wig. He wears it every year as it used to make Amanda laugh during her treatments. All the men wear pink shirts and socks, and the women are decked out in pink from head to foot. Julia and Lynda sprayed their hair pink and have pink running shoes.

Brian hands Neil a pink shirt he bought for him. "Sorry mate if I came across as too harsh on your visit. Looking out for Sis!"

Neil taps him on the shoulder, being taller. "It's okay," he wears the pink T-shirt over his singlet top. Brian sighs with relief as Lynda hasn't answered his phone calls since. Neil notices Brian's expression; he explains he and Lynda have talked it out and are okay. Neil walks him across to Lynda. "Look who I found; he gave me a shirt!" Neil says cheerfully.

Lynda smiles and she hugs her brother. "Sorry," Brian whispers to her.

"All good," she whispers back.

Neil has invited his parents and sister along; he introduces Lynda's family to his parents and Morgan. She keeps her earplugs in. Ava and Jack thank them for wearing pink shirts.

"Of course. The least we can do. We are sorry for your loss!" Robert notices their daughter's name printed on the back of their shirts.

"For Amanda." Robert tells Jack they donated to their daughter's webpage and told several businessmen. Jack thanks him. Morgan is wearing black, which doesn't impress the siblings. Lynda explains she never does anything to help her. Julia will not have this; she walks across, handing Morgan a pink shirt.

"You are in our team, and we would appreciate it if you would wear this, please!" Julia says with a smile, handing it to Morgan.

Neil walks across, thanking Julia and encourages his sister to wear it. She reluctantly places it over her T-shirt. Lynda thanks Julia, and she replies, "it's for Amanda." Donna walks across to Morgan, saying, "Thank you. It means a lot to us and the family. The charity needs all the help it can get!" she tells her daughter.

"I will for the charity, not for Lynda!" Morgan states, staring at her mother.

Neil interrupts, whispering to Morgan to try and get to know Lynda today; she's important to him. The girl gives him a stern expression while listening to her music. Neil walks across to stand with Lynda as he will be in the front along with her, being fast runners. The entire family moves towards the line-up and Lynda asks Morgan to join her and Neil. He says no, she isn't a runner; best if she walks with their parents, more her pace. Neil knows his sister dislikes walking, always asking for a ride even for a block away to the shops. Morgan gives her brother a terrible look. Lynda says to join them anyway, she will jog slower for her.

Morgan nudges Lynda's arm with her elbow as she moves away back to her parents. Lynda takes no notice and just rubs her arm, joining her siblings with Neil. Julia been training Brian for the past six months for the race. Neil has been helping Lynda at lunchtimes to try and strengthen her ankle. The four have moved to the frontline joining the other fast runners. There are groups for walkers, prams and children, catering for everyone. The dress-up group, Simon's friends, are walkers, not runners. Zoe and Liam are walking with their grandparents and Mia. Neil keeps an eye on Lynda while she's running, not wanting her ankle to suddenly collapse. He runs beside her even though he is a faster runner. As she runs along, after a little while, she changes into a jog. Neil remains by her side while Brian and Julia get a second breath and pass. Lynda laughs seeing her brother puffing hard, Neil supports Lynda's arm, noticing the bruise. "How did you do that?" he asks.

"Must have banged myself!" she replies, then changes into a walk.

Lynda says her ankle is a little sore her doctors have been concerned, telling her to take it easy today and not push it. Neil holds her hand. "Then we shall finish together with our folks." Lynda laughs, telling Neil to keep moving ahead.

"I can rest before they finish. Besides, there are mobile vans with coffees and cool drinks and food!" Lynda tells him.

Neil agrees, loving his coffee. He picks Lynda up into his arms, saying he will carry her for a bit. Lynda quickly wraps her arms around his neck, saying he's strong. Twenty minutes later, he puts Lynda down and they walk slowly along together. She talks about their holiday in a week and a half. She moves the conversation, trying to find out where Neil is planning on taking her as he's keeping it as a surprise. Neil moves her hand up, kissing it and advising her to wait; she will love it. He has taken a lot of time planning their perfect first holiday together. Neil is aware when they both go on holiday at the same time, the gossip engines will move around the entire building at work. He and Lynda's secret of being together will finally be shown revealed to their colleagues. Neil's boss already knows due to Neil asking for the time off. The boss thinking it's great having a love affair in his office as he's been trying to match make Lynda for years.

Lynda put a stop to it when Neil's boss tried to organise a date with his son. She disliked the son immensely; she politely reminded the boss that her job with his company was strictly business. The man stepped back, allowing Lynda to breathe the past year. Lynda always tries to avoid him on her monthly reporting days.

Neil and Lynda make it to the finish line, Brian and Julia clapping as they cross, asking about her ankle.

"It's okay; just need to put it up!" Julia points to their seats.

John arranges seating and food, setting up their camp with folding furniture in the family's regular spot. This is John's job as he prefers not to run or walk and likes being the camp organiser, having food and drinks ready for everyone. Neil escorts Lynda across, holding his arm behind her back for support. She sits and he places an esky under her foot. John returns carrying coffees for his Julia, Neil and Brian. "Thanks," Neil says.

"Don't worry, Lynda gave me your order!" Johns says, seeing Neil checking under the lid.

John hands Lynda her lemongrass and ginger tea; she prefers it after a race as it refreshes her. John packs it every year in a thermos for her. "How long will the folks take this year, do you think?" John enquires, as last year it took them two hours.

Neil jumps in, saying probably longer with his parents, especially if they are talking. Lynda says, "Yes, I wonder what about?" with a grin.

Neil smiles, holding her hand. Julia says, "Let's have our bits to eat; they will help our hunger until they arrive!" On opening up a container, she passes it around to the small group. Neil tries one and thinks it rather nice.

"Apricot and honey bits!" Lynda tells him.

Meanwhile, further back in the race, Mia is walking with Zoe and Liam as her mother-in-law joins Donna, wanting to talk about Lynda and Neil. Ava asks what Neil was like as a child. Donna tells Ava she is his stepmother, only being part of his life from age twelve, but she can say he was a delightful kid. Neil loves to have fun and enjoys making people happy. Ava is not very tactful in getting right down to it. She discusses the age difference being a problem.

"Not for Neil," states Donna.

Ava looks at her, "Lynda normally goes for much older men; it was a shock when she introduced us to a young man!" she says rather loudly.

Mia moves the children away, getting them to run to uncle Simon in his group. Donna stands up for Neil, saying he is a wonderful person, compassionate and knows what he wants. "Maybe it's just what Lynda needs considering how her last fiancé treated her!" Donna says bluntly, with a look of disapproval at the woman's reactions to Neil.

Ava is surprised by her answer, unaware she knew about Lynda's last boyfriend. "Neil cares for Lynda and will treat her properly!" Donna says to Ava and says she will go and walk with her husband.

Ava keeps walking and Mia comes up to her, saying she should get to know Neil before judging him. "I think their ages are perfect. Lynda needs a man who cares for her and if that means he's thirty, so what!" she tells her mother-in-law off.

Jack joins Ava, asking what's going on. She says nothing and keeps walking along. Donna tells Robert how Ava feels; he tells her not to worry. "Let Neil and Lynda sort it out!" Robert says he has changed his mind about Lynda, understanding her business skills and getting to know her on the phone during the last two weeks. "Let's just enjoy this walk and support Lynda's family today!" Robert tells his wife.

Morgan slips up to her mother; she had overheard Lynda's mother's conversation. She supports Ava saying how Lynda is not right for her brother and is far too old.

"The only thing wrong is your jealousy. Neil deserves a life with someone special. He's spoilt you too much; stop thinking about yourself for once!" Donna tells her daughter and walks off with her husband, telling him she is angry with Morgan for not giving Lynda a chance.

Morgan walks off, joining Simon's group. She is angry towards her mother and Neil. The pram group beat the fancy-dress group. Simon is just happy they finished, having fun with his friends. He walks across, clapping his folks across the line, telling his dad he's off. Simon goes off to celebrate with his mates each year.

"Don't ring me for a lift!" his dad calls. Simon waves and runs off.

Jack, Ava, Mia and the children join the family. Lynda lowers her foot on seeing them approaching. She tells Neil and her brother and sister not to mention her ankle, and they all agree. Neil walks across to his parents, asking if they enjoyed it, "Yes, good walk!" Robert says.

Brian hands the men a cold beer and they thank him. Lynda pours Donna a nice cold white wine, remembering from their first meeting the woman's preference.

"Please sit. Where is Liam?" Lynda asks. She then sees something she doesn't approve of and limps across. Morgan has him by the shirt shoulder, yelling at him. Lynda grabs Liam, wiping his face. She asks him what happened. "She picked on me. I said you and Neil should get married, and she grabbed me, yelling!"

"Look here, Morgan. You can call me a bitch, she, it, bang into me. You will not pick on my little Nephew. Leave him alone. Fight me if you dare!" Lynda raises her voice.

Lynda is holding Liam against her. Julia and Brian run across, along with Neil overhearing. Lynda only loses it when very upset.

"What's going on?" Neil asks.

"Your sister, that's what. Handle her or I will!" Lynda replies.

Julia takes Liam to his mother. Brian places his hand on his sister's shoulder, trying to calm her, but this time Morgan has pushed Lynda too far.

"Don't be so hard; she's only a teen. I think you're exaggerating a bit!" Neil says, looking down at Lynda, not seeing or hearing how his sister is to others.

"That's it until you notice what Morgan's like to me. I need a two-week break. Julia and John can drive me home!" Lynda yells up at him.

"Aren't you overreacting?" Neil replies.

Morgan is smirking. This is the first time Neil sees her, and he stares at her disapprovingly. Lynda limps off towards the family group and Neil goes to follow.

Brian grabs his arm. "Let her calm down before talking with her. Trust me, she needs time!"

Neil thanks him, walking with Brian over to the family. Lynda sits down, fuming. Neil walks across; he removes the pink shirt, handing it back to Brian and thanking him. Neil is wearing his singlet top underneath, now showing his muscular arms and chest.

"He's quite a man. You lucky girl!" Julia comments. Lynda looks at her sister.

Morgan takes her shirt off, tossing it down on the ground. Her mother picks it up, thanking Julia for loaning it to her daughter. Neil is annoyed by this, and he tells Morgan to say thank you. "Thanks," Morgan says offhandedly.

Julia whispers to Lynda, advising her not to be angry with Neil, "He's not responsible for his sister's actions." She nudges her sister to say something.

Lynda thanks Neil for coming and he moves across, standing behind her chair and placing his hands on her shoulders. He feels Lynda's stiffness. Brian gives his sister a nod with his head towards Neil.

Donna thanks Lynda for her advice on the wine and deli choice; her woman's group thoroughly enjoyed their luncheon. Everyone commented on the delicious food and liked the games, her selection helping to brighten up their day.

Ava is very surprised by her daughter being friendly with Neil's step mum so soon. "Glad they enjoyed the food. It was Ben who originally recommended the deli to me!" Lynda replies.

Neil now understood which Deli. The same one she stopped at for his special luncheon on the way to Jenolan Caves. Neil asks the family if they made enough money today for their daughter Amanda's fundraising page. Julia answers, saying yes. She just checked and there are more donations for cancer than last year's efforts. She thanks Robert, Neil and friend Ben for donations boosting the funds.

"Thank your friends at work, Robert and Ben's restaurant, Neil!" John says with a grin.

Lynda touches Neil's hand. He leans down and she whispers. "Thank you so much!"

He kisses her head, "it's okay beautiful." Neil uses the music app on his phone, asking Jack and Ava if it is all right to play the tune after mentioning the title.

"Yes, thank you," Ava says, forgetting to play it after having guests this year.

Neil plays the tune for the family to listen to. Lynda gets up and stands next to Neil, placing her arm behind his back. He does the same. She is still annoyed, but her affection for Neil and his consideration for her family is strong. The song ends; he turns to Lynda. "Talk later?"

She whispers, "Okay, maybe tomorrow at Sunday breakfast at our café." Neil accepts her offer. He leaves, telling his parents he's taking Morgan home.

Donna says, "Good." They will be home later, as the fundraiser is not far from their home at Bondi.

"Morgan, what's your deal?" Neil asks her while driving.

"I don't want anything to change. I need you, not that woman!" Morgan replies angrily.

Neil turns sideways, telling his sister she is eighteen next month and growing up. He asks how she would feel if he came between her and her boyfriend. Morgan looks out the window, surprised her brother is aware she is seeing a boy. "I love Lynda and want a new life with a wife and kids, and Lynda is that woman I have been looking for. So live with it!" Neil says, raising his voice, something he never does with her.

Morgan apologises. She tries the crying act she uses when she wants to get her own way, fooling Neil. "Not working this time. You have gone too far; you will say sorry to Lynda by text if you don't have the guts to phone and mean it!"

"No, I'm not," Morgan screams at him.

Neil drives the rest of the way in silence, really annoyed by his sister. He drops her off in the driveway. "You leaving me alone?" Morgan says, standing on the driveway.

"Yes, grow up!" Neil replies, reversing down the driveway.

Neil drives down to Ben's apartment to speak with him, informing him of everything that happened. Ben advises not to rush Lynda.

"Your sister is nice, but you spoilt her by buying anything she asked for. You always being there for her when she demands. It's your fault she's a jealous cow!" Ben says, shocking Neil by being frank.

Ben says he likes Lynda; she's good for him, not giving into him, and she is now hurting. "Today will be hard, remembering her young sister and the entire family. The last thing they needed was Morgan!" Ben looks at his mate

Ben offers Neil coffee to clear his mind, suggesting to wait until the morning to talk to Lynda. Neil says he will send a text to see if her ankle is okay. Ben asks to let him do it, and Neil allows his friend; he texts while Neil drinks his coffee.

Ben: "How's your ankle, Lynda?"

Lynda: "A little sore but feeling better, is Neil with you?" the only way he has known about her ankle.

Ben: "Yes, but cares about you, give him a chance. His sister will come around!"

Lynda: "Tell Neil I'll see him at breakfast!"

Ben: "Good, take care friend."

Ben tells Neil her ankle is feeling better, and she will see him in the morning. "She guessed you came to see me, smart woman!"

Lynda is five minutes late to breakfast, and she sits opposite Neil.

"I wasn't late on purpose, just slept in!" she replies.

"I didn't think you did; I was concerned about your ankle after yesterday!" Neil replies.

Lynda admits to Neil the doctor informed her she has a chip in the bone, which is aggravating her ankle. He frowns slightly, worrying. He asks why she didn't tell him. "I can sort it, just didn't want you to worry!" Lynda says.

Lynda mentions she's thinking of selling her car for a new one. Does he have any suggestions for brands? Neil says he will drive her anywhere she wants. Lynda informs him she has friends to visit, shopping trips with family, and he can't be with her twenty-four seven. Neil understands and agrees with her. He names a few good brands and types of cars that might suit her as she only wants a cheap and little car to fit into parking spots.

Lynda states it would be good to have a car now with her ankle! she smiles at him.

Neil is concerned she is planning on breaking up with him; he touches her hand to test her. Lynda holds his hand tightly, looking directly at him.

"I won't come between you and your sister. She is never going to accept me!" Lynda says in a sad tone.

A girl comes up to take their order explaining it will take an hour due to a huge number of customers this morning. Lynda says it's okay; she orders, "Avocado, bacon, tomato and sourdough. And eggs Benedict, one black coffee in a cup and one mug of cappuccino!" the girl walks off. Neil smiles as Lynda knows his order off by heart.

"Leave my sister up to me. I want you in my life!" Neil states. Lynda looks at him with wide eyes; this is the first time he has told her; she moves her hand, placing it under the table. "I know you're not there yet, but give us a chance, please!" Neil expresses, looking longingly at her.

"I miss you when you're not staying overnight, and like being around you. I am cautious!" she replies.

"Scared that I may hurt you? I will always care for you!" Neil answers, touching her leg with his foot and smiling.

The coffees are placed in front of them. She knows Neil is a loving, honest man after four months of being together. Lynda touches his leg with her foot; she stirs the sugar, saying she wants Morgan to give her a chance.

"Maybe if I take her shopping at Bondi and go to the beach afterwards!" she suggests.

Neil accepts her offer, a little nervous about how Morgan will behave. He suggests he will come along and go off shopping as a backup; but says after their holiday. Lynda smiles, thinking after yesterday at the fun race. Neil still wants to take her away he looks across Lynda's right shoulder on seeing Ben walking towards their table. "Hello, you two, been here long? Sorry I'm late. I ordered online!" Ben says, sitting down at their table. Both Neil and Lynda look across at each other, forgetting they invited Ben and Jennifer for breakfast.

"Sorry, slipped my mind you were joining us this morning!" Lynda replies. Ben's not worried, just happy to see they are together and talking. Just then Jennifer walks in, heading towards Lynda. Ben looks across to Neil, now aware of what's happening. On seeing the woman, he relaxes. She is nice looking.

"Jen, meet Ben!" Lynda says and he shakes her hand.

"Of course, we spoke on the phone for the business luncheon!" Ben replies, relaxing as he has been speaking with her.

"Of course!" Lynda says as she asked Jen to organise everything for her, being overworked.

Jen places her order of a cheese and ham croissant, "That's not a good breakfast!" Ben comments, suggesting something else.

Jen admits she's a little hung over from having too much wine the previous night, touching Lynda's hand. She was Lynda's biggest supporter in helping Amanda. Jen visited twice a week to help Lynda's mother with shifts. Jen finds this time of year hard, remembering Amanda and the other patients on the ward. Jen always supplied them with anything they asked for.

Lynda gave Jen a work bank card making it a donation with her boss's approval. Ben looks at Jen thinking, drinking too much with her slim body is not good. Lynda explains everything to Ben and Neil about how Jen's help was important to her family.

"I can't handle the cancer run; too sad for me!" Jen tells the men.

Lynda changes the subject towards Jen, saying she is a marvellous cook and never found a man compassionate for food. Ben looks towards Lynda, thinking she is trying to help him; he talks about his new menu for next Autumn. Jen has many suggestions, which fascinates him as she loves experimenting with flavours, she offers several ideas. The couples talk all through their breakfast, breaking the tension between Neil and Lynda. The women walk outside while Neil pays.

Jen comments she likes Ben, "Sounds just like he does on the phone!"

Lynda is glad they are both finding someone new and not in their office building where Lynda met her last partner. Ben invites Jen to spend the day with him and she accepts, saying goodbye. Neil holds Lynda's hand, inviting her to walk with him to the beach, not far from his jeep. Lynda takes his hand, and they walk slowly down the street and across the road. The beach is crowded; he sees a bench, and they make their way across, sitting down. Neil talks about his beach house, keeping the conversation casual. Lynda suggests they go and see how work is progressing. Neil's been leaving everything up to his Architect to make decisions on every detail. He walks her across to his jeep, helping her inside. He drives to Palm Beach, talking to her about anything, just keeping the conversation moving along. Lynda tells Neil not to plan her entire life; she still wants to keep her independence and let them work it out together. Neil realises he must have come across as too persuasive with his desires and not catering for Lynda. Ben did warn him. Neil will now work on it, catering for Lynda's life to entwine with his.

At the beach house, Neil is surprised to see the entire upper story gone, now a skeleton frame was in its place.

"Well, at least they're moving quickly!" Lynda states, trying not to smile on seeing Neil's expression.

She used to go with her mother to inspect houses she designed on the building sites. Lynda, understanding the process, tells Neil it is normal and will look lovely when it's all done. Lynda has faith in the builder, as her mother has used the company several times in the past. Lynda reassures Neil of this fact, taking his hand and moving him inside. Neil walks around; he really can't imagine how it's going to look like the computer graphic he was shown. Lynda looks around and notices Neil has kept her suggestions, standing next to the post. All the children's and grandchildren's names and measurements are still intact.

"Glad you have this!" she says, looking at him. "Yes, my mum would like this and you, I'm sure!" Neil replies, looking directly at Lynda, who blushes; something Neil likes about her.

Lynda looks up at him, happy he thinks so. They wander around the remaining house seeing new open spaces and the vast sunroom extension. "This is going to be amazing on winter mornings, baking in the sun overlooking the ocean!" she says with a smile, trying to visualise.

"Yes, when you stay over, we can enjoy the room!" Neil replies.

Lynda asks him to give her a week to sort everything in her mind with his sister, and her workload is heavy. She will see him on the bus every morning but not at lunch or stay overs at night.

"I'll see you next Saturday morning. Remember, we have a date!" Neil says urgently due to organising their week away which starts on Saturday.

"Yes, Saturday morning, it's a date. I just need to finish an important business deal before we go away for the week. I will be working until eight each night!" Lynda replies; she moves across, kissing him on the cheek.

The next week seems long to Neil, consuming himself in work, so not to think of Lynda as she's always on his mind. Neil sends two dozen yellow roses to Lynda's apartment to avoid prying eyes at her office. Jennifer talks to Lynda, advising if she's serious with Neil, she won't be living with his sister, just him.

"Remember that friend. He chose you, not a younger woman!" Jen tells Lynda.

Lynda nods her head, taking her friend's advice. She emails Neil, thanking him for her lovely roses, and says she is thinking of him. She sends a smiley face with hearts on the eyes. Neil sighs with relief seeing the message. Feeling better, he will be able to concentrate on his work instead of Lynda. Neil suffered a panic attack that morning, fearing he had lost Lynda due to his sister; he wanted to ring several times. He restrained himself, promising to give her the week off. On the bus, he tried to hold her hand. She was always typing on her mobile, working, but today she touched his fingers, letting him know she cared for him. Neil is now moving swiftly on his work, always finishing at eight to ride home with Lynda. He wasn't allowing her to travel so far alone late at night. Lynda agrees to this, waving goodnight to him each night without a kiss, making Neil feel unsure about how she is sorting everything out in her mind.

Chapter Six

The Holiday

Neil catches an Uber with Lynda to an airport, where a helicopter is waiting for them. He is flying Lynda to their destination, and her face lights up with excitement. She always wanted to fly in a helicopter but never had the opportunity. She turns to Neil, looking up at him.

"You listened to me?" she asks.

"Yes, beautiful, everything you tell me!" Neil responds, holding her hand.

On climbing inside the helicopter, they wear headphones. The pilot lifts off, giving a commentary of the sights below. He is taking a special route Neil designed with him. Lynda looks out beyond and down at the scenery; it is breathtaking. She is so excited she hangs onto Neil's hand.

"This must have cost a bit?" Lynda asks. Neil replies price isn't important; he wants them to have a special holiday together, their first away from everyone. "Seeing your face is reward enough!" he states, kissing her hand.

Lynda can't stop smiling, she is so excited seeing the landscape from the air. She loves to fly, being her preferred transport for overseas trips. She suffers from sea sickness, so she never travels by boat anywhere; she can only travel on the Manly ferry or lakes for some reason. Lynda thinks it's due to the scenery or because the ferry moves across the waves fast. The helicopter lands and Neil helps Lynda climb down while the pilot retrieves their luggage.

A woman from the winery greets them. "Welcome to Red Winery Estate." Lynda looks at Neil and he whispers. "Yes, we're staying here for the week, and I hired a sports car!"

The two things Lynda made on her list when he asked her during her ankle episode. The woman shows them down a pathway heading across to the accommodation. Neil carries the bags following behind Lynda; he likes her wiggle as she looks from side to side of the estate. Neil thinks he chose well, far away from friends and most family, time to get to know each other. Neil signs in, the woman hands him a card, then escorts them to their room; he ordered the VIP package. Lynda is impressed, an entire suite with a lounge room; Neil places the bags down. The woman points out services and a full fridge with coffee and tea, a selection Neil ordered. She leaves them alone.

Neil wanders into the bathroom, "Come see the bath!" he calls.

Lynda walks in and there is one of the biggest baths she's ever seen. "Room for us both!" he whispers, kissing her head.

Lynda laughs as he mentions he has booked a table for lunch in two hours. He suggests they can wander around the estate or there's a gym. Lynda kisses him with her arms around his neck, "or maybe not!" he says, holding her in his arms.

"I missed you!" Neil whispers in her ear.

"Me too!" she replies.

Lynda removes her top and bra and Neil gets the message as she strips in front of him. Neil removes his clothes quickly, admiring her naked form and watching her wiggle towards him; he lies her gently onto the bed. Neil kisses her knee, moving his hand up her leg to her hips, placing both hands on her waist, "place your arms around my neck," he tells Lynda. She does and he lifts her, turning on to his back with her body pressed against his. Lynda kisses him passionately as they move in a musical rhythm.

An hour and a half later, Neil's alarm goes off, "lunch, beautiful!" he says. Lynda unwraps herself from his arms, slipping off the bed into her lace underwear. Neil admires her body as she dresses; she turns around to see him smiling in bed. Lynda leans on the bed beside him, and he takes her in his arms. "You moving?" she asks.

"Maybe just admiring you!" he replies.

"Dress, I'm hungry!" she pulls on his arm, smiling at him.

Neil gets up and dressed. Lynda wears a dress with pretty shoes she brought, one of Neil's favourites; he wears his jeans and shirt. Taking her hand, they head down to the restaurant, which happens to be fully booked.

"Saturday visitors," he whispers to her. "We'll have the place to ourselves next week!" she nods her head, seeing everyone talking or eating.

Sounds of cutlery against crockery, voices raising and other voices more subdued. Noises of waitress taking orders, discussing the menu, people talking of activities. This all causes them problems enjoying their lunch. Lynda finds it overwhelming, like a squeaky guitar noise. Neil talks over the voices so Lynda can hear him. After ten minutes, she moves her placing and chair next to Neil instead of opposite to hear him talking to her.

The waitress returns with a bottle of wine, noticing. "Is everything all right?" she asks.

Neil says yes. Yes they like being closer to each other. She smiles, thinking they are honeymooners.

"Congratulations," she says.

"No, no," Lynda says, but too late, the girl is gone.

Neil grins, holding her hand on the table, "Let it go; we might get a cheaper meal!"

Neil is enjoying this gesture even if Lynda is looking at him curiously. "Pour me some wine, handsome!" she says softly.

Lynda reads the menu, which is extensive; she shows it to Neil and he agrees; she only wants a light lunch. "If this is lunch, what's the diner menu like?" she states.

Neil suggests a lighter lunch to keep room for dinner. She agrees and they both order chicken beet and kale salad. Neil comments the wine is different from what he normally chooses; Lynda loves the strong flavour. She tells Neil it is a lovely place and a good choice for their first holiday together. He is pleased she likes the room and estate; even he is impressed.

"Nice place for a wedding!" he says, looking at Lynda, waiting for an answer.

Lynda prefers not to discuss weddings. She touches his hand and says to just enjoy their week away. "Leave everything else!" she states.

This is Lynda's way of saying 'too soon'. Neil tightens his grip, understanding, but he's caught up in his feelings in a romantic atmosphere and is in love with her. Neil now knows of her failed partnership so he will proceed more slowly, restraining himself, not wanting to lose her. Lynda thinks she will enjoy being part of Neil's life. He is a very determined man and can be stubborn at times. She looks at her mobile notes folder on Neil's qualities, great business head. Handsome, sexy with a smiley face, loyal to his family, compassionate, caring outdoor man, fun and in control of his feelings. Neil is so far what some might say perfect. Maybe he's been hiding another personality during the past four months? Time will tell. Lynda's insecurities are showing, trying to find something wrong that isn't there.

Lynda talks to Neil about his father's situation. She emailed Robert with the real company details, and they are not selling shares at this time. Neil is grateful for her saving his father's finances; otherwise this could have bankrupted his dad.

"Glad he didn't buy any shares!" Neil says.

Lynda replies, "I can relax now; it's been stressful searching. If not for my American business associate, things could have been very different!" Neil had no idea she was finding it so stressful and he apologises to her. Lynda explains it's because of her ankle and trying to catch up on general meetings. Many company managers refuse to video conference, preferring to have face-to-face meetings, making her life difficult. Neil understands now why she's finding Morgan a challenge; with work stresses and the ankle injury complicating things for her.

"I just want this week to be us. Finding out if we fit as a real couple!" Lynda states, looking at him with compassion.

Neil looks longingly into her eyes, pulling her closer. "We do; just relax with me. I am yours forever!" he states.

Lynda feels nervous, whispering, "What if I never fall in love with you."

Neil whispers, "You really like me, missed me when we were apart. You are falling. Allow it to happen!"

Lynda kisses his hand, looking at him as her eyes thank him for being so kind and patient. Neil seems to know her better than she does herself. She relaxes during their luncheon, taking in the atmosphere. She asks how he found this winery, and he mentions his boss recommended it. "Once I researched the place, I thought it was perfect for us."

Monday, Neil arranges for a private wine tour of the

vineyard, walking down rows of vines. Lynda loves grape vines finding them so peaceful, something about the leaves. Neil is talking to Daniel, the winemaker offering to show them around as a VIP customer. Daniel escorts them while Lynda fades away, exploring by herself, casually walking behind, admiring grapes dangling. She holds one in her hand. Daniel turns around and walks back. Offering Lynda a grape, he pulls several off, handing some to Lynda and Neil. She finds them remarkably very sweet, Daniel informing her of the type of wine these grapes are used for.

Neil sees her gazing expression as if she's miles away, "Where are you?" he asks.

"In awe of grapevines!" Lynda replies.

Daniel expresses he feels that way too, walking amongst his grapes and glad he has guests who appreciate the vineyard. Daniel decides to escort them into an area normally off-limits to guests because of Lynda. Daniel pushes a huge sliding door just enough to enter a stone building. Inside are wooden wine barrels stacked high; he explains which wines are stored in the barrels, the vineyard's award-winning wine, and it is under security cameras and alarms. "The wine here is precious, award-winning, and expensive!" Daniel says, smiling at Lynda.

Neil places his arm behind her back, holding her close to him. She grins; he's a little jealous. She's never seen this before and rather likes Neil reacting this way. Daniel moves across to a barrel with a tap; removing three wine glasses from a barrel, he pours wine into each. On handing a glass each to Neil and Lynda he explains to smell first, swirl, then sip; slowly taking in the aroma and flavour, then enjoy. Lynda and Neil follow his instructions.

"A beautiful bouquet!" Lynda says. Neil just looks at her;

she apparently knows a bit about wine.

"Are you a wine buff?" enquires Daniel.

"My grandparents had a small winery not far from here. I grew up as a child having holidays with them. They taught me some things. especially trimming grapes!" Lynda exclaims.

"Child labour, yes, my kids do the same. What's the name of their winery!" Daniel asks.

"A small vineyard of fifty acres sold to a bigger vineyard ten years ago. My grandparents called it 'Sweet Valley' due to the sweet grapes they grew!" Daniel laughs, "This is a small world. Yes, I helped purchase the vineyard for this estate. Nice people, they said they were retiring to tour around Australia. How are they?" he enquires.

"Both did travel in their campervan. Now Grandad's gone, and Grandma is ninety-two this November!" Lynda explains.

"Does she still enjoy her wine?" he enquires.

"Oh yes, die with a glass in her hand!" Lynda replies.

Daniel laughs. "I will choose a nice wine for you to give to your grandma!" he says.

"Thanks, very nice of you!" Lynda replies.

"You will be our special VIP for wine. I shall place your names down in our vineyard owners' ledger. Do you know your grandparents' grapes are very important to our vineyard's success?" Daniel says.

Lynda smiles at Neil, feeling very proud of her grandparents, and all those holidays helping out was important after all. Neil is amazed by Lynda's knowledge, now in her element talking with the winemaker. She turns to Neil holding his hand, saying she will take him to visit her grandparent's property.

Daniel interrupts, saying he will organise their caretaker at 'Sweet Valley' for a visit; they will be very welcome. "Will

Wednesday be all right with you two?" he asks. "The owners kept the name?" she asks,

"Yes, never change the names. Bad luck for grapes!" Daniel replies.

"Your grandma didn't come to the fun race?" Neil says.

"She wasn't feeling up to it. Too sad for her!" Lynda replies, squeezing his hand. He understands, it must have been hard on the extended family.

Daniel uses his mobile and then escorts Neil and Lynda through another building; she comments to Neil how she loves the smell of timber barrels. He sniffs, saying, "I suppose!" not something he has ever experienced. He walks along, listening to Daniel explaining the process of wine. Lynda asks many questions, all ending back at the restaurant. Daniel has organised a table. He offers them to sit; he's chosen a special menu for them both with wine. Lynda and Neil thank him and Daniel sits with them for a while, expressing to Lynda how her grandparents' vines are special to him. He uncorks a bottle, pouring a glass for Lynda and Neil. He waits in anticipation of Lynda's comments.

"That is lovely, sweet but dry. I like this wine very much!" she tells him wide-eyed. Daniel explains the wine is made from half of her grandparents' grapes. It is their champion wine. He waves to a waiter and speaks to him. He walks off briskly, soon returning carrying a box; he hands it to Daniel.

"With my compliments to your family!" Daniel says. Please let me know what grandma thinks.

"Thank you, so kind!" Lynda replies.

"I shall leave you. Enjoy your dinner!" Daniel shakes hands with Neil and smiles at Lynda, saying, "It's been a pleasure to escort fellow wine growers around our estate."

Neil asks Lynda about her holidays with her grandparents,

now letting him in on her childhood for the first time. Lynda is so relaxed; she talks of fun times when she, Julia and Brian all trod wines in a barrel for fun.

"Granddad always allowed us. Mum was never impressed at our stained clothes and legs!" she chuckles, remembering this.

Lynda tells Neil how Brian and Simon would sneak off eating some grapes and having belly aches afterwards. She and her older siblings always stayed for several days each holiday except when the time came to trim the vines. Julia, Brian and Simon always made excuses. She, however, loved their property and always went, loving being around the vines. "I used to save leaves, placing them in my special book. I still have it somewhere, probably at Mum's and Dad's!" she states, holding Neil's hand as she sips her wine. Their dinner comes out looking delicious with flowers and a small number of slices of meat.

"Very fancy," Neil comments.

Wednesday morning, Lynda rises early, taking Neil down to a day spa; she has arranged a couple's massage. Neil is very impressed with her bold move, letting him know she is allowing them to do things as a couple. Both strip down to their undies, enjoying a nice massage with scented candles. After an hour, Neil is feeling very relaxed. Lynda asks if he enjoyed his massage.

"Very much, especially beside you. Seeing you naked always impresses me!" he says.

Lynda smiles as she walks him down to reception, where a special hamper is waiting for them. Lynda takes the car keys wanting to drive the sports car, and she ties her hair back; Neil gets the ride of his life as she likes to drive fast. Both enjoy the wind on their cheeks and the music blasting. Neil tells her to keep to the speed limit, don't want to spoil their holiday with a fine. Lynda nods and slows down. Luckily, further down the road is a speed camera, and Neil sighs with relief. The last thing he wants to explain to work about is a speeding ticket as he hired the car. Lynda slows further along, pulling into an area where campers stay and people picnic. Neil climbs out carrying the hamper; the view is spectacular.

"How did you find this place?" he enquires, looking down the valley.

"It's on the way to my grandparent's old vineyard, another hour away!" Lynda expresses.

Lynda walks further away from a tent sitting down on the grass. She lies back, allowing the sun to shine onto her body. Lynda tells Neil this is where her parents always stopped for lunch, fond memories.

Neil lies beside her, touching her fingers, "Very nice spot!" he says while looking at her. Lynda turns to him, resting on her side, supporting her head with her left arm. He asks about her greatest fears, she replies snakes terrify her and she hates mice; she can't even see them on TV. Just the sheer mention of snakes makes her shiver. She asks for his, discovering Neil has no fears of anything.

"Not even as a kid?" she asks.

"No, nothing scares me, really!" Neil replies.

"Good, you can protect me!" Lynda says.

He looks into her eyes, "Yes, beautiful. I will guard you against all predators!" Neil replies. She places a grape in his mouth, and he puts a strawberry in hers. She licks his fingers and he grins. Lynda sits up, looking inside the hamper and stating there is plenty of food to eat.

"They certainly packed enough." He takes some rolled-up meat with slices of cheese, "Tastes great!" he chews as Lynda takes a small sourdough, dipping it in Dukkah with oil.

After an hour they drive off; this time Neil is driving, not trusting Lynda's lead foot. The coordinates are already locked into the map navigator.

Neil stops at the gate. Lynda sees they have made a new sign, "Sweet Valley," with gold writing on a black background; she loves the style, a big improvement on the old red peeling paint one her grandparents had. Neil presses the button; he mentions Lynda's name. The gate opens, and he drives up to the house. Lynda steps from the car, standing admiring the house, and a couple walk out to greet them.

"You must be Lynda and Neil; I am Michael, and this is Susan. So, what do you think?" the man asks.

"Looks amazing!" Lynda comments on the house being done up for a home and seller. "We open it up for wine growers' association gatherings and special business people!" he states, inviting Lynda and Neil inside. Neil allows Lynda to enter first. The seller section is lovely with the old wine barrels; she notices the one with the kids' names on it.

"You kept this? That's me." She points, showing Neil her name in the middle.

Susan states they wanted to keep memories of the original owners who established the vineyard. Lynda nods her head, saying her granddad would have been glad as it was his idea for them to write their names on the barrel. Lynda's eyes fill with water; she wipes it away. Neil holds his arm around her back. "This is great!" he whispers.

Lynda nods. Susan invites them in to view their quarters, a new massive extension out the back. "Do you think your grandparents would approve?"

"Oh yes, Nan always wanted to build on but never did, spent all their days in the vineyard. She points out that was her mum's bedroom, now the new bathroom!" Lynda informs Susan.

Susan asks questions about the family and asks if they can take a photo with her and Neil for their records. Lynda agrees, standing beside Neil with their backs to the vineyard. Neil takes one of the couple, with Lynda.

"I can't wait to tell Mum; she will be thrilled!" Lynda says.

"Your family are welcome here any time. I'll give you our number!" Michael says, handing a card to Neil.

Lynda wanders outside to view the vines with Susan beside her; they are caretakers of the property for the estate. "How long have you been living here?" Lynda enquires.

"Ten years, we moved in just after your grandparents left. We are part owners of the main vineyard!" Susan replies.

Lynda looks at Susan, thinking she's younger than her and on a great journey; they wander down laneways. Lynda inspects the vines; she points out where she helped her granddad, running down aisles.

"All great fun!" she says.

Neil is being shown where they store the wine barrels for the main vineyard. The building is large and filled with new barrels. Michael states they have the room here to store the barrels. He points to a section ready to be used and he asks Neil if he knows anything about winemaking.

"After yesterday, I do a bit!" he smiles.

Michael laughs and explains the process of the barrels. On returning to the house, Susan prepares coffee and cake for everyone, saying how she is so glad they came to visit the old property.

"If we'd known when you booked at the main vineyard, you could have stayed here!" she comments. Neil answers, saying he was giving Lynda a surprise holiday, unaware of Lynda's family living here. This is our first holiday together, Neil states, looking at the couple,

"The beginning of many more!" Susan says.

"Well, you certainly made a discovery, Neil!" Michael says.

"Yes, what are the odds my grandparents' home being part of your estate Neil booked!" Lynda states.

"You must have connected!" Susan says, handing around the coffees.

Neil likes her statement. He looks towards Lynda, who is smiling. She, too, was happy to be home again. Susan asks questions about Lynda's holidays on the property. They all laugh as she tells them how she and her siblings trod wine.

"I always wanted to do that; how does it feel?" Michael asks.

"Squishy, but lots of fun. Granddad used the wine for family gatherings for the first harvest. It tasted rather good, my dad used to say!" Lynda is filling them in on lots of family gatherings on the property; her mum growing up in the valley. Lynda mentions her mother meeting her dad at Sydney University and having their wedding in front of the vines; she points it out. Susan says she will write that down. Lynda offers to find some photos and send copies to them for her memory corner.

"Thank you, that will be marvellous!" Susan is very excited; she's been trying to find where the family lived for some time.

Lynda expresses her mum will probably ring her. "She loves telling stories of her childhood and how Granddad planted the vines."

"Do you have a big family?" Susan enquires.

"Mum lives in Mosman, and her brother lives in WA. He has four kids. I am the second eldest of five!" Neil holds her hand when she speaks, aware of Amanda.

Lynda looks at him with lowered eyebrows. She says her

little sister only visited the property twice due to her sickness. Susan and Michael say how sorry they are. Lynda explains this is why her mother stopped visiting the property. "Could only get away sometimes. My dad drove me and my siblings up for holidays!"

"The family was happy when her grandparents sold, being too old to care for the vines. Brian, Julia and I couldn't help out with our workloads and them having family!" she tells Susan and Michael. Both understand as it keeps them busy, and they hire staff to run the cellar door and trim the vines. The days and weeks seem to move along very quickly, and she is having a baby now, so she is not doing as much.

"You are doing a fine job; the vines look very healthy. Congratulations, a baby; that will make eight babies born in the house!" Lynda tells her.

Susan and Michael hadn't thought of that and will make a note; they are so grateful to Lynda for explaining the plantings of the vineyard. Susan always wondered about the family and how much enjoyment there was, being in the house. Neil suggests they must go; it's getting very late.

"Thank you for coming. All our questions have been answered now!" Michael says. Lynda has made their day.

Neil is happy to leave. He places the roof up over the sports car driving back to the estate. On arriving, Daniel enquires if they enjoyed their visit to the old property?

"Yes, lovely couple!" Neil says.

Daniel is pleased, saying Michael is his brother and they are in this venture together. Lynda understands now why the family connection is so important. Neil has a special surprise for Lynda in the morning; he's taking her on a walking trail a little way from here. Neil wants her to be well-rested as it will take them all day, and they will be out of reach of phones. Neil knows how much Lynda enjoys the outdoors, jogging along trails.

In the morning, Lynda receives a message from her doctor saying she needs to contact him. She rings from the lounge of the suite and she finds out she must have an operation on her ankle, discovering more than a chipped bone. Lynda hangs up, telling Neil his plans today will have to change, and he decides on a nice drive around the other vineyards nearby. Lynda thinks it's best, too; the day is enjoyable buying and tasting wines. Neil buys his selection of reds, while Lynda buys whites. She includes one for Donna.

"What about your mum?" Neil enquires.

"Mum likes beer and spirits!" Lynda replies.

Neil remembers at the lunch he did see Ava drinking beer in a glass, now understanding why Lynda talks with Donna about wine. Both women having something to converse about and enjoy. Neil drives slowly back by four p.m. and Lynda enters the bathroom filling the bath with rose crystals. She lights candles and the scent of vanilla spreads out into the room. Lynda calls Neil, and on entering, he sees she is already in the bath. "You joining me?" she asks.

Neil strips very quickly, sliding in the opposite side. "You can be very cheeky when you relax!" he says, admiring her body, his feet touching her hips.

Lynda moves her foot down his leg, exciting him, "You are making it hard to resist!" Neil says, moving forward and then sliding her legs towards him.

Lynda slips along the bath, now close and facing Neil. He kisses her breast gently. Lynda runs her hands down his back, kissing his neck and then lips. Both caressing, a sensation never before experienced with each other, Lynda loves Neil's body against and inside of her. The pair make love in the bath enjoying the sensation of water.

That evening they decide to remain in their suite in their dressing gowns. Neil orders room service tonight, staying comfortable and going to watch TV. Neil talks about his childhood, feeling Lynda's ready to now tell him about her childhood. She listens while he talks and laughs at funny moments with his friend Ben and the mischief they used to get up to at school.

"I was in primary school when you were born, and I was finishing University as you were just starting yours. Here you are in my arms, handsome!" Lynda says. She holds his arms firmly around her.

In the morning, they say goodbye to Daniel, he tells them to come back soon, and Lynda's family is always welcome to visit the old property. Lynda thanks him kindly. Taking the bottle of wine he presented for her grandma. Neil shakes his hand, thanking him for the discount, and they drive off, heading back to Sydney.

Chapter Seven

The Challenge

Lynda visits Morgan at her home, and on entering her bedroom notices she is listening to her music; there are posters around the walls, a typical young girl's room. Lynda invites Morgan to come shopping with her.

"Why?" she questions.

"I thought we could get to know each other!" Lynda replies, keeping eye contact.

Morgan tells Lynda she never wants a big sister and is too embarrassed to be seen with her, due to her age.

"I would like us to be friends!" Lynda replies, watching the girl looking down at her book.

"You're too old for Neil and will never be able to have kids, old lady!" Morgan yells.

The words are harsh, hitting Lynda right in the heart, aware her sister is having trouble conceiving. She, too, fears she may have the same problem. Lynda breathes heavily but remains with her eyes fixed on Morgan. She will not allow this girl to intimidate her, standing perfectly still.

"Well, leave my room!" Morgan yells and everyone downstairs hears.

"I challenge you to a rowing contest. If you win, Morgan, you don't have to associate with me. If I win, you have to call me Lynda and accept Neil and me as a couple!" Lynda stands firm, staring at the girl.

Morgan sees her expression; she gives a sterner look and refuses. "You scared?" Lynda asks.

"Okay, my distance and rules. I win you get out of Neil's life!" Morgan replies, giving the evil eye.

"Your distance but rowing rules and no other deal!" Lynda answers standing firm.

Morgan agrees. Just then her mother enters the room, asking what's going on. Morgan happily tells her mother she is going to get rid of Lynda. We are having a rowing contest. Donna looks astounded as her daughter makes such a statement. Lynda leaves mother and daughter alone.

On walking back downstairs, Neil asks what's going on, and Lynda informs him. "Are you sure? She's a good rower!" he states.

"Morgan is not that good and never will be. Julia was the state champion, and I always practiced with her whenever she went out. I am not at her level but good enough to go against your sister!" Lynda answers without flinching.

"You only just had your ankle fixed last month!" Neil states.

"I know but must do this. Julia will help me train. I made it for the end of next month. Plenty of time to prepare!"

Neil is concerned; she hasn't been out rowing since she met him due to her ankle. Lynda looks directly at him, saying she cannot refuse now; she must face Morgan on her level. Neil doesn't like his girlfriend and sister against each other; he fears it will make the situation worse. He walks out to the back yard playing with the dogs. Robert hands Lynda a wine but she declines, saying they are going swimming.

"Don't let Morgan wreck your happiness with Neil. He takes after his mum; he loves deeply and is loyal to the people important to him. My son loves you, and I have seen the way you look at him!" Robert tells her.

Lynda looks up at Robert, tall like his son; she admits she loves Neil. Just as she says this, Neil enters the room. He rushes up behind her and Lynda jumps slightly. He places his arms around her back, kissing her cheek. "Let's go!" the house is one street back from the cliffs, an easy walk down to Bondi Beach. The last day of summer is a little cool but not enough to deter Lynda and Neil from a last swim, along with many others at the beach. Neil throws their towels over Lynda's backpack, and both strip down to their swimsuits, throwing clothes over their bag. Neil races Lynda into the water, and she dives under the waves. He goes under too, soon further out, enjoying the water. A surfer just misses Neil as he moves quickly past. Lynda swims across to him. "Are you all right?" she asks, worrying the board got his head.

"Yes, just missed me!" Neil replies, saying for them to swim across the other way. Lynda swims off with Neil close beside her. Further along she treads water, checking his head. A gash on his shoulder is bleeding. Lynda tells Neil he better get back to shore. On the beach, a lifeguard drives over to him, seeing blood dripping down his arm.

Lynda points to the surfer who nipped Neil. The guard says he will handle it and for Neil to go to the tower. Lynda picks up their belongings along the way, and inside she finds Neil being patched up.

"Not serious, just a nip and bleeding!" Neil says, seeing her face.

Lynda thanks the guards, checking Neil's bandage. She puts her shorts and shirt on over her swimsuit. Neil tells her it's all right; they both walk from the tower and he puts on his shorts, shirt and shoes. Lynda ties her shoes on too; they walk back to his parent's house for their car. Neil goes inside to say goodbye to his father and Donna; they wave to Lynda at the jeep and she waves back.

The next week Lynda goes out at five every morning, driving to the rowing club. She takes her scull out, which is kept at the club. She rows for an hour each morning. Julia joins her on weekends to row beside Lynda. Julia corrects her style and speed, Lynda finding it hard after not having any practice for the past eight months. Lynda's arms and legs are hurting, but she persists, not allowing Morgan to win without at least some sort of challenge.

"Morgan's coming up beside you!" Julia calls as she rows next to Lynda, seeing a burst of speed from her sister.

"Yes, think of Morgan and you'll be right!" Julia says.

Julia goes with Neil and Lynda to see how Morgan trains with her teammates. The girls smirk at Lynda, "You don't have a chance!" a girl states, looking Lynda up and down.

Julia walks across, watching the girls launch their large scull, some arguing as they row off. She keeps watching; Julia notices many mistakes, mainly the girls don't have a good rhythm and do not work as a team.

Julia decides to have a word with the coach, not going in the scull to train the girls, he sends someone else in his place. The coach notices Julia walking towards him, she asks him questions, and he tells Julia each girl thinks they're better than the others. Morgan is undisciplined and is the ring leader.

"She is not in the same league you were, Julia. You had talent at age fourteen!" She looks up at him.

"Do I know you?" she enquires.

"No, used to watch you train. I knew your coach. Can I ask why you never accepted the Commonwealth games entry?"

Julia answers her sister had cancer, and her family needed the money for treatment and for her to be close.

"Sorry to hear. I always thought you'd make an Olympian!" the coach replies.

"Thanks!" she says.

"Why are you here?" he asks.

Julia explains and he replies he's happy to help. He tells her all of Morgan's mistakes and says she is never a single sculler. He expresses the girl thinks she is better than she is.

"If she was, she would have been taken up by now!" he says.

The coach points to a girl on the sidelines watching he explaining she comes to watch. "I point out the team's mistakes and for her not to do the same. She is a single sculler talent like you, Julia!"

Julia asks why Morgan is still on the team if she is not that good. He explains her father donates to the school scull team. The school can't afford the sculls without his donation, and the principal won't kick her off.

"Tell your sister to be clever!" he says quietly.

Julia thanks him, understanding tactics will work against Morgan. She is now armed with information and will train Lynda. Julia walks back to her sister, smiling.

"What have you been up to?" Lynda enquires.

"Just research, Sis!" she places her arm in Lynda's, saying they can leave now. "We have work to do!" she whispers.

Lynda tells Neil they are leaving and will see him later. She kisses him and walks off with Julia. On the drive back, Julia gives Lynda instructions on using her scull to work with her. Julia takes her sister to her local gym, and she gets Lynda on the rowing machine, then weights for her upper strength and bike. After three hours, Lynda is sore and tired; she calls it quits.

"This is now your new routine. Five a.m. row, then afternoons at your work gym!" Julia tells her sister and to go on her old training diet.

"I don't think that's necessary; I'm only going up against a kid!" Lynda sees a coach developing in her sister. "Just like old times except with changed roles," Lynda says.

"Yes, but Morgan has youth and strength on her side!" Julia replies.

"Okay, Sis. You're taking this contest a little too seriously. I need to work, remember?" Lynda answers, saying she will use the gym at work and train with the scull club team during the week and weekend. Julia is satisfied. Early Monday morning, Lynda drives to the club with two girls waiting for her, pre-arranged for them to help update her skills.

"Hi, Lynda. You ready for training!" says Sarah.

"Yes, been eight months since I've rowed!" Lynda replies.

"That's nothing. Just follow us and our coach's instructions. She's on board to help train you!" Sarah says, tapping Lynda on her shoulder. They already have her scull in the water waiting for her.

Lynda thanks the girls and coach as Julia and Lynda have been club members since age ten. Everyone calls them the older team. Lynda doesn't mind, but both she and Julia are respected as they were great scullers and fundraise, supporting the club.

The morning is cool as the girls and Lynda move out along the waterways. She sees the sun rising as they row smoothly, sliding across the water. Back at the club the girls point out Lynda's mistakes and say they will use a double scull in the morning as this will be easier to instruct her. Sarah suggests an exercise bandage for Lynda to use on her foot and ankle to give it more support and strength. Lynda takes Sarah's advice, thanking her and the other girls. She rushes to help put the scull away, and driving off, she makes her way back home. Neil is showering so she jumps in, saving time and water. "Good morning, handsome!" she says.

He spins around, "Have a good row?" he enquires.

"Yes," she replies.

"Don't wear yourself out!" he says.

"Don't you dare mention my age. Remember it was you that told me age is in the mind!" Lynda replies, looking up into his eyes. He grins, "Okay, beautiful!" He hands her the sponge to soak herself as he leaves to dress and prepare breakfast for them.

Lynda is hungry after her rowing and eats a large bowl of fruit with yogurt. She goes to take a piece of toast. "No, your sister gave me a diet for you to follow!" Neil shows her.

"Not you too!" Lynda replies, reading the diet. "Is that lunch?" she raises her voice, preferring her normal lunch. He packs her an extra water bottle and snacks Julia made specially, giving them to Neil. Lynda notices instantly her sister's energy bits. Neil explains these are for after her exercises at lunch. She sees Neil's backpack at the front door.

"You going somewhere?" she asks.

"No, I'm training with you in the gym to help. Julia's given me a regimen for you to follow!" Neil informs her.

"I think I need to talk to Julia!" Lynda replies.

"No, she's so excited to help after you helped her for years with her sculling. She's having fun!" Neil says, handing Lynda her backpack.

He kisses her, showing her the time. They must rush to catch the bus with Jason, keeping him company. Neil communicates with Jason now after Lynda taught him some signing and proves to be a quick learner. Jason loves having a three-way conversation. Neil signs, telling Jason he will pick him up at home in the morning and for the next four weeks. Lynda looks his way; he signs saying it will prevent her from rushing every morning. Jason thanks Neil and Lynda, preferring to be driven to school as he dislikes using the bus. Jason thanks Neil for his advice handling the bullies; they have been avoiding him for the past seven months. Neil is glad; he reminds Jason to work hard at his schoolwork. He will progress in achieving his goals for his exams at the end of the year. Neil states the bullies will not pass exams being too busy picking on other kids than studying. Jason takes his advice and wanders off to school, happier these days than before.

Lynda comments that Neil's been a good influence on Jason; she has seen how he's more settled with attendance at school. Neil looks at her, saying he's just been giving him advice to prevent him from being bullied. All kids are entitled to enjoy school without the hassles of social media, and bullies poking fun. Jason never allows his disability to hold himself back being a smart kid. Lynda holds Neil's hand, telling him Jason's parents are grateful to him for all his help. Jason said he liked hanging out with you last Friday night on the wall climb.

"I did wonder why we didn't catch up!" Lynda says.

"Yes, I promised to show Jason how to climb; quite good for his first go. His dad came too, wanting to learn something he could do with his son. I was glad to help!" Neil said they all had a good night.

Lynda is happy Neil is involving himself in her friend's circle, something she was worried about – whether he would like or fit into her group. "Your mates are great, lots of fun!" Neil tells her.

"I'm glad. I worry because of being older than you!" Lynda

replies.

Lynda found some of his friends disapproving of her being older and not having much in common with them. One female friend told Neil she finds Lynda has similar tastes to her, which surprised her. Neil informs his group of friends Lynda has younger siblings and is able to connect with his age group.

The next weekend, Julia takes Lynda out using the club's double scull. Julia corrects and encourages her sister. Neil is watching to see how Julia trains, which is completely different from his sister's coach. He talks to Julia, wondering why. She tells him she trained with a NSW trainer who is an expert in his field. Neil notices Lynda's upper arm strength developing muscle, which he rather likes. Neil is still concerned about her ankle, even though the doctor said full strength is back. He worries especially when she's using a strap bandage for training. Neil walks across to help the women put the scull away into the club building. He picks Lynda up, saying how proud he is she's still going ahead with rowing against a young girl.

"How is her training going?" Julia enquires.

Neil replies Morgan's just doing what she normally does, just training on the Saturday mornings with her team. A smile crosses Julia's face, and Neil looks curiously at her, "What's going on?" he asks. "Nothing. Lynda may have a good chance, that's all!" Julia states. Thinking his sister doesn't take her training or team seriously.

"Is that so!" Neil replies, seeing Julia looks rather happy. She walks across to talk with Lynda.

Neil phones his dad to make sure Morgan is at her rowing practice this morning. "No, she's having this weekend off!" he states.

"Really, why?" Neil asks his dad.

"She didn't feel like it!" he answers.

"Morgan shouldn't let her team down; they'll be one short," he says. Robert replies no, they have a spare sculler who takes Morgan's place when she's not there. Neil is disappointed in his sister, telling his dad she better watch out. Lynda is training hard.

"Don't be silly, son. I like Lynda, but she hasn't a chance against youth!" Robert answers.

Neil can't believe his dad even said that. He stands up for Lynda, informing him she is training every day for their race.

"Morgan better smarten up!" Neil says, hanging up his mobile.

Lynda walks across, whispering to him, "Want to shower and have breakfast together?"

Neil whispers back, "Always, beautiful!"

Julia waves goodbye while Neil and Lynda drive back to their apartment, shower and dress. At their favourite café, Neil orders Lynda a ham and cheese croissant, something she loves on the weekend for breakfast. Neil is trying to get Lynda to change her mind about competing against his sister.

"You know this won't change Morgan's mind!" he says.

"I have to do this; it was my idea. Besides, your sister must be aware I'm not going anywhere, no matter how she behaves!" Lynda replies. She asks for a vegetable juice, and she expresses how much fitter she is feeling and how she is enjoying the extra exercise.

"Neil, look at the muscles in your arms and chest. I love we are working out together at lunchtimes!" she tells him, touching his leg under the table.

Neil is just concerned that Morgan and Lynda will never get along, but he will support them both in this endeavour. Lynda's phone goes off several times at the café; she reads the texts and then deletes them.

"Who's that?" Neil asks with an anxious face.

"Don't worry. It's not another man!" Lynda replies, smiling at him.

Neil pushes her, wanting to know as her phone goes off again. Lynda ignores him, and she looks at him. "You don't have anything to worry about. I love you!" she replies. Neil looks at her as this is the first time she has said the words to him, and out loud in public. "I love you too!" he holds her hand smiling.

Lynda's phone lights up again, and she presses the button. "Just ignore it," Neil is now very worried. He sees it light up again. Lynda reads it, her expression changing to serious.

"Why did you give Morgan my private mobile number?" Lynda asks, slightly angry.

"I didn't!" Neil replies.

"Your sister's teammates are sending me texts, not very nice ones. They must have got my number from you!" Lynda tells him, pulling her hand back.

Neil keeps saying he never gave his sister her mobile because it's her personal mobile, for family and him only.

"Morgan may be acting silly at the moment but wouldn't do that. I know her!" Neil replies.

"You always take her side; she is so spoilt and possessive of you. Everyone around you sees how Morgan is except you. Why would I make up how she treats me? I have nothing to gain!" Lynda is furious. She removes her sim card, breaking it in half and putting it on her saucer. Lynda eats in silence as she is annoyed with Neil being in denial. She tells him she never wants to come between him and his sister. Lynda states it is happening in front of his eyes; she will row against Morgan then they can discuss where they go from there. Neil is shocked by her comment.

"I will never change my mind; I am having you in my life. Morgan just doesn't understand my love for you. Trust me. I'm yours!" Neil says. He goes and pays for their breakfast and walks her down to the beach.

A peaceful place where Lynda clears her mind as it's spinning at the moment about whether to continue onwards with Neil. She fears Morgan will split them apart; they are always fighting about her lately. Lynda is not happy with the situation, only hoping Morgan sees how much she loves Neil. He tells her it will all work out and nothing will break them apart, especially their love for each other.

The next three weeks move along quickly with training, rowing at five a.m., then driving to work and exercising at lunch. Lynda is fitter than she's been for a long time and feeling rather confident she has a chance to at least be alongside of Morgan's scull.

Race day

Morgan is surprised to see Lynda turning up with her own scull and her entire family coming as a cheer squad. Morgan's teammates notice the scull and, on examining it, see it is the latest slick style. The girls are in awe, walking across to Morgan as her scull is four years old.

"You should see her scull; it's sick!" one girl says.

"You will have to row hard!" says another.

Morgan replies. "She obviously needs all the help she can get!"

Morgan steps across to see for herself as Simon and Brian lift the scull into the lake. She sees Lynda's ankle bandaged. "Sure you're up to it?" she asks, smirking.

"Yes," Lynda replies, smiling. Morgan wonders why? Lynda is using tactics, knowing the girl is overconfident.

"You can pull out. I am going to win, lest call it quits!" Morgan says to Lynda.

"It's not winning that counts; it's how you handle it and treat your opponent!" Lynda replies as she lowers herself into her scull.

Morgan walks across, saying to her folks, "I've got this!" Lowering herself into her scull, she rows off. Lynda has already placed herself in the middle of the river to avoid Morgan's tactics of pushing her opponent towards the sides. Morgan is not happy now she is on the banks ;the judge's boat arrives with an impartial judge from the rowing club Lynda belongs to and trusts her; she is in the boat with the girl's coach.

The judges use a horn and the sculls take off with Morgan ahead. Lynda is taking her time using the training Julia gave her. She advances around the corner and Julia is driving in her car, watching the pair row down the river. Lynda is now keeping in time with Morgan, which is irritating the girl. Lynda is listening to the rhythm in her head, keeping time and steady on the way back; she is working hard against a younger girl. Morgan is using all of her strength and now actually rowing properly; she is fast As she increases, so does Lynda. Morgan looks sideways, seeing Lynda alongside her. Morgan is rowing very well and fast, her speed increases. Lynda keeps her scull steady. She bursts forward, making Morgan row harder; she moves slightly forward. The two sculls are level with each other; Morgan uses the last of her strength and wins by the tip of her boat. Lynda lifts her oars sitting in the scull, catching her breath and strength; being exhausted. Morgan actually gave her a fast race. Morgan is already out of her scull with her teammates congratulating her.

She is jumping for joy excitedly.

Lynda rows to the dock and climbs out with the help of Simon. "Well done, Sis. Great row, ha?" he says.

Lynda smiles at him, and he hands her a drink. She has some, then walks across to Morgan to congratulate her. "I won, old woman. You keep the bet!" she says, forgetting herself in front of her friends and Neil. This is the first time he has caught his sister calling Lynda that, and he is disappointed in Morgan.

"Yes, Morgan. You missed the point. It wasn't about winning the race!" Lynda states, walking off.

"What then?" she yells to Lynda.

Donna, her mother, answers. "Your brother and Lynda's respect. They are now living together since last week!"

Morgan is furious, and she turns to her brother, "You can't give me up for her!"

"You are my little sister. Lynda is my life!" Neil replies, walking off to be with Lynda.

Brian and Simon go to lift Lynda's scull. She stops them and walks across to the coach. "This is my donation to your rowing club for Mia, the girl who has talent!"

"Are you sure? It's new!" he states, rather surprised she is offering to hand her scull over. Lynda explains it's her donation for the year, and she insists he takes it. He thanks her kindly, looking across to Mia, and he calls her across. The coach tells her and she runs across to Lynda, thanking her. "Promise me you will train to go all the way!" Lynda says.

"I will now!" Mia replies, smiling.

Julia walks across to Mia, handing her a card. "Get your parents to ring me. I will be happy to train you!" Mia looks at her.

The coach tells Mia she will never get a better offer. The girl runs off towards her dad, who has just arrived to pick her up. Julia walks off to join the family; Brian and Simon are so happy for Lynda to achieve her childhood dream of racing like Julia. Lynda spent years training with her sister. She never got the chance to race.

Lynda hugs her sister, thanking her for all her help. "Any time, Sis. Practice next week?" she asks.

"No, going to rest for a bit!" Lynda replies, smiling. They walk off towards their parents.

Ava, her mother, is wondering why Lynda is happy about the race. "Morgan won. Why are you smiling!" she enquires.

"Mum, the race was to show Morgan I am not going anywhere and love Neil no matter what she throws at me!" Lynda hugs her mum.

The coach thanks Lynda for the race, stating now he knows what Morgan is capable of, there are no more excuses to work with her team. Lynda says she will get Neil to encourage her more, and he says, "Good luck."

Julia comments she could be a really good sculler if she trained harder. Robert overhears; he is fuming, saying what does Julia know about rowing.

"You are talking to one of the most talented scullers I've ever seen!" the coach states.

"Julia was NSW champion for four years and would have been a gold medallist if she went to the Commonwealth Games but for her sister's illness!" Lynda says proudly up at Robert, while keeping eye contact.

Robert sees the women are in no mood to be trifled with. He steps back walking off to speak to Morgan. Lynda invites Donna and Robert to the café. She accepts, and Lynda gives her the address.

"You too, Morgan. You're invited!" Lynda says.

"Do we have to?" Morgan replies.

Donna says, "Yes."

The coach calls out to Morgan, "See you early next Saturday at the right time of eight a.m., not nine thirty!" he walks off, smiling.

The entire family drive to the café, which was pre-booked for everyone. Lynda made the arrangements after Neil said to invite his parents and sister. Morgan sits beside her mum, avoiding Neil. Morgan states she is giving up rowing, looking at Neil, and he looks at her.

"That's a mistake. You have potential the way you rowed in the race. I can help with tips!" Lynda says.

Morgan is surprised by her offer, "Really, you'd help?" she questions.

"Yes, Morgan," Julia said. "With proper training and discipline, you will become a good rower!"

Neil holds Lynda's hand under the table, his way of thanking her. "Okay, I'll think about it!" Morgan says, looking at Neil.

"Oh yes, Lynda has a new sim card, Morgan. I have a lock on my mobile now!" Neil's way of letting her know he's aware of her giving out Lynda's mobile to her teammates.

Morgan blushes, knowing his meaning. Her parents talk with each other. John and Zoe enter the café and the little girl runs to her mum. She sits, squeezing beside Neil on the bench seat. Morgan watches enviously, and he smiles at her. "You have a fan!" Julia whispers to Neil. John sits on the opposite side of the table. Neil leans to Lynda saying the family is larger now; she whispers back, "Maybe larger soon!" he gazes at her. She texts, *'talk later.'*

He places his hand on her stomach and she places hers over the top. Julia sees, "You're not?" she whispers behind Neil's back.

Lynda texts, *"unsure, waiting for blood test. I've been sick every day for the last three weeks."*

Julia reads the message she texts back. *"fingers crossed Sis. Happy."*

Lynda texts, *"Quiet, it may not be."*

Julia texts, *"Okay, with a smiley face."*

Neil is reading the messages on Lynda's phone and he places his arm behind her back. Lynda wants to keep it between them; she may just have a virus and went to the doctor. He advised doing a pregnancy test just in case.

Lynda talks about Simon's new interest to take her mind off everything. Simon has decided to go back to university to train as a veterinarian, something he's been interested in for some time. Lynda thinks that's a good idea as he loves animals and it may be less stressful for him. Neil gives his support, saying if he can help with studying or anything, just ring him. Simon thanks Neil; they both get along really well. Lynda notices Neil is a good influence on her brother. Brian and Julia support the brother as Julia states she is going to become a trainer again with the sculls. She gave Mia her phone number and hopes her parents ring her. Lynda is very happy as this is something her sister used to do, but gave up due to having Zoe.

"The club will be happy; they have missed you coaching the younger girls!" Lynda states, saying the club will have a chance again in next year's race against the other clubs.

"You have club races?" Neil enquires.

"Didn't Lynda tell you she came third last year!" Julia replies.

Neil is very surprised she never mentioned it to him. Simon says Lynda keeps things to herself.

"Yeah, Sis. You should be proud of last year, the first time you came in with the winners!" Brian says.

"Where did you come, Julia?" Neil enquires.

"She always wins the single scull, even at her age!" Simon says.

The entire family is enjoying each other's company. Morgan sits watching, keeping her eyes on Lynda; she is trying to work her out, Morgan only has to let Lynda in, and they can have a friendship. Lynda had a younger sister and never wants to replace her. She only wants to be friends with Morgan if she allows it to develop. Lynda is now letting Morgan decide.

Chapter Eight

Lynda's Health

In Neil's apartment, Lynda asks if Neil will be happy if she is pregnant. Neil stares across to her with a blank expression.

"Oh, sorry, the pill should have worked, never missed before. Must have been our holiday due to being totally relaxed with you!" Lynda replies.

Neil walks across, kissing her on the forehead, saying he will cope and he loves her. Just unsure, how I feel about becoming a father. I never giving it much thought. I enjoy being with you for the moment!" he states, surprising Lynda.

"Is that why you chose me at my age?" she questions him.

"No, beautiful, I fell for you the moment we met in my office that first day!" Neil replies, looking softly at her.

Lynda is happy. Instead of planning a wedding for the following year, she may be choosing baby items; she always wanted to have a baby. Lynda never found a man that did too, and to find out from Neil he feels the same way, she's beginning to think she attracts the wrong type of man. Neil walks across, saying he will still continue with the wedding plans, just in case she's not pregnant. He says he will have Patricia and Jennifer assist him until she feels better.

"Don't tell them about my health?" Lynda replies anxiously.

"Okay," he says. Neil thinks to himself that they hadn't discussed how they both felt about having children. After Lynda informing of Julia's troubles falling pregnant, he thought that it might never happen for Lynda.

"I will re-arrange my office hours, working from eight thirty to four thirty every day instead of my normal late hours and having Friday off. Neil agrees that it is a good idea and will change his times so he can drive them to work and home.

"I may have to work at home some nights. Is that okay with you?" he asks Lynda.

Lynda accepts now they will maybe have to change their lifestyles to cater to a baby. Neil comments he's glad they decided to live in his three-bedroom apartment as their main home instead of her two-bedroom apartment.

"You will be okay then if we're having a baby?" she nervously asks again.

"I need time to get my head around it. I love you!"

Lynda looks at him, she doesn't want to lose Neil. He takes her hand. "We'll have to think about renting your apartment for extra income! "Neil says with a smile, looking at her.

Lynda is fond of her home and wants to keep it for a couple of years. She has been reluctant to rent it out or sell; she hasn't moved all of her belongings yet and is not ready to hand it over to strangers. Lynda has lived at the apartment for the past twenty years and loves it as she re-decorated it five years ago to her taste.

"Yes, I just miss the ocean views, and besides, it's handy for friends and guests when they visit!" Lynda says, staring across to Neil, now massaging her feet.

Neil mentions he will take her to visit his aunty and grandma next week if she's up for it. The pair live in the country; his aunty cares for his aging grandma. Lynda is excited to meet his grandma as he's never talked about her. She asks what his auntie is like.

"She's an artist and makes quite good money at it!" Neil boasts of her achievements in the art world at local markets and art galleries.

"What's their names?" Lynda enquires.

"Aunty Elizabeth and grandma Alice are both characters; they grow their own vegies and have fruit trees, looking after themselves. Neil explains they are his mum's relatives, and he manages to visit them three times a year.

"Donna never mentioned them to me!" Lynda says.

"No, my real mum's sister and mother, who helped me after her death, more like my real mum, I guess. I never call Donna's parents my grandparents!" Neil mentions giving Lynda a longing expression.

Lynda feels quite honoured he's introducing her. She asks questions, suggesting they take them some goodies from their favourite deli. "Some delicacies they may like!" she says.

"Good idea. I always take them a box of wine, but that will be good too!" Neil answers, continuing to rub her feet.

"How old is aunty Elizabeth?" Lynda asks.

"Sixty-four, she is my mum's older sister. He says his mum would have been fifty-six this year if she lived. Mum was twenty-six when she had me. He tells her his aunty has two children and she will like them; they are his favourite cousins. One forty and the other forty-four, around your age!" Neil says, lifting her foot and kissing it.

"You are cheeky, handsome!" Lynda beams, blushing slightly. She loves the way Neil expresses his love for her in every way and loves him deeply too.

"Why have you decided now to introduce me?" Lynda enquires.

"You finally told me you love me, and it's time for you to

meet my real family. The day I visited your grandma, her face lit up when explaining the vineyard and enjoying the wine Daniel gave as a gift. I had a wonderful day, it made me realise you will like my grandma!"

Lynda laughs. "Yes, grandma likes her wine. I look forward to meeting your grandma!"

Lynda tells Neil she is going to lie down, feeling rather sick and tired. He's looking concerned at her, and she assures him she's okay.

Lynda receives a phone call from her doctor. She says the blood test came back negative; she is not pregnant. The doctor is concerned due to her having pain and being sick. She has booked her in for an ultrasound that afternoon around four p.m. Lynda rings Neil and he lets Patricia know he will be leaving early; he picks Lynda up at the lift, driving her to the doctor for her appointment. Lynda walks out to the lounge to tell Neil, she's not pregnant and has an appointment at Radiology this afternoon. He walks across holding her in his arms. "I'll drive!" Neil now having concerns for her health. Neil remains in the waiting room while she has her ultrasound, the operator frowning.

"Anything wrong?" Lynda asks.

"You will have to ask your doctor!" she replies.

Lynda walks out, telling Neil she is now a little concerned. She pays for the visit on her health benefits card. Neil drives them home, taking glances at Lynda and seeing she is very pale. He is worried about her. Lynda lies down when they get home and Neil rings Donna; being a woman and close.

"No use thinking of the worst, treatments these days are excellent!" Donna tells him. Try not to worry; she is grateful he turns to her and gives Lynda her best.

Lynda and Neil attend the doctor's appointment; she explains Lynda has a growth the size of a golf ball which must be removed as quickly as possible.

"It can be dangerous and the worst outcome would be cancer!" the doctor says.

The word cancer makes Lynda nearly faint, after her sister's illness. Neil tightens his grip, holding her hand. The doctor says until she has the operation, she can't tell. Lynda has been booked in to see the specialist next month.

"Lynda, let's take one step at a time; I am only giving you the worst outcome. It just may be a lump that needs removing. Have you had any trouble with these before?" she enquires as she is Lynda's new doctor.

"Didn't you read my history?" Lynda asks.

"Not all your records transferred, only the past five years!" the doctor replies.

Lynda is wondering why; she explains she's had uterus problems since age eighteen. She had quite a large piece removed by laser when she was thirty-two; the doctor told her it was just on the turn. In two weeks, she would have cancer and probably die. The doctor looks at her, concerned.

"Is there a history of cancer in the family?" the doctor enquires.

"Yes, my baby sister died five years ago from Leukemia; she had it since age twelve!" Lynda replies.

"I will get my girls to make the arrangements to book you in as an emergency for next week. I will have them contact you today with the appointment!" Doctor replies, frowning, now aware of the family history.

Lynda leaves the office. Neil is quite pale and she suggests they go and have some coffee. Neil thinks this is a good idea, he needs one after that. He orders at the café, their favourite place. The girl knows their orders, Lynda's lemongrass and ginger tea and Neil's cappuccino, and she leaves to get them. Neil asks Lynda why she never informed him of her health issues. She tells him that she hasn't had any trouble for the last four years and thought it had all gone away.

"Does this make a difference in how you feel about me?" she asks.

"No, I needed to know to be prepared for times like this. Is this why you fear falling pregnant?" he asks.

"Yes, always wondering if it will affect me falling!" Lynda replies, touching Neil's hand.

He tightens his grip. He loves her with all his heart, and now, just after finding their way together, the thought of maybe losing her frightens him.

"I don't want to lose you now after just finding you. Whatever happens, I'm in all the way!" Neil states, holding both hands across the table.

The girls serve their beverages and he suggests she work from home; just until she sees the specialist. Lynda looks across at him always caring about her wellbeing. She agrees, telling Neil Mr. Gardner won't mind; there are no meetings booked until the end of next month. Neil is relieved not to have to worry about her overworking in the office on the second floor of the same building. He can keep a closer eye on her at home as she will not overdo things, being in a more relaxed atmosphere with no one at the office bothering her. Neil looks at Lynda, thinking he couldn't live without her; he wants her forever, just needs to get his head around all the information. Neil knows now Lynda is in constant pain without letting him know. He now understands her buying so many painkilling tablets. He noticed but said nothing as Lynda has been under pressure at work, thinking the tablets were to help deal with this. He is now aware and will keep a closer eye on her. Neil caters for any unexpected situations or emergencies to work from home if necessary. Neil is now engaged to Lynda, which they have only told their bosses, Jennifer and Patricia about for the moment.

The boss rings to check on Neil if he needs anything done for him. Neil thanks him saying everything under control and Lynda is resting. Neil is very pleased he made the new work arrangement and will put it into action after Lynda sees the specialist and obviously will have an operation.

In the morning, Neil suggests they make their engagement official to their family and friends. He says to Lynda, after her operation, to arrange a gathering at Ben's restaurant to celebrate. "Ben will be happy to make all the arrangements while you recover from whatever happens."

Lynda looks longingly into Neil's eyes. "Darling, if I do have cancer, it's best if we don't make any future plans and we separate as a couple!" Neil turns pale as he stands beside her, "I don't care; I am not going anywhere. I am marrying you, Lynda!" he says, looking at her.

Lynda explains how difficult it was watching her sister and how helpless the entire family felt. "I don't want you to go through that!" she states.

Neil holds her in his arms, looking down into her green eyes. He wipes her tears with his finger. "I love you with all my heart and will stand by you no matter what life throws at us!"

"I love you so much, my darling man!" Lynda says, leaning against his chest. Neil holds her tight, never letting her go.

In the morning, Lynda rings her boss making her new arrangements. He says he will have Jennifer email her with work.

Mr. Gardner's voice sounds worried, knowing her family history. Lynda assures him she will let him know the outcome. She then rings her sister, Julia, informing her she's not having a baby but instead a lump unknown at this time. Julia's voice drops out, fearing the worst. She talks with Lynda for two hours about how she can assist Neil. Both sisters agree not to tell their parents or brothers until the results after seeing the specialist. Julia tells Lynda she will come around in the afternoon and bring her a meal, so no need to worry about cooking. Lynda is grateful to her sister as she only lives in the next suburb of Balgowlah Heights, not far. After hanging up from her sister, Julia rings Neil to see how he is feeling with the news. Neil expresses that finding out about it scares him and he now understands Lynda's health issues. Julia is surprised her sister didn't tell him; after all, they are living together. Neil informs Julia he is going to have an official engagement after everything.

"What? You guys are engaged? That's wonderful!" her voice raises with happiness.

Neil asks if Julia can help with organising the invites for the family and friends. "Oh, course I will. I'll use my computer and get onto it straight away. Neil, send me the friends' names and addresses and where you're planning on having it!" Julia says.

Neil tells Julia he must wait until after speaking with the specialist as to when the operation will be and how long for Lynda to heal after that. Julia understands. "When you're ready for me to send them, Neil, I'll do it for you!" she says. She also tells him she is nearby and to ask any time he needs help.

Julia hangs up. She likes Neil, thinking he's perfect for Lynda, and doesn't care about the age difference. He has made a big difference in her sister's life. Lynda is more alive and has never been happier than with Neil. She told her husband they were perfect for each other. Neil is grateful to Julia, she's always there for her big sister. Mr. Gardner rings Neil as he's known him most of his life. He asks if he can do anything to assist him. Neil replies just to help with Lynda's workload, as she's in pain but not telling anyone. To give him and Lynda support during this time.

"I will get Jennifer right on it. Neil, ring me any time and for anything!" Mr. Gardner answers.

Neil communicates with his dad during this time to give him strength. Robert encourages Neil to concentrate on his work. "It may help!" Robert says he knows how his son feels after losing his wife and Neil's mother.

The specialist informs Lynda and Neil she won't know anything until the specimen is tested and the results come back. She looks at the couple's expressions, and she quietly tells them this may take four weeks. The doctor is trying to ease their concerns, but now aware of Lynda's sister, she too is having doubts about the outcome. The doctor tells Lynda she has concerns that it grew so quickly in size and with Lynda being sick and in pain for four weeks before seeing her G.P. The doctor tells them the operation is booked for the following Monday.

"I have classed it as urgent!" she states. Neil holds Lynda's hand, seeing she is fearing the operation and outcome. He says thank you to the doctor as Lynda has lost her voice, and he takes her from the office. Neil tries to help Lynda not to worry without success; he keeps her quiet for the rest of the day and until the operation.

The operation goes to plan, and Neil works from home on his computer in his office, having video calls with clients. The waiting for results takes its toll on Lynda, who hardly concentrates on work. Neil spends time preparing meals and sitting talking with Lynda about work issues. Neil plays games with her, anything to keep her mind from worrying. In bed, he holds her in his arms, letting her know he loves her. He tells her their partnership can stand up without sex; having each other is more important. Neil tries anything to comfort Lynda, allowing her to rest and heal, as he notices she has trouble straightening and walking around.

The four weeks move along slowly for them both until they get the text for Lynda's appointment to see the specialist. Lynda is now healed, and on entering the doctor's office, they sit side by side on the chairs provided. The doctor asks how Lynda is feeling? She gives her the all-clear; there is no cancer infection on the specimen. She advises Lynda to have regular check-ups with ultrasounds to keep an eye on any more growths.

The doctor looks directly at Lynda, saying that after reading her history of growths and nearly having cancer in her thirties, she suggests a partial hysterectomy to stop the growths in her uterus.

"You will still have your cervix intact. It was too close this time!" the doctor says in a softer tone, especially seeing Lynda's face.

Neil takes Lynda's hand on seeing how pale she's become; the doctor says to think about it; she has made an appointment in six weeks.

"You don't have to decide now; let me know at your next appointment!" the doctor says.

Neil thanks her and takes Lynda out of the office. They drive home, and she sits in silence, crying. She loves Neil and really wants to have his baby; Neil holds her tightly in his arms with her head against his chest. Neil takes her across to the couch, sitting her down beside him. Lynda leans on his chest, and he wraps his arms around her, consoling her. Lynda calms after an hour; she is exhausted, so Neil suggests a light dinner and sleep for now. They will discuss things in the morning. Lynda agrees; she eats in silence, watching Thor, one of her favourite movies.

Neil wakes early, moving quietly so as not to disturb Lynda. He showers and makes breakfast, pancakes, he thought, today. Lynda loves pancakes with maple syrup, and he cooks, keeping them warm in the oven.

Lynda walks out in her PJs and he kisses her on the forehead. "Good morning, beautiful!" he says. Seeing her sad face, he places a plate with pancake, banana and maple syrup in front of her.

"Eat," he says, giving her a vegetable juice with lemongrass and ginger tea; Lynda eats in silence. Neil watches as he eats opposite her, drinking his coffee. Lynda looks up at him saying she wants to have his baby. Neil says he wants a full life with her and not a threat of her getting cancer. He believes it's best to have the operation, telling Lynda he doesn't care about having children.

"If you want children, we can adopt or use the eggs you froze. There are many possibilities!" Neil says, keeping eye contact with her.

Lynda is so amazed by Neil's understanding. How he is so supportive and loving her, no matter what is thrown at him.

"I love you too and want to spend the rest of my life with you!" Lynda says, walking over to him; she kisses him softly.

Neil pulls her down onto his lap. "I'm never letting you go; we are stronger together and must be brave. We will face many obstacles in life!" he says to her. Lynda tells Neil she wants to wait for another five months before committing to a final act of not being able to have a child. He accepts her decision but will keep a close eye on her to make sure she stays well.

"I know it's your body, but any signs of you being sick again and I will make the appointment with the specialist! Neil says in a determined voice. Lynda understands and accepts his decision.

Lynda is grateful to have Neil in her life, a man she's been looking for and has never been happier with. Neil suggests they go jogging together each afternoon to help with work pressure and stay fit. Lynda likes that idea, enjoying doing things with a partner. She mentions going back to rowing each Sunday with the club. Neil is happy about her decision and tells Lynda he will just celebrate his thirty-first birthday at Ben's restaurant inviting his parents and sister.

"I would like Julia and John there too if you think they will come?" Neil asks.

"Yes, they will love that. Might make my brothers jealous!" Lynda says.

Neil didn't think of that; he is still getting to know Brian and Simon. He agrees, just his folks and Jennifer; now she's with Ben. Lynda likes that idea; Neil says he will ring and arrange for tomorrow night.

Neil and Lynda go jogging and sitting in their favourite café the girl orders for the couple. She brings it across to the table, smiling. "I know your order. If you need anything else, just come up!" she says.

Neil thanks her as they go there every day after their jog. Lynda is engrossed in conversations around her. Two women discuss their long walking trail, commenting on meeting a funny tourist. One asks if Crocs can be worn on the rough trail, and the other woman laughs. One man is sitting alone, looking at his phone, sipping his coffee. Lynda looks across at Neil, thinking it's nice having someone to talk to. Neil looks at Lynda, so grateful he finally found the woman he wants in his life and she is compatible. Both enjoy the outdoors and games, he's off the market after spending years with girls who are only after his father's status. Neil always found it a disadvantage having a rich upbringing. People desire to be friends to get close to his father. Ben is the only close boyhood friend who liked him for himself, coming from a normal household.

Neil always lived on his own means of support from money he inherited from his mother's estate, which paid for his flat. And he's now paid his father back for his university degree even though his father refused to take it from his son. Neil wanted to show his father and stepmother he is independent of their wealth. Neil likes being around people who work for what they have. The reason he lived in Melbourne for so long away from his father is Neil uses his mother's surname. He returned at just the right time when Lynda was single two years earlier. They would have never met with her being in a relationship. Timing was perfect for the pair; he holds Lynda's hand, smiling.

"What are you thinking?" she asks.

Neil just smiles, saying he's enjoying the morning. She too is feeling well again. The sun is shining, and she has everything she wants to be loved for herself.

Saturday morning, Neil is taking Lynda to visit his aunty and grandma. On arriving, his Aunty Elizabeth greets him; she kisses Neil and shakes Lynda's hand. Neil carries the boxes, one with wine and the other with delicacies Lynda bought. He places them down on the kitchen bench and then moves across to his grandma Alice.

"Neil, did you bring my favourite red?" she asks.

He kisses her. "Yes, don't I always?" he says, smiling and explaining he has brought a special person to meet her.

She touches his cheek. "A woman?" she asks. He nods his head 'yes.'

Lynda walks across, greeting Alice. She's told to lean down; Alice kisses her cheek. The old lady tells her to sit on the chair, "I'm happy Neil is finally going to settle down!" she says.

Lynda smiles to meet her finally; Alice tells Neil to wander off, she wants to talk with Lynda. Alice asks how she met Neil; Lynda tells their story. Alice finds the story romantic and proceeds to tell Lynda how she met her husband when they were young.

Outside Neil finds his Aunty Elizabeth picking berries. She asks him questions about Lynda and how old she is. Neil tells her, and she nearly falls over.

"What are you thinking? She's too old for you, the same age as Tim, my son!" Elizabeth states adamantly.

"Aunty, age has nothing to do with it. I love Lynda and our ages never come between us. Lynda is my perfect match!" Neil speaks up, defending his choice.

Elizabeth says his mother would never have approved of an older woman. "What would you know what Mum would think?" Neil questions her, raising his voice.

"I was her older sister, and she never approved of older women with younger men. We talked often on the subject with celebrities!" Elizabeth is blunt.

"It doesn't matter. I am going to marry Lynda and don't need your approval, aunt!" Neil replies, walking back inside the house. Lynda sees his expression. He asks his grandma how she feels about his choice. "I like this woman, just perfect for you, Neil!" Alice says, smiling.

"Thanks, grandma, glad you approve!" Neil says, holding her hand. He only cares what she thinks, not his aunt.

"Your Mum would have liked Lynda, a nice girl!" Alice replies, making Lynda blush at being called a girl.

Lynda stands up as the front door springs open with people bouncing into the house. All his cousins are arriving; all come to meet Lynda as Neil arranged. Neil places his arm behind Lynda's back as people walk up to them. Tim walks across, shaking hands with Neil.

"Good to see you, Cous. You must be Lynda. I heard a lot about you. Good seeing Neil looking healthily and fit. This is Izzy, my wife, and Fred and Susan, the kids!" Tim says, shaking Lynda's hand.

"Hello," Lynda replies, happy to meet the family.

Hudson enters with his family, all rushing over to meet Neil. "Hi, this is Eve, my wife, Michelle and Ben, the kids!" Hudson says, shaking Lynda's hand. He gazes into her face making Lynda a little uncomfortable.

"Hello," she says. Lynda thinks Neil has a large extended family hidden away. "Do you have a lot of cousins?" Izzy asks Lynda.

"Yes, hundreds. My first cousins live in WA and Victoria; haven't seen them in years!" Lynda replies.

Neil now understands why he has never met any of her close cousins. Unlike his cousins, they have been rather close since he was a boy, keeping close after his mother's death.

"Took you long enough to get us together, Neil. I can see why you wanted to keep her to yourself, a real good-looker!" Hudson states. His wife nudges him to behave.

"I like you!" Lynda comments.

The women invite Lynda into the kitchen, asking if she likes tea or coffee, "Tea," Lynda replies.

"Good, we do too," they get the large teapot, pouring tea

leaves and hot water inside. Lynda loves fresh tea, thinking she's going to enjoy this cuppa. Lizzy and Eve ask Lynda to sit. Eve asks what kind of job she has, wanting to know all about her as Neil kept her a secret. Izzy enquires if she and Neil are planning on having children any time soon due to her age.

Neil walks in at just that moment. "I think Lynda's had enough of questioning!" he tells his cousins, taking Lynda away into the lounge room to speak with the men. "Thank you," Lynda whispers.

"Anytime, beautiful," he says.

Tim overhears him, "That's real love!" he says, tapping Neil on the shoulder, being the same height.

Tim asks Lynda how she met Neil. "I saw him on my regular bus, then at work. I arrived for my monthly meeting finding Neil replaced Mr. Jones!"

Tim says, "Is that so? I smell a rat. Neil hates travelling on buses; he always drives to work. Never take a bus he always says!"

Neil is going slightly reddish in the face; Lynda looks at him. "What is the truth, darling?" she asks with a grin.

Neil admits he knew her beforehand, at his dad's regular dinners with Mr. Gardner. "He spoke highly of your business skills, saving the company several times, and how respected you were at my law firm, with Mr. Gardner's important clients and that you were a lovely person. He couldn't understand why you were alone. I had only been back two weeks, and I became curious about this woman called Lynda.

"I listened to him and asked questions. He mentioned you travel on the bus with Jason. My boss told me I was due to have a meeting with you the next day. I asked Mr. Gardner which bus to catch and he told me. I wanted to see you for myself before our meeting. "I was mesmerised when I saw you and how you signed with Jason. I thought, what a caring woman. After our meeting, I really wanted to get to know you!"

Lynda sits on a chair, Neil sits himself on the arm, and the women carry in trays of tea and coffee pots. "About time," says grandma Alice and everyone laughs.

Neil pours tea for Lynda handing her a cup, and Izzy nudges her husband, whispering, "You used to do that," he chuckles.

Izzy asks Lynda what she likes to do for fun. She mentions she goes jogging and rowing, and she likes playing backgammon with Neil. Izzy says, "Have you beaten him yet? He's a good player!"

Lynda replies saying she won one game. "Good, about time." Apparently, Neil always wins when Izzy plays with him, so she's given up playing the game. Neil, suggest they play cricket.

"Are you sure, Cous? My team always wins!" says Tim.

Neil winks to Hudson as they normally lose. "Lynda's on my team. We might have a chance!" he says.

"Can you play, Lynda?" questions Tim.

"Some," she answers, aware Neil is keeping her batting skills from his cousin. She smiles at Neil. The two groups of four players on both sides are being chosen; they move outside.

Team one: Neil, Lynda, Hudson and Izzy. Team two: Tim, Eve, Elizabeth and Ben. Eve throws the coin; heads, calls Neil. He wins the toss, batting first; Neil sends Lynda up first.

"What's the deal?" Hudson asks.

"Lynda's my secret weapon," Neil replies. "Just watch,"

Hudson says he must see this as Tim bowls the first one over her head. "Hey, play fair!" Neil calls. Tim waves and he bowls softly. Lynda hits it down the paddock, giving her and Hudson plenty of runs.

The opposite team are not happy yelling, "Come on, Dad, hurry up." Neil jumps up and down excitedly. "Yes, yes, that's my girl!" he cries.

Aunty and grandma laugh, finally Neil's team has a chance. Tim quickens his bowling, now understanding Lynda's a great hitter. She hits the balls each time down the paddock or into the fruit trees. Tim is exhausted. Lynda walks off, allowing Neil to bat. "Don't give up," he says.

"Remember Neil, it's a fun game," she says on handing Izzy the bat. Izzy thanks Lynda because normally the men never allow her to bat. Lynda finds out why, she can't hit the ball at all, and Tim gets her out on the second bowl. The change comes, and it's Neil's turn to bowl; he tells Hudson they have to do it. Lynda can't throw a ball. "She's a hitter, not a bowler," he understands, not allowing her to bowl; until Tim sees their strategy.

"Okay, you two. Let Lynda bowl!" Tim calls along with his teammates.

Lynda tries, but the ball keeps going off to the side. Elizabeth gets frustrated. "Let Izzy bowl," she calls. Lynda hands the ball to Izzy, who is a great bowler.

Neil laughs; finally he gets even with Tim and he wins this cricket match; he lifts Lynda off the ground and around in circles. "Thank you!" he kisses her.

"Okay, you love birds, lunchtime!" Tim calls. The barbeque has been warming up and is now ready for the chicken and meat. The sounds of sizzling can be heard as Eve pours wine for the women. Neil, none for you if you're driving. The cops are out today, being a weekend. Eve hands him a soda.

Lynda pours Neil a red wine. "We are booked in the bed-and-breakfast just five minutes from here!" she tells him. "You clever girl, thanks, beautiful!" Neil kisses her.

Izzy thought that's thinking ahead, Lynda is a well-organised woman. She likes people like that as she is an organiser too. Izzy talks with Lynda, asking about her family. Lynda is quite happy to tell her. Neil watches Lynda interacting with his cousins; she's laughing and enjoying herself.

Tim is watching him. "You, okay?" he asks.

Neil tells him Elizabeth doesn't approve of the age gap.

"No, my mum wouldn't. Take no notice. All that matters is you're happy and have found someone you are happy with finally. You have been dating all the wrong girls. I like Lynda; she's right for you; I've never seen you so happy and steady!" Tim says, handing Neil a plate with steaks.

Neil carries over the large platter filled with a selection of meats, snags, hamburgers, chicken breasts and steaks. The kids take the snags with bread and sauce.

"That's enough, Ben!" says his mum on seeing how much sauce.

Lynda takes a steak, cutting it in half, giving Neil the other half, it being so big. Salads are plenty, and everyone enjoys the lunch and each other's company. After a two-hour lunch, Lynda is collecting plates when she overhears Hudson talking to Elizabeth, his mum, saying he agrees the ten-year gap is too much.

"Neil needs a younger woman to have kids with!" he sees Lynda; she walks off, leaving the dishes, a little upset about what she overheard.

Neil asks if she's okay, seeing tears in her eyes. She's a little sensitive since the news of maybe never having children.

"I love you!" she whispers.

"I know." He hugs her. "Don't worry about aunty!" he

guesses she must have commented.

The kids ask Lynda if she will play a board game with them, and she agrees, walking off with the kids to get away from the adults.

Neil speaks to his aunty and cousins. "I know some of you don't like our ten-year age difference. I don't care how you feel. It took me months to convince Lynda not to worry either. I fell in love with her and she's going to be my wife. Be nice or you're not invited to the wedding!" He looks stern as he gazes around the room at each cousin and aunty.

"I like Lynda!" Tim says and so do Izzy and Eve, both saying they think she's perfect for him. Eve gives Neil a hug. "We will never be rude to the woman you love, Cous!" She is fond of him, being around since he was in his twenties.

Neil walks into the playroom seeing the kids laughing with Lynda; they are playing twister. He laughs, seeing her getting tangled with Ben; Lynda falls sideways and Neil quickly steps in, grabbing the boy.

Lynda falls and Neil helps her to her feet. "Let's all play backgammon?" asks Eve walking in.

"I bet Neil wins!" Tim says on entering.

"No, Lynda's quite good; she wins sometimes!" Neil replies.

"Finally, we have a player!" Eve cries, happy to have another player she gets the game.

"Quad Gammon," Tim says.

Lynda likes that idea. Eve sets up all the pieces, and she puts Lynda on her team.

Eve whispers to Lynda, "I taught Neil. I better play with you!"

Lynda is agreeable; she may win this time. The women laugh, them against Tim and Neil, each couple having fun. Lynda makes light of it, laughing when Neil wins a turn. Eve and Lynda end up winning two games against the men's one win. The time soon goes, it is now five and Tim and Izzy must go; they have things to organise for Sunday. Grandma gives Neil and Lynda a hug, and Elizabeth says goodbye to them both, thanking them for the wine and deli items. Aunty asks Lynda to follow her into the kitchen, and Elizabeth hands her some homemade jams.

"I'm not sorry you overheard Hudson and me. I don't approve. You're obviously after a younger man to control. You're probably too old for kids!" Elizabeth says. "Neil chased me, and we fell in love. Whether or not we have kids is our business!" Lynda walks off carrying the jams, taking Neil's hand and saying, "Let's go." Neil says goodbye.

Tim notices Lynda is close to tears and he quietly says, "You're the best thing for Neil. We like you; take no notice of anyone else!" He kisses her on the cheek. Izzy gives her a hug and kiss.

"Don't be a stranger. Hope to see you soon!" Izzy says.

Lynda booked a cottage in the township just a five-minute drive away. It is rather nice with climbing roses across the veranda. Inside is all furnished with food in a fridge for the meal Lynda ordered. A bottle of wine is on the table with glasses. "This is nice," Neil says.

"Yes, looks like its pictures and saves us from getting into the traffic jams!" Lynda says.

She goes off to the bathroom, and on her return to the lounge she finds Neil sitting on the edge of the couch naked. "It's been five weeks and you're healed now. Can I touch you there, beautiful? I'll be gentle!" he states, holding his arms out to Lynda.

She moves close, Neil pulls down her pants and undies, and

Lynda removes her top and bra. She moves slowly onto his lap with her knees on the couch beside his legs. Neil gently moves her closer, kissing her breast, she kisses him on the lips and runs her fingers through his hair.

Lynda's hands move down his back and they move in a rhythm together, bodies heat and sweat forms between Lynda's breasts and on Neil's muscles. He licks the water, enjoying making love to Lynda, the woman of his dreams.

"You complete me as a man. I am yours forever!" he says to her; she tightens her legs around him, both caressing each other's bodies.

Neil lifts Lynda up, lying her gently onto the carpet. She lies beside him as he cuddles her, and he talks of their life together. "I think we should sell both our apartments and buy one together. What do you think?" he asks her.

Lynda agrees, something they both like instead of a bit of each. "I want to remain in Manly!" she says.

"Yes, beautiful, anywhere you want to live, I'm happy!" Neil replies, kissing her on the head. He whispers he loves her mind, smile, understanding towards others, that she is a compassionate lover and her as a woman. He holds her tightly. "My aunt and your mum's opinion are not important; all that matters is us. You have reached my heart forever!" Neil says. He gets up and walks across to his jacket, removing a small box.

Totally naked, he kneels and asks Lynda to marry him. She laughs, saying, "Well, hard to refuse you kneeling like that!" she sits up and he places the ring on her finger, fitting perfectly. "I asked Julia for your ring size!" he says, kissing her.

Lynda looks at her ring, rose gold with a diamond, something she always wanted. "Only the best for you, beautiful!" he states, lifting her up onto her feet, holding her against his body.

"My true love!" Lynda says, holding her arms around his naked body.

Sunday, Lynda and Neil visit her parent's home to tell them she's engaged. Her father is delighted, congratulating them both. Her mother gives her a hug and greets Neil. Ava is not happy with the situation; she has never accepted their age difference, thinking Lynda is better off with someone older. She admires the beautiful ring, surprised Neil has good taste. Ava is still unhappy when Simon comes bouncing into the room. "What's going on?" he asks.

"Lynda's engaged to Neil!" her mother states in an unhappy tone.

Simon hugs his sister and Neil; he lives at home due to his medical condition. Simon has remained on his meds since Neil has been part of his life, and both get along really well. He pulls out his mobile, sending texts to his brother and sister. In thirty minutes they all arrive at the house and voices are raised, kids laughing, all happy and congratulating Neil. "About time!" Julia says.

"What?" her mother replies.

"Well, they've been together for a year and a half. And look, they love each other!" Brian says he likes Neil and is very happy to have a brother-in-law he gets along with.

Ava enters the kitchen to collect good wine glasses and wine. She is slamming cupboard doors when Lynda enters.

"What is wrong?" Lynda asks.

"You have always gone for older men; your last partner was perfect. You should have never let him go; Neil is far too young for you!" Ava says, staring at her daughter.

Lynda looks up at her mother, furious. "I love Neil. He is a better man than I have ever had. He loves me for myself!" Lynda walks from the kitchen and takes Neil by the hand, saying they are leaving.

Jack, her father, asks why. "Talk to Mum!" Lynda says, crying and briskly walks out the door sitting in the jeep. Neil says he will take care of it.

Neil walks into the kitchen, asking Ava what she said to Lynda. Once he hears, he raises his voice and says, "You are a foolish woman; you don't know the circumstances of Lynda's last relationship. Your daughter and I are getting married with or without you. I will always care for and keep Lynda safe, providing for her. That is all you need to know. I love her!"

He gives Ava a stern look and he walks from the house and drives him and Lynda home.

Julia and Brian speak with their mother, saying they like Neil and will support Lynda in her marriage. All the family is divided and split for the day, leaving their father to deal with mum.

Engagement party

Ben and Julia have outdone themselves with fine food spread across two tables and a selection of wines and specialty beers. Julia organised decorations, including flowers in vases spread throughout the restaurant entrance and inside. Julia's daughter, Zoe, helped make the sign, *Neil and Lynda's Engagement* it read with plenty of glitter and flowers. The couple love it, giving Zoe kisses and hugs; the little girl is so happy her aunty and new uncle love her work. The guests all bring beautifully wrapped gifts. Jennifer showing them where to place them on a separate table. Ben and Jennifer are now a couple which has made Neil glad for his friend.

"When's your engagement!" Neil asks Ben; the men chuckle.

"Maybe in the future!" Ben replies, handing his mate a beer. Jennifer gives Lynda a hug, handing her a small gift box. On opening the lid she sees inside is a knife with a bow. "Your wedding cake knife!" Jen says.

Lynda hugs her friend, saying, "Thank you, perfect gift." Jen hands Lynda a glass of wine. They laugh and talk with Jen stating Neil is the best thing that ever happened to her. Both women see Morgan is actually smiling, standing next to her boyfriend.

Lynda's Dad makes a toast to the couple, standing beside Neil and Lynda. Jack welcomes Robert, Donna and Morgan to the extended family unit. He is happy their children have found each other and look happy together. "To Neil and Lynda!" he toasts them, and so does everyone in the room. Friends and grandparents are happy, too, commenting on how happy Neil and Lynda are together. A friend comments that Lynda will get sick of Neil in five years due to the age difference. Ben takes no notice of her, walking off to re-supply the wine on the table and checking his staff at the same time.

Guests are all enjoying the fine food. Everyone mixes with family; getting to know each other. Neil only invited family and a couple of close friends and so did Lynda, keeping the numbers down. Aunty Elizabeth makes it known to Ava how she feels about Lynda chasing her nephew until catching him. "Probably pregnant," she states. Ava stands up for her daughter for once. "Lynda is not having a baby; besides, Neil chased Lynda until he caught her!" Ava walks off, now knowing how her daughter feels when she complains to her.

Morgan bangs her glass to make a toast, and everyone turns to face the girl. Neil and Lynda are surprised, both take a deep breath. Morgan says congratulations Neil, and as an aside, she says she and Ian got engaged this morning and are marrying in

April. The guests stand with mouths open and some whispering. Robert, her father, claps, walking towards her and moving Morgan away. He tells Ian to take her home now, and the boyfriend takes her by the arm saying how embarrassed he is.

Robert makes a toast. "To my eldest and only son who has found a wonderful woman, his equal on so many levels. I am excited to have Lynda as part of our family. Raise your glasses to Neil and Lynda!"

"Neil and Lynda." Voices sound in the restaurant then everyone sips their wine.

Lynda's mother hugs her, saying sorry, and she will learn to accept them as a couple. After hearing Neil's aunt and sister, she feels guilty for not supporting her daughter. Neil moves quickly across to Lynda's side. Ava apologises to him, asking if they can start over. Neil agrees but thinks he will keep his distance for now.

Jen brings out a lovely cake, vanilla almond meal and passionfruit cream, both Neil and Lynda's favourite cake. She gives them a knife and they cut it in half; everyone cheers. Jen cuts it up in the kitchen for the guests.

Neil puts on music. "Stuck on you," describing how he feels for Lynda, and he takes her hand. Julia takes John, her husband, and they dance on the floor along with other guests. Neil declines not being able to dance, preferring not to. Brian takes his sister to the floor. Both learnt ballroom dancing, and Lynda spins around the floor.

Chapter Nine

Arrangements

The couple certainly had their challenges and believe their relationship is all the stronger and better for them. Morgan's fiance breaks off with her. He wasn't happy with her stunt at her brother's party. She has become demanding, a person he dislikes, deciding he doesn't want to marry a girl like her. Morgan is not upset about losing him, just not being engaged means her plans have gone up in flames. Neil tries to reason with her, but once again Morgan is being her difficult self. Lynda decides to avoid her entirely as she has enough to do with a busy workload and arranging a wedding in eight months. Neil has taken half the list to assist, *"guests list his half, suits for himself, best man and father-in-law, shoes, photographer and wedding invites on computer."*

Lynda's half for now, *"guests list her half, flowers, wedding party, bridesmaids and flower girl, fitness,"* the rest Julia and Jennifer are organising as their wedding gift. After writing it down, it seems more real to Lynda; she looks frustrated. Neil says they will choose the reception together and says that Mr. Gardner's wife is a celebrant.

Lynda has forgotten. "Of course, perfect. They were on the list anyway!"

Neil says he will ring and ask her, knowing the woman the longest, since he was a kid. Lynda informs Neil that Julia is helping as a gift, saying she loves designing parties. Lynda sips her tea, thinking not so bad, just a panic attack because it's not far off. She just had her forty-second birthday and now, finding it real, she is finally marrying Neil.

Neil kisses her forehead, saying, "It's just jitters!" He smiles at her.

"Our wedding is going to be totally different from any other before ours, handsome!" Lynda says, taking Neil's hand as he's walking past.

"Our relationship is real; we can concur on any situation, and we enjoy each other's company!" Lynda tells him.

Neil smiles, standing up saying he will make dinner; chicken teriyaki with rice. Lynda likes the sound of that; she loves his cooking, as she's not a cook. Before Neil, she used to get healthy and unhealthily take outs. Neil and Lynda go out jogging every afternoon to get in shape, especially for the wedding day. Not that either need to worry, both being in good shape and are fit. Neil has been looking at new apartments due to his selling six weeks ago, and settlement is today. They moved into Lynda's apartment but now hers is sold. Neil has a loan to cater to buying a new apartment; his money is in the bank today. He has arranged to view two apartments they both chose on the internet. Lynda and Neil view the first one thinking it's too small. He drives to the next location, meeting the agent there.

"Why are we back at my apartment?" she asks. Neil parks the car, and he takes Lynda by the hand, walking her up the street only six apartments block from hers.

Neil points up, "It's the top floor. I found this one yesterday, keeping it as a surprise. You love this location. I thought just maybe the one for us both!"

Lynda is eager to see the apartment now, and they take the

lift. At the top, the agent greets them at the front door, showing them around. The top floor is a three-bedroom with two bathrooms. The lounge is spacious, bigger than either of their apartments, and dearer. The balcony overlooks the beach, "perfect," Neil says, always liking the view. He moves up behind Lynda, whispering, "What do you think?"

Lynda says, "perfect," she turns, smiling at him. A modern apartment with the latest appliances, she comments to Neil being the cook. He tells the agent they'll take it, and back at the agent's office, Neil places their deposit. He gives the details of the office where he works, who will represent them, being a lawyer and having solicitors in the office. Neil rings one of the solicitors to expect the paperwork and email. He tells him to have the settlement date the same as Lynda's apartment date.

Lynda takes the day off; she is looking forward to spending the day with Jennifer and Julia. The women are going shopping for Lynda's wedding dress, giving enough timeline for alterations. Lynda decides to let the women choose their own dresses as long as they are yellow or silver, being the theme for the wedding. Neil convinced Lynda to have those colours as she loves yellow roses. Jennifer meets Lynda and Julia at the wedding shop as it's in the city. She is very excited, having never been a bridesmaid until now. Julia is overexcited, this being her big sister's wedding, she's been waiting for years. Julia married ten years ago and has been very happy with John and her darling daughter Zoe, so she's in overdrive for Lynda's wedding day.

Inside the large bridal shop is a second level for private viewings. Julia booked it months ago and the sales lady escorts them upstairs. Hanging on hooks are ten gowns in various styles. Lynda looks through the gowns choosing one. She wants an elegant and simple wedding dress. Julia likes more decorative and Jen is in the middle of both designs. Lynda tries on her sister's choice first as the dress is far too big for her.

"Never mind the size. We order in your size and can do alterations if you lose more weight. Unfortunately, we are unable to add to the gowns. You will have to buy another dress!" the salesperson says.

Julia never knew this; it's been years since she went shopping for her gown, and she had lost weight. Lynda is a size 12, so she looks lovely in anything, except the big bouncy dress Julia chose. Jen has the giggles as the gown swamps Lynda's height.

"Neil is tall. I look like a sugar plum fairy!" she states, upsetting the salesperson.

Jen's choice was next, not as bad with less fabric but still a younger style, Lynda feels. "You don't have to worry about your age. Wear what you want!" Jen says, persuading her friend.

Lynda walks out in the dress, and a young bride downstairs is looking up, asking her assistant if she can try that gown on. The assistant walks upstairs, asking if Lynda is happy for the girl to have the gown. She changes, handing it to the assistant. She rushes downstairs, eager for a quick sale, the young girl tries it on, loving the dress. Lynda, Jen and Julia can hear her gushing, the women looking down, seeing it does suit the girl. Lynda enters her change room, trying on another gown she walks out in a half silk and lace top with short sleeves as it's a December wedding and will be hot. She looks lovely, fitting in all the right places, and the skirt is slender; exactly what Lynda wants. The sales assistant walks in gushing, "You look beautiful!" she says, really liking the dress and understanding the style Lynda is looking for. She runs out, moving to another rack, choosing wedding gowns and brings two gowns to Lynda. She tries on one expensive gown entirely in French lace, looking glamorous. Lynda walks out and Jen and Julia are speechless, loving the gown on her. Julia takes Lynda across to the wall mirror moving her sideways. A small train at the back is perfect for Lynda, a gown she always dreamt of.

"This one is perfect for you and Neil!" Julia says. Lynda smiles at her sister.

Jen also agrees, along with the salesperson. "Right, I will take this one today!" Lynda says. The girl is very happy, this being a four-thousand-dollar gown.

It's now the turn of Julia and Jen to choose their dresses, and the sales assistant walks around the shop, now understanding the style the women are after. She brings in five lemons to yellow and silver dresses. Julia laughs with several designs, and yellow just doesn't suit her colouring. Lynda suggests silver or grey. Two more long gowns come out in pale grey. Julia likes the ankle length as Jen looks better in the long lemon dress.

"Perfect, you both look lovely!" Lynda says, looking at her sister and best friend. Julia says yes. Happy with their choices, they change back into their clothes. The assistant takes the dresses, she has just finished placing the wedding dress into a special fabric dress bag. She wraps up their dresses with tissue paper into a special box for each woman; she is wrapt with the large sale, and the dresses are all the right sizes! Julia walks across to the children's section. She chooses a white dress for Zoe and a silver suit for Liam.

"Do you think they will both look cute in these?" Julia asks Lynda.

Jen smiles and she moves across, picking another dress with net skirts and silk top, handing it to Julia.

"I love this dress more. Will need a yellow ribbon to put

around her waist instead of this pink one!" she states.

Lynda says, "Ah, it's so sweet, net skirts with silk tops." The salesperson goes across to the locked cabinet, removing three different widths of ribbon in yellow and silver. Julia chooses, saying this wedding shop caters for everything. Jen informs the women the shoe shop next door has a large selection of wedding shoes. Lynda pays for the gowns and arranges to have them delivered to Julia's address by courier that afternoon. The salesperson is very happy to make the arrangements after a five-and-a-half-thousand-dollar sale, and she gets commission.

The women move next door to buy shoes. Lynda chooses satin silk as Jen and Julia buy shoes they can wear again. The salesperson is happy to get out nearly every shoe she has for wedding styles. Julia is satisfied with a pair of silver strap shoes and lower heels as Jen chooses a white leather shoe she can wear with her summer dresses. The salesperson has their sizes, the last pair in Julia's size and packs them into boxes and bags for the women. Julia buys white sandals for Zoe, being more comfortable in the heat and knowing her daughter prefers to walk around in bare feet.

"Zoe should keep these on!" she says, smiling.

Lynda laughs, "let's hope so!" she replies.

The month swiftly moves along now that the wedding gowns and shoes have been chosen and stored at Julia's house, so Neil is unable to see them. Neil is about to organise his half of the list when he finds out from his boss an important client wants him to represent him in court, so he arranges for Patricia to take leave for the next two weeks to help Lynda choose a reception for their wedding. Neil offers to pay her; Patricia declines his offer, saying she has six weeks' leave with pay due.

"I will take two weeks with pay. Lynda's my best friend so

I'm happy to help!" Patricia tells him. Neil thanks her; she tells him she will have Peter be his assistant while she's gone. "He is very good at his job and trustworthy!" She is aware Neil likes all his cases kept private.

Neil is happy with her choice and she leaves with a quickened step, happy to be involved in the wedding arrangements. The entire office and building are excited to see Lynda finally happy. She and Neil have been receiving many cards from nearly everyone in different businesses. Patricia makes the arrangements to view five reception places that still have space for Neil and Lynda's wedding date. Patricia makes it fun and entertaining, playing fun music as Neil expresses to her that Lynda is a little stressed with only five months to the wedding.

The first one Lynda finds really unsuitable and can barely cater for two hundred guests, both she and Neil find it hard to cut down on the lists. Neil does not want to leave his cousins out, and Lynda does the same with friends she's known for years. The women move on to the next place, and as they read the menu, both dislike what's on offer.

Lynda says, "Rather have it at Ben's restaurant, unfortunately not large enough to cater for everyone, especially parking!"

Patricia asks whether Ben is able to cater for the wedding, hiring extra staff and delivery to their location. Lynda says yes, he did offer, but Neil wants him to enjoy himself at the wedding instead of working. Ben hardly gets time to himself with his deli and restaurant, and Neil wants Jen and Ben to enjoy themselves.

On the second week and at the final location, Lynda is looking rather pale. She tells her friend she is fine, but Patricia is not convinced after ten months ago having health issues. The women are met by the organiser; she shows them the gardens allowing them to wander around. Lynda likes the man-made lake and arch on an island to have the ceremony, all seeming dreamy. She videos the entire grounds and restaurant to Neil; he gazes at the video, liking everything. He sends a text. *"I like this one. Make a booking and pay the deposit!"*

The women enjoy themselves, and Lynda likes the atmosphere inside. Neil has arranged a new bank card to cater for the wedding expenses, which paid for the gowns and now the deposit for the reception. The costs will be paid for when Lynda gets her settlement, the money to pay for the wedding and honeymoon. She pays the deposit, and the woman escorts Lynda and Patricia into a private section of the restaurant facing the lake. She explains they just open all the folding doors to cater for any size group of up to five hundred guests.

"Enjoy your luncheon with our compliments with wine.

Patricia is happy, saying the deposit must have been a lot, "Yes," replies Lynda.

"It's perfect, though," she says, looking out at the lake and gardens.

Patricia talks about Neil's list and is looking forward to choosing the men's suits in the morning. Lynda laughs. "You haven't been shopping with Brian, my brother. He takes forever to decide on anything!" Lynda says, laughing.

Patricia laughs, saying she'll be fine. Lynda asks if it's not too much with her workload. Patricia confesses she took two weeks off, and Julia is helping with the invites on her computer.

"You girls are the best friends and sister!" Lynda comments she frowns, having pain in her stomach; she is covering it up, saying it is just wind pain. Patricia is not convinced, she fears

Lynda is having troubles again.

"Have you had your check-up yet with the doctor for your wedding!" she's being cagey, advising it would be a good idea, especially with travelling to France and Italy for their honeymoon.

"Really, people do that?" Lynda questions.

"I did before, I got married, didn't want anything to go wrong. You may need to have an inoculation before travelling. Weddings play havoc on our bodies and stress levels, it wouldn't hurt!" Patricia answers, watching Lynda's expression.

The meal is very nice and the wine is rather sweet. Lynda checks the label, and she smiles, telling Patricia they are her grandma's grapes. Lynda shows her the label of the estate she took Neil to. Patricia expresses remembering Neil telling her about the vineyard.

"Your grandma must have been very happy about how well her grapes are doing?" she asks.

Lynda says yes, very nice for her and the family. The luncheon is lovely. Both women enjoy the wine, Patricia only has a small amount being the driver, while Lynda enjoys her half glass. Patricia drives Lynda home, saying she will pick Neil up around ten in the morning. The suit shop booking is at eleven, giving them time to get into the city. Lynda waves, thanking her friend for helping with the reception venues.

Patricia stops just up the road to ring Neil with her concerns for Lynda, who is obviously in pain, advising Neil to get home early. He agrees, saying he's finished with court for the day and will leave now. Neil arrives home to find Lynda being sick in a bag. He moves beside her, kneeling and holding the bag for her. He takes it away, handing her another one and he empties it in the bin, returning with a cold wash cloth for her forehead. Neil kneels beside the bed, asking how long she's been feeling sick.

"It just came on last week and then stopped; it must have been the meal and wine I had at the reception venue!" Lynda mumbles, being sick again.

Neil is not convinced, "I'm cancelling tomorrow!" he states.

Lynda touches his hand, saying, "No, I'll be fine!" she wants him to choose his suit for the wedding.

In two hours Lynda is feeling better. She sits up, and Neil gives her Lemonade and crackers, aware it's the only thing she can consume after being sick. He is very concerned, asking if she's having pain like last time with the growth. Neil hands her one of her tablets to prevent her from being sick, as prescribed by her doctor. Lynda sleeps through the night, but Neil doesn't, keeping an eye on her. She smiles at him, seeing he's looking at her. He moves her hair out of her face and kisses her softly.

"You, okay?" he asks.

"Yes, feeling much better!" Lynda says.

"I hope it's not food poisoning; otherwise change our venue!" Neil states, being a little worried. He gets up to text Patricia to check how she feels as she had the same food.

Patricia texts, *"No, it's Lynda. Keep an eye on her; be there at ten a.m.!"*

Neil rings Julia, as she only lives a ten-minute drive away, to stay with Lynda. He advises her to say she is just visiting and checking on the venue. Julia agrees, he is not taking any chances with leaving her alone this time after coming home to her being sick. Julia arrives with Zoe, who is excited, telling Neil all about her pretty dress and shoes for the wedding. He laughs, knowing it is supposed to be a surprise, but Zoe is only eight and excited to be a flower girl. Julia is not listening, she is checking on Julia with Neil. He says she's showering, telling her about last night.

Julia tells him to go; she will take care of her sister and will ring if necessary. Patricia arrives to pick up Neil, he gets into her car and reports on Lynda; she tells him not to worry, "She's in good hands with Julia," she smiles to make him feel better, and it does.

In the city, Patricia escorts Neil to the men's shop she chose, having a large selection of formal attire. Brian and Jack arrive, and they see so many suits in various colours.

"Grey or black suits!" Patricia informs the clerk, who quickly moves across, checking the men's sizes.

The salesman has already sorted some designs for the men as Patricia made the booking. She is being organised after Lynda told her Brian takes hours to choose a suit. Patricia moves into action picking the tails as Lynda requested to go with her wedding gown. Julia sent a photo of the wedding gown to give Patricia an idea. She gets the men to try the suit on, including shirts, ties and shoes. She likes this store as it has everything for the men. Neil comes out looking really nice, being slender. Brian is a little larger in size, and Jack feels it's too tight-fitting.

Patricia is looking at the top hats, "No, way. I'm not wearing a hat!" says Brian and Jack in unison. Patricia laughs, saying no hat, Lynda's orders; they both sigh with relief. Neil looks in the mirror with the men saying they do look nice. He decides to try on the black suit with a silver tie. Patricia waits outside in the waiting room, and she comments to the clerk they take longer to change than women. He nods his head in agreement, not wanting to commit as he works in a men's store and has many clients around on a Saturday morning.

Brian comes out first, he looks better in the black suit, making him look slimmer. Neil always looks dashing, Patricia thinks, as he's a good-looking man.

Jack is happier in the better-fitting suit; he bends. "Yes, I can move in this one!" he states.

Neil looks in the mirror and agrees, they decide on the black tails with silver ties and white shirts. Patricia has to agree that all three look more like a wedding party now. The men change, and Neil buys the suits. The salesman places them into garment bags, handing one each to the men. Brian says he can't stay, having work to do at home. He thanks Patricia for organising it all for him. Jack stays and has a cup of coffee with Neil and Patricia, talking about the wedding.

Jack says it all sounds lovely. "Just give me the time when I pick Lynda up!" Patricia says she has it locked into her notes and has organised the car hire already. She uses a pad in her bag, handing Jack the date and time, and he thanks her. Jack leaves, saying goodbye to Neil, and Patricia drives Neil home. She keeps going as she must get home to her husband, Neil thanks her on arriving back at the apartment. Julia speaks with him to make an appointment with the doctor, and he asks where Lynda is.

"She's sleeping. I gave her a pain killer!" Julia says and leaves.

Lynda gets up, walking very slowly to make a cup of herbal tea. Neil is watching and frowning.

"You okay? Don't lie to me!" he questions her in a serious tone.

Lynda is looking out of the window at the ocean. "I remember my sister visiting me. Amanda taking one last look at the beach before her death!"

Lynda is feeling down. "Beautiful, don't talk like that. It's probably just another growth, nothing serious. You have the operation, and we shall live a long life together!" Neil says, holding her hand and kissing it.

Neil has had enough; he makes a booking with her doctor on the webpage. In the morning, Neil receives a phone call from Lynda's doctor, and he speaks to her about what's been happening. She says her girls will organise an ultrasound and appointment with her an hour after that. Two days later, Neil drives Lynda. She has the ultrasound and then goes to meet her doctor. The news is not good; another growth in her uterus. The doctor makes an urgent appointment with the specialist. The news is devastating to Lynda and Neil drives her home; she is still in shock. He insists she go ahead with the operation.

Lynda looks at him. "I can never give you a baby if I do!" she remarks.

"I don't care. We can figure it out later!" he raises his voice, annoyed. On seeing her face he quickly softens his voice. "Sorry beautiful. I am marrying you, not what you can give me. I want you in my life forever!" Neil says.

The specialist appointment is for a week's time, the earliest she could fit Lynda in. During the few days, Neil tries to keep Lynda's mind off her pain, concentrating her on advice with a work issue he has.

Three weeks onwards Neil and Lynda move into the new apartment, Neil hired a removalist with four men. He takes a chair over to the apartment for Lynda to sit on; he is not allowing her to work. Julia and Jen arrive, they are going to help unpack the boxes once delivered. Neil will organise all the furniture in each room along with all the paintings. The first lot of boxes arrive for the kitchen. Jen and Julia unpack, asking Lynda where to place the items. She tells them to just put it anywhere; Neil will organise it all later. Furniture arrives and Neil organises the bedrooms with the men, he then moves into the lounge and dining rooms. Late afternoon the truck is empty and the removalist leaves. Lynda is now sitting on their new comfortable couch, viewing the beach and watching everyone leaving for the day.

Zoe arrives with her dad; he has brought dinner for everyone. Zoe runs around checking rooms saying she can stay over, finding the spare room. Neil is using the third bedroom as his office; the men have his large desk and chair in place. Julia checks on her sister; Lynda finally tells her the truth about her health last year and has waited to make the decision to have the partial hysterectomy.

Julia can't believe she or Neil never confided in her, and she holds Lynda's hand tightly. She knows how much Lynda wants to have children. She's waited so long to find the right man, and now this happens.

"You can adopt. I agree, have the operation for your health!" Julia says.

"You sound like Neil!" Lynda replies, her eyes filling up with water.

Julia calls her daughter over and she whispers to her; Zoe goes up and hugs Lynda saying she loves her. Neil is watching; he smiles and he walks across, handing Zoe an ice cream he bought just before she arrived. Jen hands plates around and serves the meal. Everyone talks and laughs, all agreeing how much nicer the apartment is than either Lynda or Neil owned previously. Julia suggests they leave now, with it being seven o'clock, giving the couple time alone to soak up their new apartment.

Neil sits beside Lynda, telling her he received a phone call from the builder saying the beach house is finally finished. Lynda always told Neil that it would take a year to finish; she is happy.

"We can stay at the beach house after the wedding for our honeymoon instead of going to Europe!" Neil remarks.

Lynda looks disappointed, wanting to go to France for their honeymoon. She argues her point, saying she will be all right. She wants to visit Paris, the romantic city, and everything she has planned for a year.

"I really want to visit the Louvre Museum, Monet Gardens, Eiffel Tower and Venice!" she says with sadness in her voice.

"Don't fight me on this, Lynda. We can go next year. I'm not taking any risks. I'm scared too!" Neil replies, placing his arm around her shoulders.

Lynda holds his hand, saying sorry as he's been her rock, never understanding he was afraid. Lynda leans her head on his arm, saying, "Sorry handsome, thank you for loving me!"

Neil kisses her head, whispering, "Our lives are going to be amazing. We will travel, do outdoor activities and grow old together!"

Lynda holds his hand, looking at him and smiling. They cuddle, watching the lights around them lighting up the sky and stars shining upon the ocean.

Doctors' appointment

Neil goes with her making sure the right outcome is provided for Lynda. The doctor recommends removing the growth immediately before it grows like the last one and becomes infected. She also asks again, saying she's had a year to think about having a partial hysterectomy, advising Lynda she believes this will be the best outcome. Lynda tightens her grip on Neil's hand and he hangs on. She agrees to have the operation and Neil sighs with relief. The doctor sets the date for two days, fitting her in as an emergency and not taking any chances with her family history. Lynda has the operation and will now take eight weeks to recover. Neil cares for her during this time, arranging to work from home as he has no court cases booked. His boss makes sure his workload is lighter due to him caring for Lynda.

Neil is sitting at the dining room table on his computer when Lynda suggests they postpone the wedding as it is in three weeks, and her post-operation recovery will take eight weeks.

Neil puts an end to that, saying they will get married on the weekend arranged. "I love you and will not postpone our wedding any longer!" Neil moves across to her, holding Lynda in his arms as she cries. "I won't be able to have sex on our honeymoon!" Lynda says.

"I am not marrying you for sex or your body. I love you completely, your smile, laughter, talents and mind which all makes up you!" Neil kisses her softly.

"You are the reason my heart beats rapidly, the reason my mind races with thoughts of you all day long!" Lynda replies.

Neil tells her to leave everything up to him and Julia, they will fix the wedding. "Instead of the huge wedding, we'll just have family and a few friends on Manly beach!"

Neil rings Julia for assistance and she tells him to leave it all up to her and Patricia. The women move into action. Julia contacts people on the guest list, ringing and emailing those at a long distance and letting them know the couple is now having a smaller wedding so, unfortunately, they are now not invited. Julia explains Lynda's health issues, and they are all very sad but happy she is okay and will send gifts anyway. Patricia cancels the reception venue, losing half the deposit. Cars are cancelled; the photographer is informed of the change of venue along with the florist. Julia rings Jen to design a smaller wedding cake now, and she asks Julia to ring Ben. Julia does, and he offers his restaurant and staff for the reception; Julia is grateful, thanking him. Ben explains he's Neil's oldest friend so no problem, he will start organising everything. Patricia suggests to Julia and Jennifer to still wear their dresses and will sort something out for Lynda.

Neil walks into the bedroom seeing Lynda crying. She is trying on her wedding gown, it won't zip up, and her stomach is poking out.

"I don't fit into my wedding dress; I've put on weight without exercising!" she tells him amongst her sobbing.

"Wear anything, jeans and shirt. I don't care. I'm marrying you, not your dress!" Neil says softly, holding her close to his chest and allowing her to release her emotions.

"The doctor said rest, not get upset!" He removes the wedding dress, placing it carefully onto a chair.

Neil gets one of her summer dresses and helps Lynda put it on, then lifts her up into his arms. He carries her to the couch, he has already organised the cushions, and Lynda sits back with her head on a cushion. Neil puts on her favourite music, she's been awake most of the night due to discomfort and missing Neil. He has been sleeping in the spare room since the operation to give her time to rest without disturbing her. The music soothes her and she falls asleep; she sleeps for three hours. When she wakes, Neil is preparing lunch in the kitchen; she watches him. He turns, seeing she's awake, "Hello beautiful, hungry?" he asks.

"Yes," Lynda is so glad Neil is with her all day, having company and someone to talk to. Neil hands her a bowl of savoury rice with vegies, Lynda thanks him, her favourite. Neil adds the spices she loves. "You saw my wedding dress. Now it's not a surprise!" she says.

"I don't care about that darn dress. Stop worrying about our wedding. I'll sort it!" he replies, a little testy. He's more worried about her recovering than anything else as he hears a knock at the door. Neil opens it and a person hands him a bunch of flowers.

"They're lovely, thank you!" Lynda says.

"Not me," Neil replies, reading the note, "*Mr. Gardner is thinking of you, Lynda.*"

"Have to ring to thank him for me, please?" Lynda asks Neil.

Neil picks up his mobile, ringing him to say thank you, he walks out onto their balcony, ringing Ben for support and advice on an idea he's thinking of. He talks for quite some time, Neil explains he wants to get married before Lynda changes her mind.

Ben agrees, "Don't want her to have cold feet, especially now!"

Ben likes Neil's idea of changing the wedding. Ben tells his friend he has the restaurant sorted and Jen's making the cake. Neil is relieved and so grateful to Julia for organising that with Ben. Both men discuss Neil's idea and Jen overhears; Ben has his mobile on speaker. She interrupts, telling Neil to buy Lynda an outfit to her size now as his wedding gift.

"Thanks, Jen. That's a good idea!" Neil says, thinking of something.

Neil walks out to the lounge seeing Lynda has fallen asleep, having eaten half her lunch. He removes the bowl and lifts her up into his arms, carrying her back to bed and tucking her in; Neil kisses her forehead.

At the end of the three weeks, Lynda receives her doctor's call to say all is good with the lump, no cancer. The doctor says to have a lovely wedding day on Saturday. Lynda thanks her thinking this weekend is so close, and she is unsure what kind of wedding Neil has re-designed.

Chapter Ten

Wedding Day

Neil delivers a dress bag for Lynda at the apartment as he's staying at Julia and John's home for the night. He is giving Lynda and her bridesmaids the entire night together to prepare for the wedding in the morning. He places the dress bag on a chair.

"For you, beautiful, we are getting married no matter what. I love you!" Neil kisses Lynda, leaving her alone in Julia's capable hands.

Julia unzips the dress bag removing two coat hangers, a pair of stylish jeans, a long white silk and French lace blouse with a note.

"You can wear your wedding dress on our first anniversary. My gift to you, love Neil."

Julia says she's lucky to find Neil. "No, Julia. He found me!" Lynda replies, smiling.

Julia reaches into the bottom of the dress bag, pulling out three pairs of white leather thongs.

"Perfect for a beach wedding!" Julia says, smiling at her sister, noticing they are in each of their shoe sizes.

Lynda smiles, "Typical Neil, thinks of everything. The pants won't fit!" she exclaims.

"Yes, they will. He asked for your size. I told him just get the next size up with an elasticated waist for the jeans, be more comfortable for you!" Julia replies, holding her sister's hand.

Lynda holds the jeans up to her waist, nodding her head and saying, "perfect." She smiles at her sister. Julia organises her to have a crystal bath and says to leave everything up to her. "Now go, the hairdresser will be here in an hour!"

Jen arrives with her dress as they are still wearing their bridesmaids' dresses, except now with leather floral thongs. The flowers arrive, a beautiful yellow rose bouquet for Lynda and white roses for Julia and Jen. John brings Zoe and Liam to the apartment; John asks how Lynda is, never getting to the altar before.

"Nervous but fine," says Julia.

"Did Neil deliver her outfit? I thought it was perfect making it casual!" John comments.

"You in on this too?" Julia asks her husband. He replies Neil just asked him and Ben for their opinion, both telling him it was a good idea to get Lynda to the altar.

Zoe is very excited on seeing her little ring box to carry, and Liam admires the rings, and John leaves.

Lynda walks out dressed. She looks lovely; the blouse is long with points of lace at different ankles. "Aunty Lynda, you look nice!" Liam says happier he's wearing jeans and a shirt rather than a suit as originally organised.

Zoe is happy to still be wearing her pretty white dress with sandals. She shows her aunty the lovely silk box she is carrying with the rings. "Who brought them?" enquires Lynda.

"John just dropped off the kids and rings. You like the box?" Julia asks due to making it herself.

"Lovely. Thanks, Sis," Lynda gives her a hug for re-organising the entire guest list to wear casual clothing and something yellow or jeans if possible.

The hairdresser arrives, and seeing Lynda's outfit and very

long hair, she styles it to be full in the front with a short side piece to one side. A half-French plait down the back, leaving the rest of her hair free. Lynda hands her the tiny diamond stars Neil gave her to replace her veil. The hairdresser places them around the top part of Lynda's hair carefully, to be seen.

"You look lovely," says Zoe and her mother.

Lynda's make-up is applied, and she's ready. The hairdresser asks if she's happy. "Oh yes, just, right!" Lynda says.

"Have a lovely day. Lucky it's a hot, sunny day!" the hairdresser replies, leaving.

Lynda slips into her thongs and they leave the apartment. People are standing on balconies watching. Many taking videos, and friends from her old apartment building are downstairs congratulating her. Lynda thanks her friends from the block for coming to see her off. "You look lovely," they yell.

The guests have assembled, standing on the beach with Neil in front and Brian as best man. Both men are wearing jeans and yellow shirts. Julia positions Zoe and Liam in front of her and Jen as they are to walk ahead first. Neil still insisted on having his violinist and singers, and they begin. The children walk off first, Liam holding Zoe's hand. Jennifer and Julia walk side by side; a path has been prepared on the sand, racked and broomed by the lifeguards. The guards stand watching the wedding.

Jack is standing with his arm out for his daughter. Lynda takes it. He is proud of his daughter for finally marrying the right man. He, too, is dressed in jeans and a silver shirt for his daughter. "Are you ready?" he asks.

"Yes, Dad. I am!" Lynda says as they proceed forward, walking along the sand.

Lynda walks with her father. Everyone is in awe as she walks, seeing her looking lovely, even in her changed outfit. She smiles on seeing women and girls wearing some sort of yellow dress while the men are in jeans. Lynda smiles at her guests as she walks past, all taking photos.

Neil is in his outfit of jeans, yellow shirt and silver tie. Lynda smiles up at him; standing facing him. The marriage celebrant says her piece and then hands it over to Lynda and Neil to say their own vows.

Lynda's vows

If my heart could speak, the words would say.

My love is yours to keep for me. My love is yours....

My heart is swelling with joy at seeing your smile, which brightens my day.

My heart speaks my love for you....

Our hearts speak our love for each other.

My heart speaks to you no matter how far away you are....

The world moves around us, moving us apart at times, but always we find our way back to each other....

My heart speaks my love.

Our hearts speak our love for each other.

Let our love spread around the world to each heart to find someone near them. Let our love reach other people along the way finding each other.

My love keeps moving towards you as our hearts come together as one. Everyone's hearts beat as one.

My heart speaks my love for you....

My heart beats as one with yours forever....

A tear appears in Neil's eyes, never knowing Lynda's true love for him as she hasn't expressed it until now. He tightens his grip on her hands, smiling at her.

Neil's vows

My love for you is so precious, my darling, so powerful, so strong for you.

I must admit you have power over me. My heart beats rapidly, knowing you are mine.

I desire to be with you, growing old with you as our love is true.

Our love is ours, holding hands along the beach. Smiling into each other's eyes.

My love for you, my darling, is powerful, so strong for you.

My heart beats rapidly, knowing you are mine.

I shall climb the highest mountain to send my voice across the world for you to hear me.

I stand on rooftops singing to you to hear me.

Your strength, your kindness, and your friendship make me love you more.

I am proud of you, my darling.

My heart beats a thousand beats when you're near me. The sound of your footsteps coming toward me makes me smile.

I shall stand beside you forever, my darling.

My love for you, my darling, is powerful, so strong for you.

My heart skips a beat, knowing you are mine.

I gaze into your eyes while you're in my arms, and it makes my heart beat rapidly.

My throat swells and I can hardly speak, telling you my love for you is true.

My love for you, my darling, is knowing you are mine.

Lynda cries on hearing Neil's beautiful vows, showing his true heart. Julia encourages Zoe to move forward to her uncle to take the rings. Brian lifts them out, untying the ribbons and handing Neil his ring for Lynda. Neil slips it onto her finger.

Brian hands Lynda a man's gold ring, and she slips it onto Neil's finger.

"I pronounce you man and wife. You may kiss!"

At those words, Neil takes Lynda into his arms, holding his left arm behind her back and kissing her passionately, surprising everyone. The guests laugh and smile, all taking photos.

THE END